The Day Earth Disappeared

The Day Earth Disappeared

By Genesis Pilgrim

Genesis Pilgrim
© 2020. All rights reserved.
ISBN: 978-1-7333145-6-5
www.genesispilgrim.com

Cloak, veil, fade
The spirit can break free
Reach up and hold the ground above your head

I believe in you

Contents

Foreword

In the following book I present the actions of the Mahanaim task force entrusted with the mission of repairing the Earth. The Mahanaim task force was led by me—Genesis Pilgrim.

When leading the Mahanaim task force to Earth via the Luminary Watchhand, I later discovered this movement itself passed beyond Mahanaim's chronological timeline. This is difficult to understand—and painfully so, but suffice it to say these events within Earth occurred at some time between Earth's 21st Century and 5000 A.D.

The disappearance of the Earth from the Luminary Watchhand sometime thereafter caused a shift in chronological time as viewed in the 4th Dimension. So, perhaps the best way to view this—until we make more discoveries—would be to view the following as a description of events which preceded the final disappearance of the Earth and its presumed warding within a higher dimension—most likely the 7th Dimension or even higher.

TO MAHANAIM: A follow-on mission will be conducted to provide a patch upon our shared Luminary timelines—opening the Luminary Watchhand for our return after completion. A separate transmission will be sent detailing my plan for the follow-on mission to provide the patch. DO NOT send a rescue team—as I fear such a mission might end in peril.

TO EARTH: If you receive this transmission, perhaps this book can help prepare you for tribulation. While our contact remains severed, know my task force is moving quickly to set conditions for the timeline patch. We have a plan to accomplish this from our position atop the Luminary Watchhand. Although we cannot reach you now, we will maintain vigil until reunited. In the meantime, STAND FAST. Help is on the way.

CONCLUSION: It pains me to write something where I cannot offer full details concerning the specific time of events. Please excuse my inability in this regard.

This book may present challenges to your understanding. I advise discernment in reading its contents. If you would like to learn more about a specific phrase or topic contained in this book, I recommend you consult the page index at the end of the book.

Sincerely,

Genesis Pilgrim

Commander,
Mahanaim Task Force

<u>Prelude:</u>
Spaces & Patterns in Time

"Kai, write this down please . . ." Genesis asked.

Often the pilgrim was struck with thoughts which would overtake his mind. Being driven by these thoughts as gifts from the ethereal dimensions beyond, Genesis was always quick to capture them whenever they appeared. This was one such occasion.

Kai moved quickly—removing an arcane device from his backpack. With the device in hand, Kai nodded, signaling his companion.

Genesis began: "Any time-traveler will tell you…*er*, I guess I'll tell you, that the 5th Dimension—the time-travel dimension that is—is more about *spaces to be filled* and *patterns to be followed* than it is about specifics."

Genesis was a humble man. Although a Visionary, the pilgrim often imagined—quite inaccurately—that there were a grand company of others possessing the same remarkable abilities. Although he had never met another time-traveler, the pilgrim contented himself in the thought that he merely did not know any because they were *too busy*… doing time-travel.

Genesis continued, "Well, I estimate it isn't accurate for me to say 'any time-traveler will tell you,' because not many time-travelers are inclined to write books. Usually those individuals are off doing time-travel. So, you might never find one with the propensity to attempt explaining this stuff to anyone who doesn't already understand it firsthand. Nevertheless, here I am."

"Yes—*here you are*," Kai repeated, giving himself opportunity to catch up his notetaking.

The pilgrim pressed forward: "*I want* to explain this because *I want* people to understand. I am not comfortable with the thought of anyone being held captive by the first three dimensions, so if I can impart knowledge to help people escape, I will do so."

Genesis took a deep breath: "So, as I was saying…*time-travel is more about spaces to be filled and patterns to be followed than it is about specifics.* The sooner one grasps this, the sooner the fabric of Creation comes into focus.

"You see, everything in creation follows a certain pattern of rhythm. Not to complicate things too much, but somehow the higher dimension patterns move onto the lower dimensions. And, in the dimensions where time is linear, the patterns existing in the higher dimensions are somehow folded out onto it.

"Sure, I guess my explanation only leaves you with more questions—for which I probably do not have answers. After all, I am human. I am in the process of working to figure this out.

"But in my various travels throughout linear time—that is time in the first *three-dimensions*—I can tell you it is quite common for details to somehow shift at certain points. However, even after details shift, the story remains the same.

"Weird, huh?" Genesis offered in rhetoric.

"I'll give you an example . . .

"There might be a *Bridget Jones*, but then after a time jump or two, and a return to the same general spot, I can find there is still a "Bridget Jones," but she might be called "Janet Smith."

"So, these shifts in details show although specific details can be altered in linear time, the "spaces" and "patterns" they occupy—when indeed it is a *vital* space or pattern—cannot, by any means, be altered.

"In other words, things in the lower dimensions subject to linear time absolutely *must* follow the patterns set within the higher dimensions. Even if names can change, or specific days on which events occur can shift slightly, everything in the lower dimensions are subject to the *fate* decreed in the higher dimensions. And linear time marches toward the fulfillment of higher patterns.

"Always.

"Why am I telling you this?" paused the pilgrim in rhetoric.

"Well, with my heartfelt fondness for ancient religious texts, I sense I have a moral responsibility to teach others when I have been entrusted with knowledge. And, remarkably, within ancient religious texts—the Bible in particular—I see *pattern expression* is shown quite clearly in prophecy.

"For example, when the Bible states that something happened in Heaven, or was spoken in Heaven, this means that somehow that Heavenly event or spoken Word would be fulfilled in the lower dimensions of linear time on Earth.

"There are no exceptions. This is why prophecies *always* come true—even if they take many, many years.

"I have found this to be true. Interestingly, when visiting certain points—and viewing the "spaces" and "patterns" that keep sticking, no matter how much is changed around them, this highlights those immutable patterns which must be understood as a part of a grander scheme from a *higher* dimension.

"Another way of putting this . . .

"If I go to one location and time, and record everything, then I leave and return, I need only consult my notes from my first visit to determine what was truly significant in that setting. Upon my return, if I note all the patterns which remained, then I can deduce that those are the patterns based on the *higher pattern*. But if I find other details were changed, then this means that those specific details were not a part of the higher pattern.

"And, by putting my finger on what remains the same and what changes, I can feel the Heavenly pulse as it surges within the linear time of Earth. I can see the higher dimensions as they appear in the lower dimensions. I can see the 6th Dimension of the Heavenly pattern within the 3rd Dimension."

Genesis reflected further: "In the 21st Century I remember hearing people deride the Bible—saying it is not falsifiable. But now, having achieved and working with 5th Dimension capability, I feel I have arrived at a scientific method of testing Bible prophecy—allowing me to see after various jumps what keeps sticking.

"And within these simple observations a skeptic could deduce that somehow there is something which is tethering events in linear time—forcing them to move with a spiritual *fate* toward certain ends.

"Cool, huh!?" Genesis exclaimed as he clapped his hands.

"I certainly think it is," Kai added as he scribbled ferociously on his device.

Without regard for the lagging Kai, Genesis continued: "It is a really funny thing to consider... Let's say I were able to find the most die-hard skeptic—a person who denied everything supernatural, a person who is a naturalist. I could take that person with me on a journey through multiple jumps to the same place and time," Genesis paused at the absurdity of what he just said—considering how to backpedal . . .

Before Kai could answer, Genesis resolved his fumbling of concepts: "Well I guess if I took a skeptic with me on a journey through time, then he probably would no longer be a skeptic!"

Kai interjected, "He is a *die-hard skeptic* after all, Genesis. So, even if you showed him the *spiritual* 4th Dimension, he might still deny the supernatural."

Genesis chuckled, "Yeah, I guess this person wouldn't be a good skeptic if he gave in *too* soon. But for a moment, let's imagine the skeptic remained a skeptic."

"Okay."

Genesis continued, "Then all I would need to do is bring that skeptical person back and forth to the same location—having him record *detailed* observations every time we returned. Although this would be a painstaking process, the skeptic would reveal in his notes the very patterns declared by prophecy. In other words, repeated travels and comparisons would show that somehow— amid incredible differences—that certain patterns *kept sticking*. And this would leave any rational person with the striking realization: *All things in the lower dimensions must follow patterns decreed in the higher dimensions*. No exceptions. Therefore, time-travel could be used to *prove* the existence of higher dimensions. With enough jumps it would be impossible to explain away the things which stick. Therefore, I can prove the existence of higher dimensions through 5th Dimension time-travel."

"I think I get it, Genesis. Although I wouldn't volunteer to do *repeated* time jumps." Kai shuddered as his mind was transported back to his first experience of time-travel—when the pilgrim sent him to retrieve Genesis (if that even makes sense).

Kai's shudder then morphed into a mystifying state, causing a confusion to pass over his mind. Then, just as quickly as Kai dropped into his momentary confusion, he emerged from it . . .

Kai completely lost his train of thought and was hoping to have the pilgrim coach him back on track . . .

"What's your point, Genesis?"

"Well, my point is that *minor points*—that is points which are not prescribed by a higher dimension pattern—don't matter to a time-traveler. In fact, to be a good time-traveler, one must learn to quickly let go of the inclination to think in terms of *exact* names or *exact* dates. You see, many of those things change—and as soon as you can write them down, you find that they already changed."

In a sprint of thought, Kai caught up, offering an astounding observation, "It gives you a great appreciation for the accuracy of ancient prophets in the Bible, Genesis. Despite all the shifts in unnecessary details, somehow the prophets were able to describe the *exact* Heavenly pattern which *must* come true."

"The student becomes the teacher," Genesis jested, motioning a feigned bow before Kai.

Kai laughed, "I have heard you talk about this stuff so much, Genesis, *I* could write some books!"

Genesis clapped back, "If you are complaining about your present mission, Kai, I have some ideas for *other places* I could send you." Genesis raised his hand to his brow: "Speaking of that, I know of a team which needs a leader to—"

Kai interrupted, "No, I'm good, boss." He waved his hands in front of his face—batting away Genesis' words. Kai was content with his current mission and found no need to invite upon himself further hardships in far off lands.

Genesis laughed. He had no intent of sending Kai off on another mission. Nevertheless, he found pleasure teasing him so.

The pilgrim returned to the conversation: "Kai, this is the major point: Whenever I talk about time-travel, I don't use *exact* names—because they change. There are only a few names which are an *exact* part of declared Heavenly prophecy which must remain the same."

"Example?"

"Cyrus, king of Persia, who was prophesied *by name*. He *might* be one example of a person whose name would always remain the same—because it was declared from Heaven to be so. In other words, the name of that person in the 6th Dimension is 'Cyrus,' so all lower dimensions were compelled to adopt that higher pattern."

"So, you checked up on Cyrus?"

"No—it's just a guess."

"For now that is," Kai drawled—in jest at first, then recoiling from his thought, realizing it possible the pilgrim planned to move through those points in the past.

"*For now*," Genesis repeated, raising his eyebrow—perhaps as a mental nod to his future self, momentarily letting down the guard of his poker face, hinting at the cards within his grasp.

Kai didn't doubt much of anything anymore. There was a time in which Kai used to question the pilgrim's reach. Now, Kai held within himself a general acceptance of Genesis' abilities—confident the pilgrim could always *find a way*. And, within this thought Kai found security.

Genesis continued, "But like I said, Kai, names usually don't stick. So, "Betty Charles" can easily become "Betsy Ross." "Anthony Carver" can easily become "George Washington. Therefore, it might be best to refer to individuals with *nicknames* which capture their qualities or the *positions* they occupy in society. After all, it is far more likely those qualities will stick more than the names, and certainly the society positions would stick—as they will always find a person to occupy them. So, the names don't matter much."

"Why, Genesis?" Kai asked.

"Well, if you remember our previous discussion about human nature, Kai, I explained how a human being is much more than just his physical appearance. A human contains within himself a spiritual infinity."

"I think you called it *Inversely Proportional Dimensional Consciousness* theory, Genesis," Kai recalled.

Genesis was surprised at Kai's memory. Genesis often felt confusion as words jumbled in the corridors of his own mind. Genesis paused momentarily, playing back Kai's words to see if they matched his own memory.

"Yes, that was it, Kai! I called it *Inversely Proportional Dimensional Consciousness* theory. … When thinking about the eternal worth of each human it makes sense that we should avoid putting too much emphasis in the "name" of an individual. After all, many names are haphazardly assigned to children by their parents or guardians. Many names mean nothing and offer nothing significant to the individual who is named. Nor do they adequately contain within themselves the ability to fully capture the eternal capacity and infinite worth of the individual."

"I see."

"Yeah, when we have a proper perspective of the importance of each human, being made in the image of

God, we are able to let go of the fluff. Indeed, if any name *does* matter, it is the one assigned to an individual by God Himself. Sure, to the person who is held captive by linear time in the 3rd Dimension, his name can become meaningful throughout his lifetime. But in the grand scheme of eternity, humans outlive their names—many times in fact. So, in the scope of eternity, the particular name assigned to an individual by his parents at the beginning of his first phase will ultimately pale in comparison to the mission and purpose he will achieve in the endlessness following his initial lifespan."

"Wow!" exclaimed Kai, "Is that why your name changed?"

Genesis nodded, "I know it is a lot to think about, but it is an important point: Humans were designed to completely transcend—we were designed to be eternal, spiritual beings. And, eternal spiritual beings aren't tied down by the haphazard assignment of verbal labels— names that is—often picked by parents just because their parents, *liked how the name sounded*," Genesis motions air-quotes with his hands to bracket the phrase as it fluttered from his mouth.

The expression and words touched Kai, "That makes sense when you explain it like that, Genesis."

"Yeah, it really does," Genesis agreed, then went a step further to solidify his point, "Kai, in the 21st Century there were people who named their children all types of nonsense—where they would just jumble together letters and sounds and whatnot. None of it made any sense, yet parents would place these bizarre names on their children. It certainly worked for humans who were content to remain evermore within the 3rd Dimension, but upon breaking free we soon realize that all that stuff is left behind. As a human moves into a higher dimension, he is left to see the pettiness in the things behind him. Sure, some things in the 3rd Dimension were good—especially those things connected to faith, courage, hope and love— each offering glimpses of the spirituality of the 4th Dimension and beyond. But all the nonsense of the 3rd Dimension eventually washes away as we jump out of it."

"So, I guess it might be best to drop names altogether in a book about a time traveler in linear time?"

"Yes. Because the names of 3rd Dimension Earthlings change. What is important is the *pattern* and the *spaces* which are filled by those people. If anyone moves, someone will fill the necessary role within the pattern because the pattern *must* be fulfilled. So, it would be a far better practice to label the *necessary roles* rather than the people themselves."

"Genesis, you mentioned dates too?"

"Yes, dates often don't stick. So, any time-traveler who is intending to offer an accurate description to others would be wary of using *specific* dates."

"Why?"

"Think about it, Kai. Just to help it to make sense, think of the higher dimensions as Heaven—just for simplicity's sake…Is there linear time in Heaven?"

"No," Kai guessed.

"Right, Kai. Time does not move linearly in Heaven. When people are protected by the presence of the Creator, there is no need to fear anything—and thus no need to think in terms of *moment-to-moment*. Therefore, people in Heaven can just simply exist for all eternity—never worrying about what might happen in the next moment."

Genesis continued, "Thus, Kai, if the "pattern" upon which linear time on Earth moves is based on Heaven, then this proves that the *hours, days, minutes, years* and so on—in Earth—are not sticking points for the Heavenly pattern. Things from Heaven simply unfold on Earth's linear timeline, shifting and rippling their way into fulfillment."

"Ah," Kai sighed with realization, "I see."

Kai raised his hand to the side of his face—as if to gently guide the new thought to his brain:

"This is why you don't say events will occur at a *specific* time."

"Yes. And, extending this thought further, this is why prophets avoided doing so as well. In some cases, prophets might have offered *estimates*—like Jeremiah saying there would be seventy years until the return of his country's exiles—but in most cases the *exact* day of an event is seldom a sticking point."

Kai wrapped up Genesis' points . . .

"*So, all who travel here, abandon the use of names and dates.*"

In his past travels, Kai developed a fondness for pirates—and he offered his response with the stereotypical pirate voice, squinting his eye and motioning his arm as if grasping a pint of ale.

Genesis laughed, repeating Kai's point, "Yes, all who travel here, abandon the use of *exact* names and dates."

In his delivery, the pilgrim mimicked Kai's pirate expression, gaining from Kai a volley of amusement and a blurt of laughter.

As the room settled, Genesis concluded, "In this book, names are generalized—with people being given names which best represent their *pattern role*. And

Earthlings are referred to by use of nicknames, rather than their actual names. Also, since *dates* are not something which sticks, they are omitted. So, what you will be left with, if you are receiving this book in linear time, is a general gist of events. Watch out for the pattern and guard yourself against the great deception which may arrive in your generation."

With that, Genesis completed his thought and Kai stowed his recording device.

As they moved forth from that moment, a thought hung in the air where they stood—as if organizing itself amid the buzzing of the words which swirled about its two visitors. A shadow fell in their wake as they departed. That place, now unoccupied, was overtaken by gloom. The ethereal oil of gloom settled, slowly spreading out across the Luminary Watchhand above the Earth.

As Genesis and Kai made preparations in Mahanaim, the Sun and Moon above the Earth were left with gloom as their only companion. They sank and waned—longing for the arrival of the promised company. The Earth continued to cry out. There was no comfort amid the discord; no relief to the stirrings within.

Gloom descended.

<u>1</u>:
Diagnosing Earth

"Harmony!" exclaimed Genesis as he stepped away from the game table—placing his hands on his hips.

"Not fair!" blurted Kai—looking at the *Bumble* gameboard in dismay.

"All done, Kai. How long did it take me?" Genesis snickered.

"There should be rules about this! You can't use time-travel!"

"Says who?" asked the pilgrim defiantly—flipping over the game box. "Nothing on here says I can't use time-travel," Genesis laughed.

"That's not the point," objected Kai with a playful smirk. "If you do this all the time, then what is the point of anyone playing against you?"

"Perhaps you should wear a tin-foil hat, Kai," offered Genesis in jest. "Then I wouldn't be able to read the *Bumble* story in your mind."

"*What!?* Now you are reading my mind too!? Double-unfair!"

"I didn't design the game. Its not my fault if they made it too easy. Maybe they should start putting aluminum hats in the box."

"Would that stop you?"

"No," the pilgrim laughed. "I want to see you wear the hat though."

It was a funny exchange for sure. Certainly, the designers of *Bumble* never predicted how gameplay could be exploited by *time-travelers*. Indeed, at the game's creation there existed only musings of the 5th Dimension on Mahanaim. And, to my knowledge, no one predicted a further dimension of reality would contain within it the ability to move throughout time itself. Thus, Genesis Pilgrim posed a challenge to the game of *Bumble*.

Now, in the Luminary System of Mahanaim, people are fanatical for the game *Bumble*. And why shouldn't they be? *Bumble* was a marvelous game which was limitless in its creative capacity. *Bumble* provided a playful means for individuals to compete against one another through an interactive, speed-based game. Players even designed stories for their games—allowing Bumble to pique the interests of nearly any type of human.

So, why is *Bumble* important to *our* story?

After his mysterious arrival in Mahanaim, perhaps the area through which Genesis' ability became most apparent was in the game of *Bumble*. In the Mahanaim *Bumble* competitions, Genesis instantly achieved master player status—demonstrating his ability to un-do *Bumble* stories in record time.

When viewing his performance in the *Bumble* tournaments, many commentators would scratch their heads—uncertain how his exceptional performance was possible.

However, you must understand these things from Genesis' perspective. As silly as it may sound, Genesis never knew he was breaking any "rules"—indeed there were no such rules to be broken. He simply knew the game gave his mind respite in this new place. His mind was often overtaken with sadness and overwhelming confusion as he came to grips with his new surroundings in Mahanaim after being transported from Earth. Being unaware of his condition and neglecting to share it with anyone, Genesis nearly suffered from a condition called Perception Overload.

But the game of *Bumble* offered Genesis the way out.

At first, Genesis began playing *Bumble* in many different places. And, recognizing his talent, he was quickly recruited to compete in tournaments.

What was it like watching Genesis compete?

Well, after being provided with the pre-read material for a *Bumble* game, he would instantly achieve "harmony" or "discord" to complete the game. In fact, in many cases, the only thing anyone saw Genesis do was call out "harmony." So, from their perspective it appeared Genesis *instantly* altered all game pieces with his mind.

Of course, that is a ridiculous notion. Nevertheless, it was the only way people could make sense of the hooded and cloaked pilgrim. *How else could he instantly complete games?*

Remarkably, games appeared much different for Genesis than they did for his observers. For, from Genesis' perspective, a game was a painstaking process—where he spent much time studying and painstakingly moving the pieces. They told him to achieve *harmony* with the game pieces *as fast as possible*. And that is what he did. Without realizing it, his movement was so fast—from a linear perspective—that he moved *backward* in time through the events. As he was drawn in by the game's story line, his mind somehow created a vessel to carry the gameboard. And, being so consumed in thought as he cracked the *Bumble* story, the pilgrim subconsciously separated himself from the physical world—only looking up at the end to declare "harmony" at the game's completion.

So, you must understand how confusing this was for Genesis—being told he possessed some power of which he was truly unaware. Thus, the emergence of his new identity was something he achieved quite by accident—not requiring a teacher, but stumbling upon it as a gift within himself.

****

Now we find the pilgrim alone within his castle. In the heights of a tower corridor, the pilgrim reclined in solitude.

His reflections on the past continued to swirl in his mind, as his brain handed his consciousness a never-ending series of past snapshots.

As Genesis idly observed the train passing in his thoughts, one car at a time, he gradually became more aware of the reality he faced: In the midst of his mind's cycling it would be impossible to sleep.

In many similar circumstances the pilgrim would effectively ward off the train within his mind as he sipped a warm beverage. He would focus on willing each part of his body into a state of deep relaxation, gently giving way to ever deepening stages of sleep. The train of thought would gently merge with his dreams.

However, this evening he was particularly drawn in by the passing cars of thought. In the parade the pilgrim's consciousness perceived a pattern. But the pattern, although unquestioningly there, was somehow elusive. Genesis reflected—aware of an approaching *realization*. He focused his mind upon it so it might not escape his notice.

Over many years, the pilgrim learned patience— *within himself.* He began to view the parts of his body as speaking to him, some in an altogether foreign language. But, for the sometimes nonsensical "language" of his subconscious, the pilgrim learned to be mindful of trains.

He often thought of his subconscious as pulling different snapshots out of an album, then handing them one at a time to his consciousness. So, the language of his subconscious was one *unspoken*, but rather *shown*. As is the case with most conversation, at times the snapshots were idle, showing nothing of note, bearing no perceived connection. But at other times, when it was left to Genesis' mind to "guess" at the connection between the snapshots, he could find within them a message—a type of marching order to direct his next steps over the coming days.

So, the sorting done by his subconscious was most useful, and something he grew to take *quite seriously*. In case his conscious mind missed something, his subconscious would give him a "second chance" to benefit from the data it stored.

His sleeplessness on this particular evening beckoned him to leave behind Mahanaim. As Genesis slowly roused himself, redirecting his blood within his groggy limbs, feeling his breathing rate and heart rate begin to slowly dance in anticipation of movement, he reflected on an old saying . . .

"Trying to sleep" is an oxymoron.

Genesis chuckled to himself as he jostled himself from his sleep attempt. It was clear his subconscious was trying to hand him something very valuable, so he chose to board the train ahead of him—determined to travel where it would take him, to see *what* it wanted to show him.

Genesis opened his eyes on the Luminary Watchhand—atop the Earth. Looking down at that jewel of Creation, the pilgrim's heart was stirred for his homeland—from which he was parted in some mystery occurrence.

As he gazed at the glistening jewel, Genesis pondered his departure. His gaze was pulled deep within the colors of the jewel. His eyes attempted to trace out locations in the below continents—somehow connecting those visions with memories long forsaken in the halls of his mind. Much was lost and the jewel to him seemed equally majestic and cryptic.

Although he spent a lifetime within its ethereal boundaries, to Genesis the jewel of Earth seemed *closed* to his mind. He gazed at the lands and oceans—barely eking any memory of his past. He felt conflicted—as if he had never been there.

Genesis' heart was moved to grief bordering on Perception Overload. His brain felt caged—as if he were being called to loosen it immediately from capture within itself. His heart sank and beads of sweat raced down his reddened face. His mind was breaking—collapsing in upon itself in confusion which held back an ocean of ethereal despair.

In a miracle of this moment, Genesis' mind was ushered from its descent into Perception Overload. He felt anew the weight of the Luminary Watchhand pressing upon his feet. He held fast the Watchhand using his outstretched legs and the staff in his hand. The Watchhand swirled about him as it came to rest once again beneath him. Genesis reentered himself—still finding his eyes gazing at the magnificent jewel beneath him. He breathed deeply—freeing himself from the grasp of the previous moment.

Centered, the pilgrim looked down upon the Earth—as if seeing it anew, somehow transformed from its appearance just a moment earlier. To him, the jewel looked akin to a *Bumble* game piece—suspended above its zone. Being so accustomed to the thoughts of "harmony" and "discord," the pilgrim's mind naturally interacted with what appeared to be a *Bumble* game piece before him.

If the Earth below were a Bumble game piece, thought Genesis, *all I see within it is discord.*

His life had recently been a blur of *Bumble* games—so he found in this moment he was using the game itself to evaluate the entire Luminary System of the Earth.

Genesis reached out his hand—as if to *feel* the Earth. His mind raced to diagnose the Earth through his senses, just as he would diagnose a gameboard.

First, he noticed the Sun and Moon in their circuits. Their patterns were skewed—clearly off-balance. It felt as if the Sun and Moon were out of step with one another. Their breaths were labored and forced—exhaling and inhaling at unpredictable intensities. Genesis thought the breaths similar to the gasping and pronounced snores of a sick man and woman with sleep apnea. Thus, the Sun and Moon jostled themselves about on their circuits.

So great was Genesis' dismay of the Sun and Moon, he feared a great throe might shake them loose from the tracks beneath them—sending them as rollercoasters spiraling from their rails.

His heart broke within him, being consumed with compassion for the sickened lights above the Earth.

Second, the Earth's sky *glistened*—as if bursting when touched with the gentle light of the Luminaries passing through the ether. It was as if the sky was *resisting* the Sun and Moon—causing reflections.

Now you must understand how this would have *felt* to Genesis—as a master *Bumble* player. Understanding the play between the Sun, Moon and Earth, each relies on the process of *give-and-take*. Picture this as each inhaling and exhaling through the ether—to give and to take from its counterparts. The sickness of the sky, however, prevented such breathing—as a toxic substance in the sky was somehow pushing the "breaths" of each off their courses, breaking contact between the Sun, Moon and Earth.

Third, Genesis felt the ground and seas beneath were a cacophony of wails and cries—as they implored the Luminaries above for rescue. However, Genesis could feel relief was never delivered with the passing Moons. For the sky itself despised the moonlight—not granting it passage to the despairing Earth beneath. So, the land could *never heal*—being cut off from the healing of the Moon's monthly wax and wane. There was nothing to take the grief; nothing to impart grace.

Thus, the Earth was left destitute by the evils of humanity. The sky and seas were poisoned. The ground cut and bleeding. The Earth *forgot* the Sun and Moon—so complete was the breaking of contact between these ancient companions established by the Creator. The loss of healing put the Earth in a state of shock—searching to find beyond the ethereal ward of the sky some relief. Seeing glimmers of light beyond, it cried ever louder in distress—if only to reach *something* capable of granting relief. But being incapable of reaching relief, the Earth was left to its grief, consuming itself in despair.

Certainly, you might not understand these things. However, Genesis *felt* it. His outstretched hand formed upon it a pink ethereal thread which extended within the Earth's jewel below. The pink thread drew in the cries of the Sun and Moon. As the thread gently passed through the firmament, it refracted into an aurora—which swept over sky, land and seas. And, in turn, Genesis' mind greeted part of the Earth—responding to them with kind reassurance.

With this, the train within Genesis' mind rolled into its station. Just as Genesis was gifted to adjust the pieces on a *Bumble* gameboard, so also could he use his gifts to *adjust* the Earth!

As he stood on the Luminary Watchhand with arm outstretched, Genesis' mind moved back within the walls of his Mahanaim castle. He reflected on the boundless gifts of his many companions who were drawn to him from throughout his new homeland in Mahanaim.

With that thought, Genesis felt a surge of power coursing through his hand and arm—as if the Earth beneath sensed his mind, offering consent unto it.

> *The Earth needs help*, Genesis thought
> ...*We will help*.

The Earth was overjoyed to hear this voice—so long had she cried out without answer. She sensed empathy within the pink aurora—the hand of one with long-lost gifts imparted by the Creator to provide succor.

The thread provided connection to a *true* source of healing, unlike the many men who forced themselves upon the Earth, sky and seas with their fell so-called "solutions"—each only adding ills to future generations.

At the thought of her long-awaited, now imminent restoration, the Earth burst into tears—so overtaken with joy at the dispelling of her despair. As she remained enamored by this thought, Genesis moved himself back within the walls of his Mahanaim castle to make preparations. The pink thread followed in his wake— linking his Mahanaim castle to Earth in intention. The aurora remained in the Earth's sky as a promise—held fast by her as a pledge for the moment of Genesis' return with his company.

2:
Mahanaim Task Force

The next phase in our tale finds us within an immense castle in Mahanaim—located near the border of the Pax and Non-Pax Lands.

This castle is the home of Genesis Pilgrim and the capital of his "Mahanaim task force." The surrounding areas near the castle are built up into gentle hamlets in the deeply forested areas. Differing greatly from others areas of Mahanaim, the *Bumble* prodigy, Genesis, decided long ago to make his home somewhat reminiscent of Earth's Medieval Europe.

Why?

Well, I guess you would have to ask him to know for sure. However, based on several factors we could certainly arrive at some good guesses . . .

<u>First</u>, the economy of Mahanaim—and its culture—differs remarkably from the economies of Earth. Whereas Earth's economy is based on fiat currency and the pursuit of monetary wealth; the people of Mahanaim do not use *empty* numbers. Rather, the people of Mahanaim each pursue ventures fitting with the skills and gifts within himself. So, to be *wealthy* in Mahanaim is to have full-reign to seek after fulfilling self-pursuits based on one's own desire.

Get it?

In Mahanaim, happiness and fulfillment = wealth. No fiat monetary numbers required.

<u>Second</u>, because energy is *freely* available to all Mahanaim citizens through the Ether Grid, there is no need for citizens to work tirelessly at pointless occupations. Each citizen has his place within society where he deems fit. And the Ether Grid sustains him in that place. To explain this simply, when power is free, there is no pressure to work at pointless ventures.

<u>Third</u>, due to the first two points, each Mahanaim citizen is free to find productivity in the desire of his heart. Although this might not work on Earth—as a place

beset by only *physical* thinking—we find on Mahanaim the people desire to contribute. Therefore, each tinkers diligently to discover new things and to create necessary things to support others.

Fourth, because of Mahanaim's emphasis on *Frontiers*—that is *upcoming challenges to humanity as a whole*—the citizens have within themselves a fervor to pursue solutions. Perhaps this is a major motivating factor for individual citizens—as they view *themselves* as necessary to save future generations. Indeed, this is why the division between the Pax and Non-Pax was created. The clear demarcation between the two allow Pax areas to be focused upon expert-based innovation—allowing Mahanaim to make its best effort to prepare for future Frontiers. The people of Mahanaim often work diligently in the Non-Pax, then later bring their discoveries into the Pax to share with others.

It certainly is difficult to explain such things, however. I imagine most people might not find interest in the culture of other worlds. But if you are such a person *who does*, I hope my explanations were helpful.

How is this relevant to our tale?

The four things discussed above each had a hand in rapidly building up the numbers within Genesis new community—which he began to call the "Mahanaim task force." And, when you understand the perspective of Mahanaim citizens and the Mahanaim culture, the castle of Genesis Pilgrim makes sense.

For, within that castle and the surrounding hamlets, the pilgrim gathered unto himself a large community of skilled individuals. Each person who came to Genesis found within the castle and its hamlets happiness and the ability to freely pursue his own self interests amid a thriving, supporting community.

At first, Genesis attracted the attention of many due to his rapid successes in the *Bumble* tournaments. The fixation of Mahanaim upon *Frontiers* led many to see within Genesis a time-travel skill which might be a blessed gift from the Creator—perhaps even necessary one day for the saving of Mahanaim itself. So, you must understand, many desired to be a part of *whatever* was happening in and through Genesis Pilgrim.

Due to his *Bumble* victories, Genesis was deeded a large portion of land, which for him was most suitable— being located near the border of Pax and Non-Pax. In Mahanaim, the Pax areas are highly regulated because they are areas where all serious business is conducted; whereas the Non-Pax areas are wholly unregulated. Now, the Non-Pax areas still have laws to provide justice for the people. But those areas do not have the strict regulations on speech present in the Pax.

This topic will be discussed in more detail elsewhere. But for now, this is a good amount of *introductory* information. Suffice it to say, the location of Genesis' castle provided a good home to many in his company whose skills required frequent visits into the Pax, while simultaneously providing for relaxation and individual research in the countryside of the Non-Pax.

If you want to better understand Genesis' castle company, allow me to use some Earth parallels...

In Genesis' first lifetime upon the Earth, he served as a U.S. Marine First Sergeant. So, he used his vast military knowledge to assemble and train a castle army. He gathered unto himself a band of Mahanaim citizens— whom he trained as warriors. Now, he did not *personally* train them. The two commanders, named Centurion and Zeg-E, oversaw training with the guidance of the pilgrim.

In this way, Genesis quickly became akin to a *Roman general on Earth*—gathering around himself *his own* army. And, as will be discussed elsewhere, although they had no reason to fight on Mahanaim, Genesis ensured his castle army would be matchless among all charted Luminary Systems. He used Centurion to cover *physical* aspects of training; while the Visionary Zeg-E developed profound abilities within the soldiers—even including shape-shifting!

And, since Genesis *was* a first sergeant, he ever sensed the importance of professional development. Within himself he still desired to lead others—giving them the tools they need to succeed in their professional goals. So, you must understand, for anyone on Mahanaim, Genesis was a great boss. Indeed, he wanted all those in his company to be *successful beyond imagination*. As each individual pursued his heart, Genesis worked to recruit more individuals to continue to progress the *big picture*.

Therefore, if you would like to imagine the daily activities of Genesis, picture him travelling to different parts of the castle and the surrounding hamlets to visit his people. With each interaction, the pilgrim would ask his people *what he could do to enhance what they were doing*.

It is funny to consider that the means through which Genesis succeeded on Mahanaim was through a game called *Bumble*. And now, throughout his castle and surrounding territories, Genesis moved similar to a *bumblebee*—cross-pollinating and tending to each individual as if they were each a blessed flower.

When not busied travelling and tending to his people, Genesis diligently worked on his own pursuits. In the Pax, Genesis registered himself as the Accessions Commander for Ancient Israel, Earth. So, while each individual in his castle tinkered, mused and worked, Genesis pored over ancient documents in his own quarters.

Continuing in our Earth-based comparisons, within the castle of Genesis, a large corridor was assigned to the master-tinkerer named The Goat. Think of him as a

Mahanaim *Dr. Frankenstein* type of man. In his youth, the Goat worked as an explorer. And now, in his old age, the Goat levied his many years of exploration to become a master inventor. Indeed, his many years of exploration imparted unto him vast knowledge from nearly every area of the charted Luminary Systems.

So, how was this helpful?

Well, Goat led efforts to outfit Genesis' castle army with the *best* equipment. As Centurion and Zeg-E trained the soldiers, the Goat would constantly design and test new equipment with the soldiers.

And, within the castle of Genesis, we find many more such characters. In a high towered area of the castle, a Visionary named Boggles kept herself secluded—busying herself with observations of the Luminaries and experiments with the Ether Grid. Within those secluded towers, Boggles quietly gained for herself knowledge and ability which far exceeded that of even the Mahanaim Pax!

Now, whenever you have an army, we all know "logistics" is queen. As Sun Tzu taught on Earth, an army that runs out of supplies is stopped in its tracks. However, at the helm of logistics, Boggles' advanced Ether Grid methods ensured there was *always* ample energy to grow food and transfer supplies. And, since Boggles' reach extended into other Luminary Systems, supplies would *never* be a problem for Genesis' army.

Never.

Therefore, one could make a case for Genesis' castle army being the most inexhaustible, terrifyingly-capable infantry of all charted Luminary Systems throughout humanity's history. But for the moment, I digress. We will discuss them in more detail later.

Then you can decide for yourself.

Looking further within the castle, we find many of the people in Genesis' company were profound indeed. Truly, people like Boggles might be far beyond your conception. For, unlike others, I have no tale I could tell you of Boggles' backstory. If I tried, you might laugh—being so incapable of understanding. So, if you wonder why a person such as Boggles would be content secluding herself for an entire lifetime, *hold that thought*. There is much about her now which you might realize as we speak of her in later chapters.

Of course, we could weary ourselves with the examination of *every* individual within Genesis' company. But I trust in our following tale, we will have opportunity for such examinations.

Needless to say, once Genesis determined his calling to "repair the Earth," it was a quick transition indeed. He registered his mission to Earth in Mahanaim's Pax—officially notifying Mahanaim's government of his intent to depart and later return.

Once registered, Genesis prepared rosters and equipment. He designated a *remain behind element* to guard and continue to operate the Mahanaim castle and its hamlets in his absence.

At the appointed time, Genesis and his *Mahanaim task force* departed—enroute to the nearby Earth Luminary System.

According to Mahanaim records, no such feat was ever attempted—*the repair of an entire Luminary System*! So, within the Mahanaim Pax and Non-Pax alike, the people were abuzz with the news.

The people thought, *Surely, if anyone can do it, the Bumble prodigy, Genesis Pilgrim, can!*

On the appointed day the people of Mahanaim sent off Genesis and his company with great fanfare. Some mourned at their departure. Others were hopeful. For, if ever Mahanaim were to face a similar Frontier as Earth, perhaps the experience gained during this mission could provide a template to do likewise for the future generations of Mahanaim.

As time passed, Mahanaim eagerly anticipated news—which arrived regularly from Genesis' Luminary Watchhand camp established atop the Earth's Luminary System. Mahanaim children dreamt of one day being like the great Genesis Pilgrim and those in his company.

And, while Mahanaim remained abuzz with fluttering hearts as they discussed the latest news from the

Luminary Watchhand camp, the company of Genesis moved to bring their detailed plan to fruition.

The future of the Earth depended on them.

<u>3</u>:

Mahanaim Army

The light of the Moon from the nearby Earth gently illuminated the translucent ground of the Luminary Watchhand.

Atop the suspended arc stands the second-in-command of the Mahanaim infantry. His name is Centurion. He is a stern man—battle-tested and direct in all his dealings. He is a man of few words—often preceded by a cadre of associates who go before him to accomplish his will.

Now, we find him as wont—before the assembled formation of the Mahanaim's army. In the fading darkness as evening gives way to the first hints of sunlight, the soldiers appear as shadow warriors—each holding a ranged weapon.

As Centurion moves into his central position before the army, hundreds of shadows shout in unison—letting forth a *battle cry* which shakes the ground. Immediately, in turn, each subordinate leader salutes Centurion—providing an official report on attendance.

With a glint of his visor, and a short command, each leader rushes from his position to Centurion—who provides coordinating instructions for the upcoming day's events.

As I said—Centurion is a man of *few words*. So, *few*, in fact, he seldom spoke in *complete* sentences. His instructions are punctuated—compelling his sergeants to *reflect* on his words.

He has a deep accent, which hitherto has not been accurately defined. This serves to increase the *mystery* of this commander. In areas where he may lack, Centurion gains balance through his reliance upon a cadre of subordinate *sergeants*—who creatively implement their own strategies to accomplish Centurion's instructions.

Thus, we now find Centurion—huddled with a group of his sergeants. Words are exchanged back and forth as they work together—forming a plan, allowing for mutual support of each unit and shared responsibilities within the Mahanaim infantry.

Meanwhile, in the background, stand the assembled *shadow warriors*...silent.

Now, I suppose, this might be a good time for me to share with you some of the specifics about the Mahanaim infantry. So, please, walk with me to the assembled troops...

There are some things you *must* understand. As previously discussed, the Mahanaim Luminary System itself has no need for militaries, armies and warfare. Indeed, such things are foreign to Mahanaim culture.

So, *where* does *this* army come from?

As discussed in an earlier chapter, this assembled army is part of Genesis Pilgrim's Mahanaim castle army. When Genesis left Mahanaim enroute for Earth, he took with him a large portion of his castle army.

Indeed, *whenever* Genesis assembles a task force, he brings with it an army which will best suit the mission. Therefore, the Mahanaim infantry we find today on the Luminary Watchhand has been prepared *specifically* to support the mission of Genesis' task force within the Earth Luminary System.

So, how are these soldiers equipped and what do they do?

Hold your horses and I'll tell you!

And, keep your voice down so you don't disrupt Centurion's meeting!

In each soldier's hand, you see a ranged weapon. If you look closely, you see each weapon differs from others in appearance. This is because the weapons have different capabilities. This is owed to the Goat's penchant for tinkering. As the designer of these weapons, *The Goat* thought it best to provide a wide array of different weapons. And many weapons have been designed specifically for the *exact* soldier who wields it. Perhaps it was the Goat's creativity which guided him to do so. But suffice it to say, each soldier has a weapon.

So, what are the weapons used for?

Similar to a stun gun or a pistol, the *ranged weapons* are capable of being either *non-lethal* or *lethal*. Of course, the application of *deadly force* is always a last resort and typically authorized only in self-defense. After all, the non-lethal functions are quite effective at neutralizing targets through a range of differing effects. Some of the effects are quite creative—yet designed with purpose to prevent *permanent* damage to the target.

We have found nearly all situations can be resolved quite effectively via application of non-lethal force and subsequent negotiations. So, we prefer to get our "enemies" to this stage, rather than resorting to any *permanent* solution. Of course, our "enemies" appreciate this kindness in our military approach.

As a basic run-down of equipment, each soldier has various personal equipment at his disposal—including visors, sound equipment, cloaking devices, and so on. I guess if you want a quick explanation, suffice it to say, each soldier has equipment to widen the range of his perception. This makes Mahanaim soldiers excellent watch-standers—possessing the ability to "see" things well beyond *normal* human limits.

Now, let's talk about some *other* things…

As I have said, the citizens of Mahanaim are *quite different* from citizens on Earth.

How?

Well, you see *on Earth*, humans are generally imprisoned within their lower 3rd Dimension perspective—viewing *everything* as *physical*. In other words, the mind of an Earth human is connected merely to his brain. Thus, the Earth human tends to think of everything as "physical." If you are not familiar with this, let me assure you, it is quite boring.

However, the citizens of Mahanaim have a *deeper* grasp of those lower dimensions—1st, 2nd, 3rd, and some, like Genesis, can even reach *beyond* into the further dimensions, such as the 4th or 5th. And, when a person is 4th Dimension capable, the lower dimensions are able to be perceived in far different ways.

So, how does this apply to these soldiers in front of us?

Glad you asked!

Although many of these soldiers are not 4th Dimensional—and certainly none are 5th Dimensional— these soldiers are *thoroughly* 1st, 2nd and 3rd Dimensional.

What does this mean?

Well, they can channel different dimensions of their being—toggling in and out of certain manifestations. And, with this ability to *toggle in and out* of different dimensions of being, the Mahanaim soldiers gain some *powerful* battlefield enhancements.

In other words, you might seem intimidated when viewing these soldiers in "human form," but if provoked or necessity requires, these soldiers can *shift* themselves into a baser form to better confront challenges presented.

Look here…

Each soldier is wearing what appears to be a cloak which is stitched to offer maximum movement during physical activity. However, what you will quickly notice with closer inspection is that each cloak has different bunches and extra folds of cloth and hard material. Many of these variances are in different positions—and no two cloaks are *exactly* alike.

Suffice it to say, the variances of each soldier's cloak have been tailored to his exact manifestations of being. The *ranged* form of every soldier is his *human* form. So, while firing a ranged weapon, a Mahanaim soldier will remain in human form.

But if a Mahanaim soldier *needs* to go hands-on against an enemy, he immediately *shifts* out of human form into *another* form—channeling either the 1st, 2nd, or 3rd Dimension of his being. Therefore, the cloak of each soldier is designed to fit *both* forms of the soldier. Thus, the cloak of each soldier allows for an immediate securing of human gear so that nothing is lost in the transformations back and forth.

This means the soldier can fire his weapon while in human form, then immediately shift to *another* form. You will notice the weapon of each soldier is *tethered* to his body. This allows it to be automatically stowed when the soldier changes his form. This makes transitions into different forms seamless. A soldier can fire his weapon, then in a flash assume an animal form to chase or evade his enemy. Then he can flash back into his human form just as quickly.

Get it?

I know this might seem bizarre—especially if you are not familiar with the different *dimensions*. But don't worry, you'll figure it out. I have faith in you.

I guess perhaps one of the first places you might become accustomed further with the Mahanaim army might be in viewing how they support Genesis and his cadre…

I'll give you a clue: The military "dogs" aren't "*dogs*." And, you would find those "dogs" are also as smart as humans…*exactly* as smart in fact.

"Can you guess why?" I ask with tongue in cheek.

And, I won't spoil the surprise, but *dogs* are just the *beginning*.

As we end our tour of the Mahanaim army, let me offer you a bit of advice:

Whatever you do, make sure these guys are always on your side!

And, for any enemy's sake, let's hope they do nothing to provoke Centurion—because his form is something *far greater* than the form of a dog.

Last, if the Mahanaim army is *shooting*, those *humans* can be reasoned with.

But if they *stop shooting*—run!

4:
Scouting Earth

The late morning Sun shone brightly overhead—showering Lewis in white light. Somehow it was different than he remembered it. His eyebrows fell as he searched his memories. Lewis recalled the Sun appearing more golden than it now appeared. But just as quickly as the "thought" emerged, it left him.

He now breathed in deeply as he stretched his arms to the sky. He felt great—so great in fact, he felt as if he could stretch his arms far enough to reach the clouds over him. The stretch was so complete it transformed into a *yawn*, followed by a motivated *shout* . . .

"Hooo!"

The shout rustled the wilderness around him—as if shaking the birds from the bushes and trees, peppering them into the sky above.

Lewis shot his arms left and right, twisting his trunk—then lifting his legs, each in turn. He felt rejuvenated—as if he just flipped the circuit breakers of his body. His body now limber; his mind focused on his task.

Lewis reached into his pocket—freeing a roll of paper. Unrolling it, Lewis' finger traced the words, until they arrived at their destination. He paused for a moment—drinking in the instructions written on the page. Then, re-rolling the paper, he placed it back within his pocket.

"Come on Mage, let's go!" Lewis called out.

A moment later, his expedition partner emerged—map in hand.

"Lewis, do you have everything you need?"

"Yes, it certainly appears so. We will want to get back soon so we can report our findings."

"Okay, that sounds good. I'll signal the Anchor," Mage stated as she fidgeted with a device on her wrist.

The map—now under Mage's arm—flapped in the gentle breeze.

"*Beep, beep, zip,*" whispered Mage's device. As if responding to the beeps, Mage looked up: "Transport is on the way. Just waiting for noon."

Lewis nodded.

Mage looks down—now turning her attention to properly stowing away her map. Then, she began looking over her gear—ensuring everything is in place. Over the last week, Lewis observed Mage's extreme attention-to-detail.
She certainly is meticulous, he noted—a characteristic most desired in an explorer.

Lewis and Mage stand quietly. As the wind passes, it returns to Lewis' mind a thought he held just a moment earlier. Lewis' eyebrows fall once again. He winces—as his thought beckons him saunter past Mage.
As she watches Lewis climb a hill—Mage supposes Lewis was simply following a hidden rabbit trail within his mind.
He certainly is inquisitive, she noted.

Mage—still stowing her gear as she climbed—arrived at the top of the hill to find Lewis, looking upward at the sky.

"So, whatcha looking at?" Mage asked playfully.

"Mage, it looks different."

Mage's eyes darted back and forth—working to trace out the object of Lewis' attention.

"*What* looks different?"

"*Everything*," Lewis answered. Lewis searched his mind—attempting to locate and put the right words together. He felt as if he was wrestling a jigsaw puzzle. Finding nothing further to describe his thought, Lewis reluctantly yielded to silence.

A moment passed with both explorers standing atop the hill looking at the sky.

Lewis broke the silence—

"Mage, I guess it is just how I *feel*. I know this world, but it all seems so different. Earth seems as if it was knocked off balance. It appears everything is still here just like before—only it is all *different*."

The breeze halted and Lewis' words hung in the air.

In their two-man team, Mage was the one who was brainy and thorough; while Lewis balanced her attributes with his boldness. Whereas Lewis was comfortable charging into a thought; Mage was cautious as a detail-oriented planner.

Carefully considering Lewis, Mage worked to distill his thought into a workable form . . .

"Lewis, what do you see and feel which seems 'off-balance?' Can you explain?"

Lewis always appreciated the concern Mage showed him. It was as if Mage constantly moved to funnel Lewis toward progress. In other words, Mage was the peanut butter for Lewis' jelly.

"That! Right there!" Lewis exclaimed dramatically, motioning with his hand arching over half the sky. He had a knack for comedy—so he tended to act out his interactions in over-the-top ways.

"*Uh huh*," Mage replied—watching Lewis dance in front of her, arms jutting out, pointing to the north, south, east and west.

"Can you be *more specific*?" Mage offered with a laugh.

"The whole half of the sky is white—like a *flipping* light bulb without the filament."

"What do you mean?"

"Mage, point to the Sun—show me *exactly* where it is in that white glowing."

"The sky's too bright to see it."

"That's my point, Mage. This half of the entire sky is as bright as the Sun, but it is *white*."

"Oh, I see," Mage answered with a finger resting on her temple.

Lewis' knack for drama extended to his explanations, "Mage, it is like the sun is a scoop of butter. As I remember it, the Sun would always be that single pat of *golden* butter. But now when we look at the sky it is like the pat of *white* butter is spread across about half of the sky every day. We can't point to the Sun most days and it is like its energy is dispersed *throughout* the sky."

Mage appreciated Lewis' explanation. She reflected on her casual observations of the sky over the duration of their scouting mission. She now remembered seeing this, even though she didn't take conscious note of it.

"Now that you mention it, Lewis, the sky does look . . . *different*," Mage agreed. "Come to think of it, the sky *does* look like a light bulb without a filament. I don't remember it looking like this before."

"*I know, right!?*" Lewis rhetorically exclaimed. His mixed emotions coalesced into a gulp. He swallowed hard—thankful for Mage's level-headed agreement, yet conflicted with what this could mean.

Lewis often mused at the calculated manner in which Mage approached *all* things. At first, he expected her to dismiss his "sky talk" as nonsense. But now his mind was reeling. Mage confirmed Lewis' observations weren't just *in his head*.

Lewis' mind swirled and his vision tunneled. He suddenly realized he hadn't breathed for a while, so he took a deep nasal breath.

The hair on Mage's neck stood on end. She always *hated* the sound of Lewis' deep exasperated breaths. She heard them *often* at nearly *every* juncture of *every* journey as her fellow explorer toggled with his inner thoughts.

Mage shook herself free of her preoccupation with Lewis' breath. She broke the moment of silence:

"The sky certainly is eerie."

As the words left Mage's mouth, she shivered. The cold air from sky overhead cascaded down the hill in a faint fog. It felt as if the weather shifted.

Suddenly the two explorers were united with a shared perception—as if their hearts blazed a silent message to one another:

"This is *not* our home."

Thus, the scouting mission which preceded the Mahanaim task force's arrival came to a close. The two chief explorers—Lewis and Mage, who lived their first lives upon Earth, arrived at the same conclusion of Genesis Pilgrim...

The Earth was different—a mere wraith of what it once was. And, even to those ungifted in the grand *Bumble* perceptions of the pilgrim, the brokenness of the Earth was apparent in at least a veiled form.

Mage and Lewis spent their last minutes on Earth in silence—surveying the sky as they waited for the noon transport. Although their hearts reeled at what this revelation could mean, both became certain the "solution"—whatever *solution* might be—was beyond their assignment.

After all, they were *explorers*—charged with *exploration*. And, although Lewis' heart broke with his realization of the broken sky, he was left to stew in his helplessness. Surely, he could make a report of his observation, but he would do so only as a parting shot before being presumably whisked away to another far off mission.

What will happen to Earth? Lewis reflected.

As he pondered, tears welled in his eyes as he fondly recalled his past life in this good place. And, in those thoughts, Lewis—for the first time—felt the gentle stirrings of the Earth as she signaled her despair. The Earth so often called with no one to hear. But now, with Lewis' feet pressed intently on the surface of the ground and his heart tuned to that voice, the Earth found a friend. The Earth spoke to Lewis without speech—and the message was clear in the moments before the transport arrived:

Lewis, remember me.

Thus, Lewis and Mage ended their scouting mission. Upon the report of their findings in the Luminary Watchhand camp, Genesis' "Mahanaim task force" made final preparations to commence the Earth mission.

****

Of course, at this point you may have some questions . . .

Perhaps *many* questions.

I sure did.

Considering the scouting mission of Lewis and Mage on the Earth, you may be left wondering about *security*. After all, as you will see, during the other missions upon the Earth, it was common for Genesis' teams to take with them a *security element* of some kind.

So, what's the deal with the lonely explorer missions? Why were Mage and Lewis sent out by themselves?

Well, at this time it might be best to clue you in on some helpful details about Mahanaim's military . . . specifically, how Mage and Lewis were protected during their meanderings about the Earth.

Let me introduce you to a shadowy figure . . .

Her name is Zeg-E. We discussed her briefly in Chapter 2. On this particular day we find her staring at a hilltop through the aiming apparatus of her ranged weapon—scanning the area around Mage and Lewis.

Zeg-E reaches into her pocket, then places a disk into her mouth. The disk is pushed aside by her tongue—coming to rest betwixt her teeth and cheek. She feels her pulse slow as her vision tightens. A warmth passes through her arms—giving an airy sensation to her fingertips as they caress the trigger assembly of her firearm.

As Mage and Lewis crest the hilltop, Zeg-E toggles position—instantly *teleporting* to multiple sides of the hill to gain a fuller perspective.

Actually, it might not be accurate to say Zeg-E "teleported" to different locations. Sticking with my original statement, there are many things you might not understand about people from the Mahanaim Luminary System. And, Zeg-E is certainly a mystery.

It would be much more accurate to say Zeg-E "occupies" multiple physical locations at once—simply shifting her consciousness from one physical location to another at will.

Now, we are left to simply ponder at the significance of such an ability—or how it could be used most effectively by a sniper like Zeg-E. Perhaps this ability to disperse oneself through multiple physical locations makes "sniper" a good fit for one with Zeg-E's skill. After all, when her consciousness is in one location, it might be helpful for the other locations of her body to remain motionless as she leaves them—simply staring through the scope of a rifle.

Actually, I have reflected on this quite a bit and how I would use this skill if I were Zeg-E. I reckon it might be best for Zeg-E to rapidly shift her consciousness through her multiple bodies—ensuring each "body" is always sighted in and ready to shoot at a target.

Then, when moving forward from one location to another, it would be a simple issue of bounding forth—one body at a time, shifting one's consciousness from one body to another, setting each one in position.

In fact, when reflecting on Zeg-E's ability, we find it is a most helpful skill—where she could even cover her own withdrawal or advancement through an area by laying down *her own* cover fire.

I reckon this is how Zeg-E does it. But frankly, I have no idea. Of course, if I had such an ability, I might be clunky and make mistakes. When moving from one physical location to another, I might stagger to remember the details of each body's location.

But I am quite sure Zeg-E has no such problems because this skillset has been all she has known.

Like other Mahanaim soldiers, Zeg-E's clothing and equipment are nearly identical. She wears a veiled cloak and carries with her a ranged weapon—preferring to use "stunning" shots to neutralize targets. So, if she were found among other soldiers, it is likely she would be indistinguishable—which is just how she prefers.

Perhaps the only distinguishable mark on Zeg-E is a small plate of inscribed metal held tightly around her neck by two bands.

What does the necklace say?

Who knows?

But, legend around camp has it the plate has inscriptions on the front and back—which are used to identify the one carrying it. And, the story has it that this is the same "tag" which identified Zeg-E from the time when she was a little girl.

It is a sad story actually—and one just as mysterious as the sniper who is before us.

It is told Zeg-E is from an unknown Luminary System—perhaps one that is currently recognized as "uncharted" by Mahanaim. She was reported found as a young girl in a city called Zegopolis in a region known as District E. If this is true, her name certainly makes sense—tying her back to her origin in this place. And having no name nor records, Zeg-E could find an anchor of sorts by holding to this place with fondness.

But it is unlikely you would get Zeg-E to speak to you about such things.

Like many of the Mahanaim soldiers, Zeg-E is a lady of few words—preferring solitude and the quiet accomplishment of her mission. Although Zeg-E is the official commander of the Mahanaim army, she often leaves her second-in-command, named Centurion, in charge. After all, Centurion is a strict disciplinarian and a stickler for details. So, after receiving orders from Genesis or Goat, Zeg-E would often briefly discuss matters with Centurion—who in turn would assign soldiers to specific missions. And, then, Zeg-E was "free" to pursue *other* ventures.

So, why am I telling you this?

Well, in all cases where it might "appear" Genesis and his people are vulnerable to attack, please always be mindful of Zeg-E. Genesis or his people might "appear" to walk alone, but if threatened *for even a moment*, a hail of fire from a *single* sniper could descend upon enemies from *many* directions.

So, how many "physical locations" can Zeg-E occupy?

Who knows?

Sure, if you or I—who are personally unfamiliar with this ability—were to be endowed with this measure of grace today, it is likely we might only be capable of managing maybe three or four physical locations at once. But, in Zeg-E's case—who has practiced this unique ability *for a lifetime*—I am sure the possibilities are quite endless. Maybe even twenty or thirty positions!

So, how does she find that many rifles?

I reckon that is a part of her practiced ability—to simply re-manifest her personal items with each physical location of her body, using the "projections" of each item at each location.

Certainly, Zeg-E is in the running for the most unique and helpful ability among the Mahanaim task force.

So, today, we step back from Zeg-E—leaving her as we found her: Quietly staring through the scope of her rifle, rolling the disk to the side of her mouth.

There is one thing I *do* know:

I'm glad she's on my side.

5:
Earth Politicians

The silence of the auditorium was broken as Genesis and his team entered the room with a *buzz*, then a *SNAP!*

The politicians—who just a moment earlier were astir with conversation—now speechless. No matter how many times the pilgrim appeared, it still demanded attention.

Some of the politicians were disheartened, however, being long desensitized by Hollywood *extra-*

terrestrials—aliens who arrived in three-dimensional UFOs, landing, then slowly walking down long ramps from their aircraft. Somehow—no matter how spectacular was Genesis' emergence from the 4th Dimension—there were still humans who were left desiring something more akin to the movie portrayals.

But Genesis was not an alien. He was simply a man like any other man. And, perhaps in this way, he and his team were *even more remarkable* than the Earthling ideas of "aliens." For the concept of aliens really was not that fantastic. After all, *aliens* in popular lore were still wholly dependent on the lower *three dimensions*—having UFOs made of *physical* matter and supposedly arriving from other "planets." But these planets were nonetheless in popular thought still considered to be *three-dimensional*, *physical* places, contained in the far-off realms of the *physical* "universe."

Although the politicians still held to some of those beliefs—in aliens, UFOs and whatnot—Genesis and his team thought them ridiculous, having seen for themselves the true position and outward characteristics of the Earth, Sun and Moon.

Indeed, there were vast differences between the worldview of the pilgrim and the Earthlings. Whereas the Earthlings desired for Genesis to "fit" their preconceived notions of the extra-terrestrial; Genesis held within his mind a well-developed understanding of the full *spiritual* reality *beyond* the 3rd Dimension. Therefore, Genesis grew weary with such thoughts of "aliens" and endless "outer space"—knowing they were responsible for keeping the minds of humans held captive, never capable of "seeing" anything beyond the physical...imagining that even the far off "planets" were similar to their own limited conception of Earth. And in this, the *physical-minded* Earthlings erred—most grievously.

Perhaps it would have been best for the politicians to abandon all such Hollywood thoughts—simply seeking to understand the appearances of Genesis based on their own merit. But this is the struggle of all such people who are entrenched in physical deception. They *cannot* see—even when the truth is placed before their eyes. Had the politicians carefully reflected, they could have easily understood the nature of reality. For the buzzing appearance of the pilgrim and his council revealed their ability to *altogether defy the physical*—transporting themselves within and without at will.

Indeed, Genesis and his team held no trinket nor *physical* device—further indicating that their transcendent ability was not one controlled by *anything physical*. Rather it was the *mind* of the pilgrim which was transcendent—and through their association with his mind the members of his company were capable of travelling with him throughout time.

So, all these things were made plain...most plain...if only the politicians cared to examine what they saw, piecing it together.

But they did not. Truly they could not. Sadly, this was a trend among those held captive by the cage of the first three dimensions: They were ever seeing, but never coming to the knowledge of the truth. Whereas those held captive walked by *physical sight*; Genesis was subject to a higher Law...he learned to walk by *faith*, not by sight.

Nevertheless, the details held within the visions of Genesis' appearances indicated most clearly that the Law of the higher dimensions is one governed by "transcendence"—not covering physical space, like a UFO bumbling its way through an empty vacuum for light ages (a most laughable thought for anyone who has achieved 4th Dimension capability). And, since the Law of the higher dimensions allows for the complete transcendence of lower dimensions, this means that human advancement is based on *spirituality*—not *physical* things.

However, I digress.

Here stands Genesis: With his cadre, before the politicians in the midst of a grand auditorium. In the brief moment after their arrival, the *crackling* of their jump within the 3rd Dimension subsided. Waves of energy rapidly raced to find their place—and once satisfied, passed into the spiritual Oblivion beyond, concealing the source of their arrival, awaiting their next command from the pilgrim.

While the politicians were held captive by thoughts of such grand, unexplainable appearances; Genesis and his team were much too busy to be distracted by such things. Whereas lesser men desired to gain such power for themselves; the Mahanaim task force was on a mission—simply moving from one point to another to accomplish a set purpose.

And today that purpose compelled Genesis to venture into this large room.

Perhaps it was Genesis' unconcern for power which guided him to gain such incredible power in the first place. After all, other men often desire power—like how the politicians loved to be treated with special honor among their citizenry. But Genesis despised such things. Having gained for himself all types of honor in his previous life and upon Mahanaim, he fully grasped the depths contained within human praise and fully understood its limits—its spurring of blind, fallen ambition. And, in such grasping, the pilgrim learned the praises offered by men accomplish no good purpose. Thus, the pilgrim detested such things. He had no desire to gain glory in the realm of captive humanity. So, whenever approached with praise or compliment, Genesis was most wary of the potentially sycophant purpose of the complementor. But even more important, Genesis was wary of the corruption of his own heart if allowed to receive personal praise unguarded. For this reason, Genesis found it best to altogether dismiss such thoughts when he saw the compliments and praises of others welling up in their eyes in the moment before they began to deliver the words. And, in those moments, the pilgrim always moved to hasty retreat—countering the fell effects of praise before they could take root within him.

Thus, in this moment, Genesis quickly began his address, giving no opportunity for his hosts to settle from the magnificent appearance, nor for praises to form on their lips…

"Ladies and gentlemen: When last we departed, we left with an agreement to reconvene to discuss matters further. Today, our desire is to present a detailed plan showing how we will repair the Earth."

Genesis gestures toward one of his companions—who is holding a large stack of papers, as if to verify the preparations are in order.

Genesis' companion anxiously nods in approval, as if seeking to unburden himself with his ungainly stack. Satisfied with the non-verbal signal of the companion, the pilgrim finishes:

"We are ready to do that now. We can leave these documents with you for your review."

"*Not so fast*," replied Mr. Sly, being incredulously uncordial with his guests, "We have questions which need answering."

Being the ranking member of the political assembly, Mr. Sly had the Earthly authority to withhold the approval of the political council.

"Certainly," replied Genesis, much to the noticeable chagrin of his burdened companion—as he shifted his weight from his shoulders to his hips, with a crackling of his knee. The stack of papers weighed heavily in his hands. He gasped with the realization that his unburdening would be delayed.

Seeing the dismay of his companion, Genesis smirked and shook his head—coughing back laughter at the hilarious frazzling of the man with the papers.

Without concern for the stack of papers, Mr. Sly began anew…

"*Genesis*—if that is what we are to call you—"

"Yes, that's fine."

"Okay, *Genesis*, what is it that *you* and your people intend to do to *our* planet?"

"Rather than give you an exhaustive *verbal* answer, I will provide this *detailed* plan," Genesis stated with a gesture to the stack of papers, "This will allow you and your political counsel to read it thoroughly for yourself, in addition to consulting with experts to do feasibility analyses." The cloaked pilgrim nodded, "I am confident this plan will hold up to rigorous scrutiny."

"Well, that is not what I asked, Genesis. I want you to *explain* to us what the written plan states."

"No," the pilgrim cut.

"*What do you mean, "No!?*" countered Mr. Sly. In his ornate council chair Mr. Sly felt as if the authority of his entire country rested upon his contentment. Within his hand his gavel rested, being held with purpose. In many earlier meetings before the arrival of the Mahanaim task force, Mr. Sly would use his gavel most liberally to bracket sessions—compelling speakers to move according to *his* agenda. The gripping of his gavel indicated Mr. Sly desired to do the same in *this* meeting—holding the altogether vain thought that anything three-dimensional, *let alone a silly wooden mallet*, could bend and break the will of an opponent who travels through time at will.

Genesis was defiant, and his next statement was directed at solving a long-time problem with the political system of Earth…

"Mr. Sly, there will be no easy answers. I will not provide *Cliffs Notes* to politicians who are too lazy to be thorough. This is *your* Earth, and you will have the discipline to read through the plan *in its entirety—for yourself*. Then you will understand. Only when you make great effort to emerge from your own ignorance will I answer your questions. But in the meantime, you have some reading to do."

Without a pause, Genesis motions to his companion with pointed finger indicating the exact place on the table where the documents are to be placed.

Genesis' companion traces a line from the extended finger of the pilgrim, walking toward the intersection of the line to the table which opposes it. The companion makes his first step up the flight of stairs to the large council desk before him.

"Hold it!" retorted Mr. Sly, almost slamming his gavel out of habit, yet restraining himself at the final moment. Sly objected to the pilgrim before he understood why. There was something about Genesis which Mr. Sly found annoying—or at least it appeared that way. Perhaps Mr. Sly didn't like the idea of anyone in his auditorium who held authority which superseded his own. And certainly, if that was the case, Genesis held such power— for his power was not based on any appointment by human whim or popular vote, but by a *power* which altogether transcended the physical fabric of the created order.

Realizing Mr. Sly was stuck—being unsure of his objections, Genesis decided to peer into Mr. Sly's mind, addressing his objection at its roots.

"Mr. Sly—"

Genesis was interrupted by Mr. Overcompensate—a slender politician seated to the right of Mr. Sly.

"Genesis, we have many scientists, ecologists and intelligent people. We have everything under control. There is no reason why we would need an exhaustive plan from *you* and *your* team. *We* can repair the planet on our own," Mr. Overcompensate orated from his aloof position with a dismissive wave of his hand.

Genesis answered, his attention now divided between both Mr. Sly and Mr. Overcompensate:

"Gentlemen, first it is important for you to understand, Earth is not a 'planet.' In fact, it is something different altogether. Since you do not even understand the *nature* of the Earth, your idea that *you* will somehow muster the ability to *fix it* is ridiculous. So, please allow me latitude to offer a brief answer."

Mr. Overcompensate's eyes darted across the room, then fell fixed to the table before him as he cleared the lump in his throat. Mr. Sly's face, now red, still hinted at the loss of words within his mind. Still grasping his gavel, Mr. Sly motioned with his free hand—signaling Genesis to speak further.

Genesis continued, "Ladies and gentlemen, this brief exchange highlights a severe problem with the political system of the Earth—which ultimately has led to the degradation of the Earth's environments. Understand this…

"The problem with Earth's politics is that it does not appoint actual *experts* to solve problems within their areas of expertise. Rather, Earth's politics appoint people who *do not* possess requisite knowledge.

Mr. Sly felt compelled to speak, yet somehow, he was restrained from within—being unable to do so. The room remained quiet as the words of the pilgrim danced before the council—piercing hearts, beckoning change from those capable of it.

"In the entire realm of Earth's politics there are very few experts, but many smooth-talkers. Many politicians begin their careers as lawyers. Now, let's consider the role of a lawyer: A lawyer *never* has to be right; he just needs to be capable of *convincing* a jury or judge into believing his words. And, it is in such a position we find ourselves today. Despite my presentation of a detailed plan to fix the Earth you have destroyed, you want me to give you a summary because you are too lazy to do the work for yourself—to use your own time wisely to build your own knowledge of the Earth's problems by carefully weighing the testimony of true experts.

"Concerning the state of the Earth, there are no Earth 'experts'—whether scientists, ecologists, or whatever—who hold superior knowledge to my Mahanaim task force. We alone know and understand the *true* condition of the Earth. Yet, despite our clear mastery of these things, your senior council member, Mr. Sly, decides to use a lawyer-tactic—turning this most necessary meeting into a battle of wills. But I did not travel through time to banter nonsense with undisciplined people who do not take the time to read plans for themselves.

"Therefore, do not be deceived. The only pathway to the repair of the Earth during your generation is found within these papers," Genesis motions to the stack, now appearing before Mr. Sly, "And *you* will find the discipline to fulfill your calling as public representatives. *You* will read and study. *You* will prepare questions. And through that diligent study you will prepare yourselves to speak intelligently on the topic during our next meeting."

An observant person *might* have noticed the crackle which occurred as the papers vanished from the hands of Genesis' companion. In a blue bolt, the papers re-emerged from Oblivion, finding themselves on the table before Mr. Sly. So quick was the transfer of the papers, it was likely missed by all in the room—occurring with the blink of an eye. Perhaps the most observant would note how the papers were transported apart from the companion who held them. And, if there was one such observant person within that auditorium, his eyes may have been opened briefly to another glimpse of transcendence…maybe even one more convincing than the first appearance of the team. But who are we to say for sure?

Nevertheless, as Genesis spoke, Mr. Overcompensate listened attentively. During the brief exchange, he was struck with a realization—a feeling as if he spoke out of turn. A sincerity welled up within him. Desiring to take back the abruptness of his earlier dismissal, he gestured to the pilgrim…

"Genesis, I apologize for what I said. You and your team *are* appreciated, and we welcome your leadership. I can speak for myself in saying I need to learn more about this topic: *Repairing the Earth*, as you call it."

"Well, thank you, sir. I am here to help," Genesis replied cordially—always eager to move forward with people, preferring forgiveness and teamwork to accomplish mutual goals.

"Mr. Overcompensate, it pains me to see the Earth in its dire condition—crying out for help. So, it is tough for me to have such a strong desire to offer assistance in an uncharted venture. I know this is new to you ladies and gentlemen, so I will do my best to be understanding as we develop a solution together. But to be upfront, I am requiring *all* the Earth politicians to act like experts— examining this issue diligently *for themselves*. Then we can solve these problems together."

Mr. Overcompensate now felt settled, having a position from which he felt comfortable asking another question…

"Genesis, if you don't mind explaining more, I find your discussion of politics intriguing—particularly how expertise and politics interact with one another."

Genesis was always guarded against sycophants. This led him to carefully weigh the intentions of Mr. Overcompensate. Finding him inwardly genuine, Genesis decided to expound further...

"Mr. Overcompensate, I can offer more perspective on that issue. Perhaps if I explain more about politics, you and your council may better understand our perspective."

"Yes, please!" Mr. Overcompensate shifted in his seat. Despite the fact that Genesis a moment earlier *tore into* the political council—an event from which Mr. Sly still held silent, as if using all his strength to balance his motionless gavel in his hand—Mr. Overcompensate and the rest of the politicians were still enamored by the otherworldly appearance of Genesis and his team. And, in this miraculous occasion, the politicians wanted to take full advantage—learning all that they could from the time-traveler before them.

Genesis began, "My task force is from a Luminary System called 'Mahanaim.'"

"What is a *'Luminary System*?'"

Genesis sighed and felt defeated at this immediate emergence of an incredible red herring—a red herring which in fact challenged the entire worldview of all the people seated before him.

Such was the nature of the 4th Dimension and Beyond: No matter how well it was explained, those held captive by the first three dimensions held within themselves a powerful *ward* of sorts. Genesis was all too familiar with this show-stopper, which would always pull the consciousness of a person so trapped from conversation. Genesis would see firsthand how the nature of the first three dimensions would pull and close off its captives from the acceptance of anything beyond its own borders. It was a most powerful magic of the physical realm—an automatic demonic power which ever tethered the minds of those held within, pulling them back, causing their minds to lock when approaching the barriers of the 3rd Dimension: A person's eyes would glaze over as his mind was pulled back to thoughts within his own physical cage. Cognitive dissonance would bar the minds of 3rd Dimension humans—preventing them from shaking themselves free of its hold.

The question of Mr. Overcompensate hung in the air. The anticipation of the politicians rose as they viewed the motionless pilgrim before them. Genesis had a habit of becoming *lost in thought*. In Mahanaim, people grew accustomed to *waiting* for the pilgrim. They recognized

this was a part of the inner operation of Genesis—
something which needed to be simply accepted. Many
believed Genesis needed to think more deeply as a trade-
off for the miraculous power which resided within him—
as if such power commanded an inner division of his
consciousness. And, perhaps, this was true. Nevertheless,
it was a known fact: If one ventured to learn from the
pilgrim, they would need to have the discipline to wait for
answers to emerge.

Silence rested upon the auditorium. Those
accustomed to a constant rustling of noise became
restless, yet somehow held in reverence—fearful to break
the silence, unsure of its purpose.

For those within Genesis' council, they were often
left with thoughts of what to do with such moments of
silence—as they awaited responses from Genesis. Many
of those on Genesis' team thought these moments as
times where they were being likewise beckoned into their
own time of inner reflection. So, they simply did what
Genesis did—they allowed the peace of the moment to
wash over themselves, retreating for a moment in inner
reflection until the moment when they were likewise
beckoned back to the conversation.

Somehow the silence of the pilgrim ever reminded
his companions that the "power" of Genesis was not
inferior to him. Rather, the power of the pilgrim was
beyond him—something with which he made constant
effort to align himself. And, in this inner aligning the
power of Genesis was somehow sustained. Therefore, in

times of silence, the team of Genesis also held themselves in silence—some even bowing their heads in reverence within themselves, beseeching the Creator to grant them wisdom and power for the Frontiers ahead.

It made for a most bizarre contrast: Whereas Genesis and his companions remained silent and motionless—save for the bowing of some heads in reflection; some of the politicians began to stir nervously, pulling their cell phones from their pockets or fidgeting with the items on the table before them. And, in this simple example, perhaps one could witness the root cause of those who achieved transcendence: Reverence and inner reflection in moments of silence rather than an anxious stirring with the physical. In a sharp demonstration of irony, the Earthlings took in hand a device called a "cell," rather than reflect on the magnificence of the present moment. Indeed, there is no better way to illustrate the dire entrapment of Earthlings within the physical dimensions.

Genesis reemerged from his mind, finally answering the question of Mr. Overcompensate. Carefully accounting for the warding of the 3rd Dimension, Genesis delivered his words, trying to avoid losing his listeners…

"A 'Luminary System' is a land consisting of its own luminaries."

"You mean you are from a *planet* called Mahanaim?" Mr. Overcompensate asked further, "In which galaxy and star system is Mahanaim located?"

"Mr. Overcompensate, I do not want to miss you on this point, but the *stars* are completely different than what is thought on Earth. For example, Earth is not a *planet*. And Mahanaim isn't a *planet*. The Sun is *not* a giant ball of gas, and the Earth is *not* travelling around it."

Mr. Overcompensate's eyes immediately glazed over and the rest of the politicians were noticeably distracted. Apparently, all of them jumped in the river to view the red fish—the 3rd Dimension ward was working its fell purpose of distraction.

Genesis again retreated momentarily within the thought of the powerful ward of the 3rd Dimension. He mused within himself, considering if he ever finds a way to help these people, he must find a way to dispel the warding of the 3rd Dimension. Genesis noted within himself that careful explanations are not capable of helping a trapped person break free.

So, Genesis carefully files this thought within the halls of his mind: *I must find a way to dispel the ward of the 3rd Dimension to reach those held captive within its cage.*

Genesis quickly created distance from the distraction of this point...

"Never mind that for now, Mr. Overcompensate—about planets and the nature of the Earth."

Mr. Overcompensate nodded reluctantly as confusion remained upon his face.

The pilgrim continued, "Suffice it to say, our politics on Mahanaim are quite different from Earth's politics."

"How so?"

"We use a system called Pax Law to promote the use of expertise and ensure rights for citizens."

"You mean Pax Law—like the *Pax Romana* of the Roman Empire?"

"Well, it is based on that general idea, but it is very different."

"How?"

Genesis appeared momentarily distracted. He gestured toward one of his counterparts, who in turn gestured back to the pilgrim—as if inviting him to continue speaking on the topic.

"Well, here goes," Genesis shrugged, "In Mahanaim we have two types of governed lands. One is called 'Pax Lands' and the other is called 'Non-Pax Lands.' Both types operate under their own list of laws, and citizens are free to choose where they desire to live. But whenever a citizen is located in a Pax Land, he is required to follow Pax Law."

"Interesting."

"Yes, it is a good system for many reasons," Genesis continued, "It is good because citizens can choose for themselves their own level of governance. In other words, Pax Law extends consent to individuals rather than compelling people against their own will. So, a person who does not desire to live under the governance of Pax is free to abide in a Non-Pax region."

"Understood, Genesis. Pax Law extends consent to citizens. What else?"

"Well, in Pax areas, 'white noise' is prohibited."

"What do you mean?"

"In order for a person to speak on a topic in Pax Lands, they must hold credentials of expertise on that specific topic."

"So, there's no free speech?"

"There is—in Non-Pax Lands, people can say *whatever* they want. And, as a result, whenever you are in Non-Pax Lands you generally distrust what people say— meeting their comments with skepticism. After all, in a Non-Pax region, you might be talking to a person with expertise, or you might be talking to a crazy person who is attempting to mislead you. In fact, many people prefer living in Non-Pax areas for this purpose. Many people enjoy the light-hearted banter and lively social interaction. But in Mahanaim, we separate these things from our regions which are dedicated to society's advancement. This is why Pax areas prohibit bragging, bullying and fishing for compliments among other forms of meaningless rhetoric. In fact, in Pax areas an individual cannot ask another individual to do things for him because requests need to have *direct benefit* to the person accomplishing the task. The only exception to this is when a person has consented to an apprenticeship—then the teacher can assign tasks to his apprentice. But beyond this, veiled attempts to get others to do work *for you* are not allowed. A person must be *direct* in asking another for something. In other words, no *fishing*—whether for compliments, personal benefit, et cetera."

Genesis trails off, recognizing the deep nuance contained in the articulation of these points, so he digresses—settling for a summary instead:

"Whenever people go into a Pax area, they must follow Pax Law, but they are free to go to Non-Pax areas anytime. A person can move freely between both types of regions. Make sense?"

"Yes, it does—actually."

Genesis continues, "In Pax Lands, a person must *carry his credentials*—demonstrating he has *expertise* to speak on a specified topic."

"I see."

"Yes, it makes a lot of sense when you think about it," Genesis pauses, "In fact, I believe our society's advancements can be traced to this system of Pax Law."

"Why?"

"Well, when you have areas where *only* experts can speak with other experts it drowns out those who lack expertise. So instead of people bickering and being led down false trails by smooth-talkers, they can focus instead on innovation amid a group of their peers in a field of their expertise."

Mr. Overcompensate nods.

"So, to answer your question about free speech, Mr. Overcompensate, in Pax Lands only experts with credentials speak on their areas of expertise. Sure, Pax Lands lack 'free speech' in the sense that crazy people cannot lead people astray. But if one wants to exercise that type of misleading *free speech*, then they are free to live within Non-Pax Lands. This can be done while creating a haven for creative innovation among experts within the Pax areas."

"So, who checks to make sure a person is validated to speak on a topic in a Pax area?"

"Well, that is the beauty of it . . . the system runs itself. No one needs to check on *everyone's* credentials."

"How do they do it?"

"Simple: In Pax areas all persons who venture to speak on topics are *required* to maintain on their person a copy of their credential. And, when engaging another in conversation, the other party may ask to see the papers or proof from the other person. Then the other party chooses for themselves how far they will listen to the person based on the proof they offer. No one needs to walk around and check everyone's credentials," Genesis chuckled, "Instead, experts just verify the expertise of those with whom they speak. And they determine for themselves *how far* they are willing to accept the words of the other person. For example, if a heart surgeon were to speak on a medical topic, you would first view his credentials. Then, as he spoke you may decide to *only* listen to what he has to say about the human heart."

"But what if he starts talking about other organs—the kidneys, liver and so on?"

"Well, in Pax areas, there are penalties for those who speak on topics where they do not hold *actual expertise*. So, as the heart surgeon spoke, it might be necessary for him to briefly mention how the heart interacts with the kidneys or liver. But in doing so, the heart surgeon would need to state to the other person that his expertise does not cover those areas. So, there is a constant check on speaking *too far*—because both the listener verifies expertise and also the speaker is wary of going too far, warning his listener when he is approaching the outer limits of his expertise."

"Wow."

"Yes, it is a great system—and we owe our society's vast advancements to it," Genesis cemented the point, "In this example, the heart surgeon and his listener could then consult a kidney expert to expound on how this field of medicine interacted with the study of the human heart. This is how true advancement is accelerated—when humans are allowed to dedicate their entire lives to the study of specific areas, then *only* those perspectives are upheld and mutually supported. Whereas on Earth, many smooth-talkers pipe up to offer their non-qualified views to deceive others; the Pax system on Mahanaim accelerates advancement by drowning out all such smooth-talkers who *could* deceive others."

Mr. Overcompensate asks further, "How long does a person need to study at universities to become an expert?"

Genesis laughs, "Mr. Overcompensate, to grasp Pax Law you would need to remove such Earthly thoughts. Colleges and universities on Earth would largely be considered as Non-Pax—containing within themselves mostly white noise bickering and nonsense. In fact, there is little about Earth's universities which would meet our Pax standards."

"Okay," Mr. Overcompensate drawls inquisitively, still looking for clarification.

Genesis continues, "*Experience* qualifies a person as an expert. Reading about a topic can substitute in the case where a person doesn't hold experience—and reading certainly is the first step in the pathway to becoming an expert in *some* fields. But reading alone— even when done in a prescribed course of study in a university—does not make oneself a Pax-level expert."

"Got it. So, Pax areas use apprenticeships?"

"Yes, that is pretty much it," Genesis agrees. "Of course, an expert may assign reading to his apprentice, but in the development of Pax experience, the emphasis is on experience—not necessarily *college degrees*. And this is vital in fostering an environment where experts can break into Pax experience for themselves."

"What do you mean?"

"Well, one of the problems with Earth's reliance on college degrees is that it *hinders* expertise."

"How?"

"When universities hold sole credentialing ability, individuals in charge of the universities can sway the direction of entire academic fields. In Mahanaim no one possesses this type of power. And, as a result, the policies of a university and their choices to grant or withhold credentials cannot stifle advancement. Whereas college leaders on Earth may decide to annul a person's work; in Mahanaim if the person did the work, it continues to be valid—with the person still holding the same weight of testimony."

Mr. Overcompensate appears lost.

Genesis clarifies the point, "For example, let's say a man studied and recorded thousands of observations on mushrooms. Well, if the person were pursuing a biology degree on Earth, then the college administration could decide at any time to withhold the Ph.D. degree from this individual. In fact, the college administration may dislike him for personal reasons, or they may disagree with the conclusions he reached in his dissertation on mushrooms. So, they move to stonewall him from this field of biology. Get it?"

"Yes, I'm tracking."

"Well, in Mahanaim, no one has the power to invalidate this man who spent thousands of hours recording observations on mushrooms. No matter what, his observations still stand and cannot be taken away from him by the whims of anyone."

"How so?"

"In Pax areas this specific man would always be able to speak about mushrooms, despite the fact that he ruffled the feathers of other biology experts. Those who listen to this man's observations on mushrooms would always be able to evaluate his thoughts based on his past accomplishments. Make sense?"

"Yes, it actually does. A lot in fact."

"Mr. Overcompensate, this concept extends further, and is actually a great blessing to our people. A person can be born and raised in a Non-Pax area. But if that person desires to become an expert, he can do so—independently."

"How?"

"In Earth's past this was the path of many inventors—as they started by simply tinkering *on their own* with various items. And over time they built their own knowledge independent of anyone to validate them. But, in your present day, your universities stifle this process—telling such people they must possess years-worth of useless degrees, all used to lock people out of certain fields of study. But this was not the case for humanity's past."

"Yes, that is true. Many of our inventors were self-taught, just putting in the hours for themselves."

"Yeah, Earth would be wise to remember such things. In fact, listening to such people who possessed self-taught, disciplined expertise would allow Earth to immediately break free of many things which hold it captive. I am certain of this."

Genesis wants to move on, but in a flash another point emerges within his mind. The pilgrim has a habit of speaking too much and losing his listeners. Thinking it likely he already lost all the people in the room, he offers another point…

"Mr. Overcompensate, on Earth, gone are the days where actual experts are given a platform to teach because all platforms are governed by those who do not possess actual power. For example, consider the Lord Jesus. Let's evaluate Christ based on Pax standards."

"Okay," Mr. Overcompensate smirks.

"Well, the beginning of the Lord Jesus' ministry was significant, and in forty days He became an 'expert' based on Pax standards."

"How?"

"Before the Lord Jesus began to speak about issues of the soul, He first fasted without food and water in the desert for *forty* days." Genesis pauses, offering a question: "Have you ever known someone who could accomplish such a feat?"

"No, Genesis, I haven't. People cannot live without water for more than a couple days," Mr. Overcompensate scoffs.

"Yes, *that is what you are told*. And, perhaps that is what you have witnessed. So, when a man has an experience where he lives for *forty days* with neither food nor water, this *immediately* qualifies the person to speak as an expert on the topic of *what sustained Him during this period*. So, within Pax Law, Mahanaim holds a system capable of offering a platform to *all* people who are experts. The process is not hindered by silly ideas of universities and colleges. Anyone can become an expert. And when a person is an expert, we listen to him based on his expertise."

"I have never heard anything like this before, Genesis."

"Sir, it is why your Earth is in such disrepair. Your political system and universities stifle expertise—making it impossible for those with solutions to speak loudly enough to be heard atop the bickering and nonsense of non-experts. In fact, your political systems are all ran by those who are 'convincing' to non-experts."

"Huh?" Mr. Overcompensate's mouth dropped. He thought he was getting the point, but now was lost.

Genesis, realizing it likely all his words would sail beyond the captive imaginations of humans before him, resolved to continue nonetheless. Although he arrived to simply drop off documents, Genesis was now driven by purpose. He longed for these humans to understand—even if it were only a small piece of the puzzle.

The pilgrim focused his comments further on Mr. Overcompensate—driving them within his mind…perhaps the only political mind in that auditorium who was able to receive his words.

Genesis continued, "Mr. Overcompensate, think about it this way: When your political systems elect officials, the *voting majority* consists on non-experts. And, non-experts are easily duped and led astray—hence they are *non-experts*.

"So, who best to deceive a non-expert? A lawyer of course—a man who is practiced in the social art of being *convincing*, creating compelling cases before juries and judges. After all, a lawyer never needs to be *right*. The lawyer needs only be *convincing*," Genesis pauses, then checks for acceptance, "Do you see the problem with such a political system ruling society—a system put in place by non-experts, consisting primarily of those whose only skill is being able to convince others of nonsense?"

Genesis was surprised by his own explanation. In his mind he recycled his own words—verifying they moved the conversation in a relevant direction. Needing to say nothing further for this point, the pilgrim waited for the room to settle.

Before the contemplating Mr. Overcompensate could respond, Mr. Sly emerged from his red-faced exile atop his throne…

"Genesis, I do not like what you are implying. You are saying we politicians are swindlers."

"Yes," Genesis agreed. "That is what I am saying."

"Well, Genesis, I would say based on your own 'Pax' standard, we who have borne the leadership of our countries are alone qualified as 'experts' to make decisions. Therefore, you would not be qualified to offer us any advice when it comes to governing our Earth."

"That is an interesting perspective, Mr. Sly, but one which is full of problems."

"How so!?" Sly retorted atop his crossed arms.

"Mr. Sly, in Mahanaim it is likely none of you who sit in this auditorium would be qualified to run *anything*. Convincing non-experts to vote for oneself is something altogether pointless in Mahanaim. And, if you desire for Earth to move beyond its disrepair, you would be most wise to heed those who can demonstrate *actual expertise*," Genesis motions to his team next to him, "We are a team of *actual experts* who have the ability to alter the path of Luminary Systems for good. But your path is a reckless one—where you are lost and are deceiving others to follow you into deception."

The point was a powerful one, yet for all his inner-striving and many years spent debating to win cases, Mr. Sly was *compelled to argue*—regardless of whether he was right or wrong. After all, this politician spent years of his life defending violent criminals—arguing to remove them from punishment, setting aside his own personal morals to do so. And in many cases, he succeeded to horrible results.

Genesis saw this within the mind of Mr. Sly. Then, the pilgrim felt a rising in his throat and a tightening of his chest. Such corruption—so far removed from the pilgrim—now made him physically sick, feeling the decay of such thoughts as they corrupted his mind with their arrival. The pilgrim dispelled his mind from the intrusion—powerfully rebalancing his consciousness on its purpose in this auditorium, and resettling the physical affects felt within his throat and chest. Having reset himself, Genesis completed his point, now addressing all the 3rd Dimension prisoners before him…

"Ladies and gentlemen, evaluate the expertise of those standing before you. Determine for yourself whom you should heed. If you desire to keep Earth entrenched within its current problems—ever desiring to fix things, but being unable to arrive at *true* solutions—then keep doing what you are doing. But, if you desire to advance human societies on Earth, repairing your problems as you usher in a golden age of restoration, then you would be wise to heed those standing before you who have accomplished such things."

With those words, a spiritual veil was lifted from that auditorium—if only a brief respite from the 3rd Dimension darkness which would soon again rush in to consume the ethereal light. Those who were capable of seeing, actual saw—maybe even for the first time. And, with this new sight, many determined within themselves whom they *should* follow: They felt their minds compelled to follow the pilgrim and his team.

As the room bathed itself in reverent silence, some politicians eagerly glanced at the large stack of papers before Mr. Sly. Those touched by Genesis' words felt a longing within themselves to read the words of those who travelled from Beyond for the purpose of helping them. Some were touched by thoughts of love. Others were affected by thoughts of utility and *actual solutions*. And some others were moved by visions of how this new future within their grasp could transform the lives of their people for good.

<u>6</u>:

Overcompensate

Mr. Overcompensate stood alone in a large field, with a single black car parked on the gravel road behind him.

And, had a countryman ventured down that gravel road, he would have been taken aback by the sight of a well-dressed politician in the *middle of nowhere*.

Mr. Overcompensate glanced down at his watch, then looked up. Only twenty more minutes.

Mr. Overcompensate chose to arrive early for this meeting with the pilgrim. After their previous meetings, the politician held a special curiosity for the dramatic appearances of Genesis and his team. On this morning he desired to once again witness the crackling of hidden electricity as the fabric of the ether folded in upon itself to let loose its traveler.

However, Genesis—having a knack for both prediction and humor—planned to *sneak up* on the politician. Having already used the "standard" arrival pattern several times in the presence of these Earthlings, Genesis and Kai were cooking up a plan...

"Genesis, this is going to be funny!" admitted Kai, as the pair stood on the path of the Luminary Watchhand.

"I know!" chuckled the pilgrim, "He's going to be like, *Whaaat!?*"

"Yes, we will get him for sure," Kai laughed. Genesis' companion grew fond of practical jokes during his previous mission. And, although this joke would be a much-muted "prank" in comparison, Kai looked forward to defying the expectations of the serious politician.

"What do you think he's doing now, Genesis?"

"No doubt about it—he is standing in the field, looking up. Probably recording a video."

Kai scoffed—remembering the odd affinity of Earth humans for their *cell phones*.

As Genesis and Kai amused themselves, a third person stood near them. Boggles Arachnine—the Luminary expert of the Mahanaim task force—blended into the background hues of the Watchhand. Today she stood at the Anchor location to precisely time the portal transfers "to and from" Earth.

Boggles cleared her throat—drawing the attention of the duo before her…

"Genesis it is time for final checks."

The pair perked up, eyeing their gear and paperwork to ensure all required items were in hand.

"Ready to go!" Genesis responded enthusiastically, "See you when we get back."

Boggles' head nodded in acknowledgement—with pulses of light reflecting on the multiple lenses on her glasses.

Kai shuddered. There was much he didn't understand about Visionaries. At this moment he wondered about the purpose of Boggles' many lenses, devices and stacks of charts. She was most bizarre— moving around with herself a mobile work-station with all her accompanying "star data." In a moment's notice,

Boggles could speak about nearly *any* Luminary System on the *entire* Outer Darkness plane.

How did she do it?

Who knows?

But Kai was right—it certainly was bizarre.
And amazing.

In fact, Boggles would oft speak about Luminary Systems *far beyond* the borders of the *furthest* charts in Mahanaim. So, to the ungifted mind, they would say Boggles worked "in theory"—speaking of things impossible to know or understand. Yet, the more stunning reality, was that Boggles could actually *see* beyond the charts—*feeling* for herself the exact movements of the Luminaries as they danced upon the invisible threads of the Outer Darkness plane.

"You ready, Kai?"

"Ready," Kai echoed.

Genesis placed his hand upon Kai's shoulder with a loud...

SNAP!

In a flash, Genesis and his companion arrived on that same gravel road behind Mr. Overcompensate's car. The pair opened their eyes—their minds drinking in the details around them.

First, feeling the shift in light. Then, the air with suspended dirt drifting from the road. And, with that brief orientation on their surroundings, Genesis spotted Mr. Overcompensate.

Genesis and Kai glided across the field, sneaking up behind the politician. The two moved in a "combat glide" posture—rushing in a silent crouched manner to the well-dressed man who stood oddly in the empty field.

They arrived and moved within arms-length of Mr. Overcompensate. They stood motionless and silent—waiting for the politician to notice them.

The moment passed.

Mr. Overcompensate looked down at his watch. Then he looked up—still oblivious to the close presence of the pair behind him.

Genesis scoffed at the idea of using a "watch." He noted in his mind how utterly detached Earth humans were from the Sky Clock above them. After all, the movement of the Sun and Moon above the Earth could tell humans all they "need" to know about "time"—with more precise measurements being tracked by the movements of the other Luminaries.

Genesis' mind was fixed upon the "watch" of the politician as a point of profound contrast—when just a moment earlier he stood next to Boggles, a Visionary who feels time through the Luminaries themselves.

Boggles would never use a watch! Genesis reflected. *I wonder what she would think if we brought her a watch?* Genesis thought. Just then, Genesis broke the silence with a blurt of nasal, scoffing laughter—bringing himself to uncontrolled amusement at the conflicting perspectives of the two worlds.

The startled politician spun around—seeing two veiled men so close they were nearly breathing on him!

Mr. Overcompensate let loose a yell as he stumbled backward then forward, losing his balance and rolling *head-over-heels*.

As he flipped, the politician's notepad and other articles jostled free—as if fleeing from his alarm in every direction.

Kai laughed, then recoiled from his laughter—helping Mr. Overcompensate back to his feet.

"Genesis, it's you!" Mr. Overcompensate stated as he brushed grass from his overcoat.

"Yes—and it's you," Genesis echoed, "We arrived for our meeting."

Mr. Overcompensate moved quickly to *pretend* as if the fall never took place. Having brushed all grass from his pants, he resumed his normal professional posture with a gentle downward tug of his tie.

"Genesis, we agreed to meet here. Everything is on schedule as required in your detailed plans provided to the council. We couldn't be happier with our arrangement between your Mahanaim task force and our political council."

"That's great news," Genesis exclaimed, "I'm glad to hear everything is going well. I'll be sure to communicate that to our people…that they are doing a great job."

Mr. Overcompensate scratched his head and paused. Genesis perceived something was on his mind.

"Do you have something you would like to discuss?"

"Yes, I do," Mr. Overcompensate admitted, unsure how to phrase his question. Having reflected, he began:
"Genesis, I want to thank you for your earlier explanations of Mahanaim culture—particularly Pax Law. When you explained those things, I learned much."

"Well, I am glad our discussion was helpful," the pilgrim smiled, "We are here to help—and anything we can do toward that end is our pleasure."

"I do have another question," the politician trailed off, then resumed, "On Earth, 'funding' is one of the biggest problems facing politicians. Often it takes a long time to secure funds for projects—and there are many hang-ups which occur in those processes. Frankly, after seeing the vast effort of Mahanaim here on Earth—with all your personnel and equipment—I am stunned at the thought of how that is possible."

"What do you mean?" Genesis asked with a blade of grass in hand. He had a habit of fidgeting with things—and when in the woods, sticks, rocks, and leaves, often found their way into his grasp.

"How in the world did you get the funding for *Earth's repair* approved on *Mahanaim*? I don't understand why that decision would be advantageous for the people of Mahanaim. Nor do I understand how that decision would have been approved. Maybe some advice could help me and other Earth politicians as we work to fund our own projects in the future."

"Sure. I'll answer the best I can," Genesis agreed. "You see, the main difference concerning money on Earth and money in Mahanaim is that Earth works on a fiat system—that is a fake, credit-based system. But Mahanaim prohibits the use of credit or interest—which is called usury."

"Okay, but how did Mahanaim get there? And how does it work without credit and interest?"

"Sir, in Mahanaim, energy production is essentially free—with the Luminaries being used as sources of free energy. People harvest the energy provided abundantly by the system put in place by the Creator. And, as such, there is no 'real' need. People are free to dedicate their lives to the pursuit of their callings. And, since there is no need—and each family can provide for itself through the abundance provided by the Luminary System—there is no need for a fiat, credit-based money system. People simply harvest their goods—whatever they might be—then trade with their goods in hand.

"Think back to the beginning—in humanity's early days in agricultural-based societies on Earth. The problem occurred when people were separated from the 'free energy' means within the Earth's Luminary System. Then, as a result, people stopped trading with 'on-hand' goods. Instead, those in 'banking' positions began to tell farmers they could get 'advances' on their upcoming year's harvest. In other words, if I am a farmer, and I need wood to build a barn, yet it is Spring and I don't have crops to trade for wood, then a banker would tell me he would give me wood *now*—in exchange for a written pledge stating my *upcoming Fall crops* would be given to him."

"What's wrong with that, Genesis?"

"Well, once people began to take advances and credit, interest payments were levied. In other words, the farmer who gets wood to build his barn in the Spring would have to pay more in return," Genesis paused, then summarized his point, "The entire financial system of Earth became *fake*—where no one deals with *actual* physical goods. Instead, on Earth, everyone started passing '*I owe you*' notes to each other. Everything became fiat."

Genesis expounded further, "You see, originally the Creator's Law forbade credit and interest being placed upon the upcoming year's harvest. In the *Harvest Festival of Firstfruits*, God's people were required to first bring a 'sheaf' of that year's harvest to the tabernacle as an offering *before* their family could use any of it. So, the system of God's Law prevented the placement of claims or credit being made against upcoming harvests because God was to get His share *first*. And, that couldn't happen if people allowed claims to be placed upon the harvest before it was grown. Therefore, God's people were required to only deal with the goods which were *in-hand*. Or, at least that is what was *originally required* in that

Law. Mahanaim operates under a similar code—although they arrived at that conclusion in a different way."

"So, what happens when people fall into bad times?"

"People in Mahanaim are compassionate—living in abundance, so they *give* rather than *lending*," Genesis explained, "You know—giving without expecting repayment, where one hand gives freely."

"Well, I guess people could afford to *give freely* if energy were 'free.'"

"Exactly, but it is easier than you think. You just have to let go of the strangle-hold industry has on the public—pushing energy sources which are pricey to deliberately keep people in bondage. Once a Luminary System learns to harvest the power provided by the Greater and Lesser Lights of its system, all these things fall into place."

"I don't know where we would start."

"I do," Genesis offered—enthusiastically seizing upon the politician's veiled concession, "In fact I could take you to *her*."

"To whom?"

"Well, if you want to know *exactly* how to harvest Luminary energy, I could bring you to the foremost expert in this area. We just saw her a moment before we came here!"

Kai nodded with a sarcastic look on his face—communicating an inner realization with Genesis on the absurd thoroughness of Boggles. At that time, both Genesis and Kai's minds were drawn to an earlier experience—where Boggles entrapped them for a seemingly endless monologue on her charts.

How Boggles could make one's head swirl and ache—as if draining the life from those before her! She could spin a thread around the minds of her listeners—explaining nearly every aspect of every known Luminary.

Now, it wasn't that Boggles was boring…far from it. Rather, Boggles was abundantly passionate and gifted—a Visionary gifted far beyond the capacity of others.

Nevertheless, this was now the plan of Genesis—to lure Mr. Overcompensate to Boggles Arachnine, so she could teach him things which he would never learn otherwise.

Mr. Overcompensate nodded in agreement, "Where can I meet her?"

"We can bring you with us to the Luminary Watchhand."

"Okay, that sounds good—"

Mr. Overcompensate trailed off, looking down at his watch. A tuft of grass and dirt protruded from the watch's face—appearing as if sandpaper were scraped across it.

"Oh no! . . . My watch!" Mr. Overcompensate screeched.

Genesis stepped to the side of the politician, looking down at the watch cradled by the wrist and hand of the well-dressed man.

"That's no big deal!" Genesis retorted, "We can fix that—no problem. In fact, Boggles might even trade you something *better* for it. I bet she has never seen an Earth watch before."

"Wait . . . She is a master at astronomy, but she's never seen a clock!?" Overcompensate blurted.

Genesis laughed, "You'll be surprised…Watches are trinkets, Mr. Overcompensate. Boggles will show you Time itself."

<u>7</u>:
Free Ether Energy

"You see, Genesis, in order to fully establish Earth's power grid, I need the sky cleaned," explained Boggles—the task force's Luminary expert.

"As is *always* the case, every Luminary System possesses *all* the power it needs. And it can be gleaned quite harmlessly from the Greater Luminary and Lesser Luminary of the system."

"So, the Sun and the Moon are *all* that is needed?" clarified Genesis.

"Yes. Here's my report—showing sufficient output from both the Sun and the Moon. They are very healthy, boss," said Boggles with a smile of satisfaction. She held endearment for all Luminaries—regarding them as her dearest friends. Indeed, Boggles' heart was warmed. To give a *full bill of health* for the Sun and Moon was a heartfelt moment for the kind-hearted Boggles. She beamed with the pride of a doctor declaring a patient cured of a profound malady.

"Of course, Genesis, in order for humans on Earth to gain *full* use of the Sun and Moon through an Ether Grid, we will need to return the *sky itself* to optimal composition."

"What do you mean?" Genesis had a good idea, but he positioned his question to elicit a professional diagnosis from the expert before him.

"Well, my measurements have detected high measurements of aluminum, barium and strontium— along with other artificially-increased compounds. These cause magnetic and electrical disturbances in the Ether. So, these things will need to be filtered away before the Ether can be fully used by the people."

"Simple enough," Genesis said as a clasped his hands together—as if to capture the mission, "Amie, are you getting this?"

On Genesis' left stood another shorter figure, a young woman. As the task force's aviation leader, Amie was in charge of the air fleet—a large group of aviation machines piloted by crews. Although Boggles could identify the problem and provide information, it would be Amie's job to plan and conduct the aerial clean-up efforts.

As Genesis spoke, Amie scribbled frantically—jotting down her notes. After a pause and a short nod at Genesis, Amie turned her attention to Boggles…

"My dear Boggles, can I have a copy of your paperwork so I know *exactly* what compounds must be filtered?" asked Amie with a smile. She was considerate—always going out of her way to show appreciation for others on the task force.

Boggles blushed—being moved by the kindness of Amie's entreaty.

"Of course, my *dear* friend," Boggles answered as she handed a stack of papers to the woman before her. Boggles' goggles bobbled in the faded starlight behind her, bouncing light off the papers.

"Thank you," offered Amie with a bow, "Do not be troubled, Boggles, I will see to it that your skies are treated with the utmost courtesy. We will greet the Sun and the Moon in your name. It is our blessing to join with you in this mission to return dignity to these greatest gifts from the Creator."

Boggles lunged forward, embracing Amie with a hug—sweeping her off her feet.

"Finally, Genesis, you brought me someone who gets it! Someone who loves the Luminaries as I do!" beamed Boggles as she held Amie high with a backward-bowed back.

From Genesis' perspective it was a most ridiculous sight: The tiny Boggles straining to hold Amie—barely lifting her dangling feet off the ground.

Amie was surprised—never expecting such a warm embrace from Boggles, and certainly not expecting to be lifted off the ground! Amie simply allowed for the over-the-top display to pass as she hovered above the ground.

Finally returning to her feet, Amie replied…

"Thank you, Boggles! If you would like, please feel free to stop by the air command center at any time. I will be there directing and monitoring the progress of our crews. I would love to give you a tour—especially after you worked so diligently to gather this information," said Amie—gesturing at the papers in her hand.

"Yes please!" conceded Boggles eagerly, "I will stop by soon. I just need to finalize some other observations here," motioning at the observatory behind her.

****

In the darkness of the aviation command center, was a slender, shadowy figure. Zeg-E, the commander of Mahanaim's army sat reclined—stretching her slender body atop a chair, with her feet resting on a table. As she sat in the darkened room, with the glow of display screens depicting the map locations of Mahanaim's aerial fleet, Zeg-E held in her hand a long blade.

When not engaged in a sniper mission, Zeg-E liked to keep her hands busy—tinkering with one item or another. Currently, the object of Zeg-E's "tinkering" was a knife. In a most bizarre, yet subtly skilled fashion, Zeg-E was using the blade—so long as to be considered a "sword" rather than a "knife"—to manicure her fingernails.

The curtain of the tent swung open as Amie entered the aviation command center. Amie carefully checked the tent flap behind her—ensuring it was secure.

Although Amie had little to distinguish her from other humans—she was most notable in her attention to detail and knack for being *thorough*. Indeed, this is why she was selected to lead Mahanaim's *sky fleet*—a large group of flying machines piloted by crews.

"*Zeg-E!*" gasped Amie, "Sorry I didn't see you there. How are you, my friend?"

Although Zeg-E seldom spoke to others, she felt comfortable around Amie—as if in the presence of a sister. Zeg-E held out her manicured hand—examining her work.

"Peachy. How are you, Amie?"

Amie exhaled—holding in her hands a disheveled stack of papers...

"My sky fleet and their crews have worked hard to prepare for this mission," said Amie as she waved the papers in her hand, "Now we are *finally* here."

"That's great! What's that stuff?" asked Zeg-E with a gesture of her knife at the papers.

"It's the list of contaminants we need to remove from Earth's sky. It was the last piece of the puzzle we needed for planning purposes."

"Cool."

Zeg-E's body was tired from her previous missions on Earth—and it felt as if she were being rejuvenated sitting in the chair, stretching herself as if to soak up as much energy as possible from the Luminary Watchhand beneath her.

Suddenly, a thought struck Zeg-E…which she immediately shared with her friend:

"Oh, am I disrupting you, Amie? If you need to focus on your preparations, I can leave."

"No, Zeg-E. You are always welcome. Stay as long as you like," Amie replied with a smile—which was answered in kind.

Amie drifted to her table in the center of the tent. She set down her papers—beginning to shift various items on her desk as the room fell silent.

Time passed as Zeg-E continued to fiddle with her knife. Amie meanwhile pressed various buttons on her console at regular intervals, punctuating each series of pressings with the flipping of paper sheets. Finally, her course of *pressing and fidgeting* passed, leaving Amie content to lean back in her chair.

A moment passed. Amie's eyes drifted back to the shadowy figure to her right.

"Zeg-E, I am curious about something."

"What's up?"

"Well, I notice you are here *often*—and I always appreciate someone of your skill being nearby. In fact, having you near makes me feel *safer*," explained Amie with a shrug settling her words.

"That's a good thing!" jumped Zeg-E.

"Absolutely it is. But I was wondering—" Amie trailed off.

Zeg-E bit, "Wondering about what?"

"Well, whenever I meet and get to know people, I like to learn things about them—you know, stuff about what makes them tick."

Zeg-E motioned with her knife toward the items on Amie's desk, "Aren't you busy?"

"No. I finished everything I needed to do. Now I am just waiting until my brief with the pilots and aircrews," Amie took a breath, "I think *now* would be a good time for chat."

"What's on your mind, Amie?" asked Zeg-E— appearing aloof as she held out and examined her other hand, searching for imperfections.

Amie laughed aloud as she imagined Zeg-E removing her boots to give herself a pedicure with the ridiculous *sword/knife thingy*.

"*What's so funny!?*" Zeg-E blazed, nearly dropping the blade.

"Nothing," Amie giggled, "I was just thinking how interesting you are."

"Huh!?"

"Here you are *the commander of the Mahanaim army*," gestured Amie in a jesting imitation of the regal posture of a military leader, "Yet around me, you completely drop your guard—giving yourself manicures!"

Amie laughed again: "I keep waiting for you to ask me to do *make-up* with you or something."

"*Ha-ha*," answered Zeg-E sarcastically—crossing her arms with feminine defiance, further baiting her counterpart, "*Very* amusing!"

"If you must know, *Amie*," sassed Zeg-E in a drawl, "I never had a sister and you are *kinda* like *that* person."

Shrugging her shoulders, Zeg-E added: "Of course, I can't manicure my nails around the soldiers because I am the *commander of the Mahanaim infantry*!" As Zeg-E delivered the words, she did her best to imitate Amie's impression with those words just a moment earlier. However, Zeg-E—lacking much of the grace usually endowed upon women—was incapable of dancing as effectively through the words.

Immediately sensing her counter imitation fell flat, Zeg-E resorted to putting her hands on her hips and sticking out her tongue with a grunt.

In kind, Amie replied—raising her hands to her ears and shooting her tongue back at Zeg-E.

Then, as if somehow connected—the two girls crossed their arms in unison. After glaring at one another, they both broke into smiles.

"Geez, Amie! What do you want to know about me!?"

"Well, start by telling me *something interesting*. I heard all types of stuff about you, and there is a bunch of *mystery* surrounding you. Is what they say true?"

"Who is *they*?"

"You know…*They*."

"*They* talk a lot, don't *they*?"

"*They* certainly do," answered Amie with a chuckle.

"And, what...pray tell...did *they* say about me?"

"*Well . . .*" sighed Amie—doing her best to pique Zeg-E's interest. Seeing her eyes light up with anticipation, Amie backpedaled—putting herself firmly in command of the conversation.

". . . *maybe I shouldn't tell you*," finished Amie with a wink—barely visible in the darkened tent.

"Huh!?" objected Zeg-E, "Now you have to tell me!"

"Alright, alright," teased Amie—selecting her words to playfully bait Zeg-E further, "*They* say you have mysterious powers."

"Mysterious powers!?" shot Zeg-E, sitting conflicted with arms crossed yet a smile which betrayed her.

"Yup, *mysterious*," Amie repeated—this time while gesturing her hands as if *casting a spell* toward her newly adopted *sister*, completing the impression with a mystical sound: "*Woooooo.*"

"*Honey*, there is nothing I do that is *mysterious*! I do all simple stuff that anyone *could* do. It's their fault *they* don't listen to me carefully enough. Maybe if girls *like you* would stop sassing me and just pay attention, *they* could learn a thing or two!" Zeg-E finished— imitating Amie's mystical finger flailing, "So you can take back your little, '*Woooooo*.'"

"Well, entertain me, *Zegs*," entreated Amie endearingly, "Just tell me *how* you do your thing as a sniper." Amie scoffed, "I don't really know anything about military stuff, and I am interested to know what makes you so special and different from me."

"You are special, Amie. You are respected. You are a good leader and a good organizer," Zeg-E offered in candid encouragement.

"But among the task force, I am clearly *way* out of my league. And, I get that—and it's okay. I'm a hard-worker, but I don't have any super powers or anything per se."

Zeg-E wheeled closer to Amie: "You have heart though, Amie. And that *is* a super power. Because when your heart is right you can find the ability to do great acts of courage. Your mind is sharp—and it is no wonder why you have been selected for your position."

The tension of preparation for Amie's great mission weighed upon her heavily—especially within the camp, as she lacked a confidant to vent about the stress of such matters.

Perhaps this was the reason *why* Zeg-E was intuitively drawn to Amie's aviation command center. As a military commander, Zeg-E could sense *many things* beyond the perception of others. And, at this moment, Zeg-E's intuition led her to provide a personal connection where one was *greatly* needed. Zeg-E patted Amie's hand, then drew her into a hug as tears welled from her eyes…

"It's okay, Amie. I know you are a great person because your heart is connected to your mission. Your tears show how important this mission is to you. And, more importantly, your tears show you are the right person for the job. There are many people who do things. But people seldom care so deeply for the things they do," Zeg-E paused, "I believe in you, Amie."

The moment passed as the two girls embraced.

Amie was the first to withdraw—now feeling most comfortable with Zeg-E, no longer seeing her as a *dangerous soldier*, but as a person who was *deeply empathetic*—like her—with the ability to draw great strength from within.

Amie wiped the tears from her face carefully—recomposing herself, mindful she was now in the presence of a person with whom she could always drop her guard.

"Zeg-E, I have time before I need to go to my brief, can you still tell me about *you*? I am *very* curious about *you*."

"Do you want personal details like where I was born or do you want me to tell you about the *mysterious* stuff?"

"Ooo, let's talk about the *mysterious* stuff!" Amie's heart fluttered with anticipation. She longed for something fun to give her mind much-needed respite from her regular duties.

"*Zeg-E, tell me about all the things you don't explain to other people!*" insisted Amie with giddiness—as thoughts of the previous moment faded. She often wondered at thoughts of Zeg-E and how she accomplished many of her feats. And, now, in this most remarkable moment, the sniper and army commander offered to appease every wonder which previously captivated her mind.

"Okay!" said Zeg-E with a hand wave—as if restraining Amie from grabbing onto her.

Amie—satisfied—leaned forward in her seat as if to snatch every word from the air.

"Well, most people don't get it when I explain *how* I *see* things, but I'll give it my best shot for my good buddy," said Zeg-E with a smile.

"Whereas others would be inclined to look at physical things and think of them as physical—I feel the vibration of all things around me."

"You mean when things move?"

"No—all the time I sense the vibration of things around me."

Amie was puzzled.

Zeg-E searched for a better explanation. Mindful of Amie's earlier gracefulness in movement, Zeg-E attempted a better explanation…

"Amie, to me, everything is like a big dance. And, everything everywhere is playing a melody of its own. Rather than looking at things, I 'feel' my way around everything—putting my body in places where there is harmony. And, when I feel dissonance, I glide my body past it or re-shape it to fit what I need. So, for me, all things are like a dance. By staying in tune with all the different melodies, I can feel dissonance rising before something physical occurs."

"So, you can predict the future?"

"Kind of," answered Zeg-E, "but not long-term stuff. Have you ever heard the saying, '*Mind precedes matter*?'"

"Yes."

"Well, it might not be the best way of putting it, but that saying does well in capturing *how* I interact with all things around me. Before I move my body, I place my mind. And, I view all physical things in a similar way. Everything is vibrating—playing its melody. I simply dance my way in harmony, leading my body with my mind."

"I see," said Amie with a nod, "I like how you explain that—like a big dance! How beautiful!"

"Yes, it is beautiful!" Zeg-E agreed. She was touched by Amie's reflection on the simplicity of beauty rather than pondering the advantageous nature of her abilities. To Amie, a *super power* was a means of experiencing beauty; not a means to gain personal advantages.

"So, how do you teleport from one location to another? I heard you can do that."

114

"*Teleporting* wouldn't be the right word."

"Why?"

"Believe it or not, I have the ability to occupy many different physical locations at once—and I can shift my mind between the different locations my body occupies."

"Wow! I wish you could take me with you and show me!" Amie said enthusiastically, then wondering if it would even be possible.

"I cannot place myself anywhere. I have to place my body in locations where I find or create harmony. And, as I keep finding locations with harmony—where all the melodies are in tune with one another—I can insert my body into that place," Zeg-E paused, not really sure what to add. She continued: "Once I place my body in a location, I do better if I keep that body location motionless—essentially joining in the melody of that location."

"That's probably why *sniper* is a good job for you."

"Yes. Being a proficient sniper is all about observing and waiting. And when I set up more and more positions, each visor sends back information to Goat at the Luminary Watchhand camp."

"How many positions can your body occupy?" Amie inquired quietly—leaning in closer as if to receive a guarded secret.

Zeg-E was reluctant to answer—abstaining from the appearance of boasting. However, she carefully and quietly offered with a giddy smirk...

"About forty," Zeg-E giggled like a little girl—as if sharing secret candy with a schoolyard friend.

"Amazing!" answered Amie.

"Yeah, it is kinda tough though because when doing this I don't keep a tally. I just know it is *about* that much because Goat told me he had that many video feeds from my visors."

<u>8</u>:
Sky

"That looks cool," Genesis mused aloud.

Before the pilgrim was a vast video display—depicting the location of *every* flying ship within the sky fleet. On the display the sky tracks formed a web pattern across the entire Earth.

"Yeah, it does look cool," answered Amie, "If you look closer, Genesis, next to each ship is its number—used in radio communication." Amie continued, "I must confess, however, I had nothing to do with the flight

117

routes…that was all Boggles." Amie gestured toward the Luminary expert next to her. Amie was humble—always looking for opportunity to direct praise to others rather than receive it for herself.

Amie shifted in her seat, leaning back under the steady light of her desk lamp.

Boggles' glasses reflected the subtle light of the lamp—causing beams to dance gently before her.

"Thanks, Amie," answered Boggles with a bow.

The three stood silent for a moment in Amie's command center, gazing at the sky fleet as it drifted on the video display. The sky ships appeared to dance with one another—as if directed in concert.

Genesis reflected on the pattern of the ships' movement. Within the pattern was something quite profound—a grace which could easily escape notice. However, knowing the sky routes were designed by Boggles, Genesis was keenly aware the pattern was *somehow* tied to the awesome movement of the Luminaries throughout the Outer Darkness plane.

In the passing silence of that moment, the pilgrim's eyes darted about the video display—attempting to decipher the hidden "code" of the tracks.

Within the tent, Boggles grew restless, longing to return to the company of her blessed friends—*The*

Luminaries. Boggles broke the silence—snapping Genesis from his fruitless venture…

"If you guys think the *video display* is cool," Boggles teased, "How would you like to see the *big picture* for yourself?"

"**I would!**" answered Amie as she pushed herself from her desk—eager to step away for a brief respite. Her eyes ached from the darkness of the command tent—being insufficiently illuminated by the lamp.

"Where are you taking us, Boggles?" asked Genesis.

"A couple steps outside the tent. I want to show you how I designed the ship routes using the Luminaries."

She reads minds!? Genesis thought to himself with a subdued chuckle.

"Alright," Amie said as she stood. She grabbed a device, tucking it under her arm. Nodding at her assistant in the tent, Amie said, "Be right back. You have the radios."

"Got it, boss."

Boggles was the first to leave the tent, followed by Genesis and Amie. Boggles felt confined within the tent—as if she needed to *hold her breath* within it. Breaking free from the tent, Boggles immediately drew power from the Luminaries around them atop the Watchhand. As she sauntered to the edge of the Watchhand, Boggles drew strength from the Luminaries with each breath—as if reviving herself from her brief separation within the tent.

Seeing Genesis walk off in the company of the two ladies, Kai roused himself from his post outside the command tent. He ran to catch up with them—being unsure where they were going. Arriving near them, Kai slowed to mirror his pace with the three.

Startled at Kai's rush behind them, the device nearly slipped free of Amie's arm. Glancing back at the huffing Kai, Genesis shook his head with a smirk.

Arriving at the edge of the Watchhand, Boggles removed an item from her satchel. With a couple *clicks* and *snaps*, a tripod emerged before her. Beckoning with her hand, Boggles invited the others to stand next to her. Reaching onto her glasses, Boggles popped out *one* of the many lenses.

As explained elsewhere, Boggles held a propensity for being *thorough*. And, as the Luminary expert, she held extraordinary knowledge. Boggles began…

"Depending on how much you want to see, I can start by showing you *one* view of the Luminaries. This will help you to see how I designed the sky tracks." Motioning to the many lenses on her glasses, Boggles finished: "If you want to see *more* after that, then I can keep showing you *more*," she offered proudly.

If you were to meet Boggles, perhaps you would be most taken aback by the contraption upon her face—with its most bizarre arrangement of viewing apparatuses. So, doubtlessly, the prospect of having Boggles present *every* view was overwhelming for the humble Amie and the pilgrim.

Genesis laughed jovially: "Can we start with just the *first* view, Boggles?" He bowed out of respect, smiling beneath the brow of his forehead.

"Sure!" Boggles replied enthusiastically, inwardly reveling in her vast wisdom, thankful for the esteem her *Visionary ability* granted her. She was always grateful for the opportunity to teach others—and seldom she had *eager* students. Her wisdom in regard to the Luminaries was outmatched. And, when she spoke of her dearest friends, her words had a habit of overtaking the minds of even the most astute. So, in many regards, within Boggles there was a conflict—where she knew *very much* of the Luminaries, indeed bordering upon *everything*—yet she lived in a world where none had the ability to conceptualize her words beyond a mere utilitarian level. Yet, for the most part, her wisdom left her so occupied by a pursuit within herself under the Luminaries that she ever grew less concerned with her disconnect with others.

Nevertheless, in this moment, the great Boggles contented herself to simply teach Genesis and Amie. Confining her explanation to how she derived the sky routes, Boggles pressed forward.

Snapping the *single* lens in place on the viewing device atop the tripod, Boggles spoke: "Alright, Amie, Genesis . . . *and Kai*," Boggles said as she dramatically shifted her head to see the pilgrim's companion behind him, "On the video display in the tent, you saw each flying ship moving in a certain route. Now, those routes are connected to the Luminaries as seen *within* the Earth. So, another way of saying this is that the flying ships are each moving from one Luminary to another as seen from within the Earth. Look here…"

Boggles motioned to the viewing apparatus, placing her hand on Genesis' shoulder—as if to guide him to the viewer.

"You can see from this lens the trails of light which beam from all the surrounding Luminaries upon the dome of the Earth's Luminary System."

"Wow!" Genesis exclaimed, "That looks amazing! I wonder how that one lens is capable of focusing *only* on the beams travelling to Earth."

"Well, that would require a lot of explaining, Genesis, so maybe later I can talk to you about the lenses."

Boggles controlled the viewing, trading Genesis for Amie—and last, beckoning Kai forth to see things for himself. As Genesis and Amie attempted to orient themselves anew amid the new vision, they pondered the beams of light. Their ponderings were halted by Kai…

With his head attached to the apparatus, Kai asked, "Boggles, what is the purpose of the flying ships travelling to the light?"

"*Ooh…* Good question!" said Boggles, cracking her knuckles, directing her answer toward Genesis and Amie—as it would seem awkward to talk to the *back* of Kai's head.

"As you guys can see, the Luminaries—or stars— are located very far from the Earth's Luminary System. The light connects each Luminary System—which is how we can access them from one another via the Luminary Watchhand."

As she spoke, Boggles performed what looked like a dance—stretching out her arms to draw the attention of her companions to the *other* Luminary Systems. When she made mention of the Watchhand—she stomped her foot…as if to remind them of the ground upon which they stood.

Kai glanced up from the viewer, reluctant to step away from it—desiring to be the first to see the next thing.

Boggles continued, "Each Luminary System sends threads of light to other Luminary Systems. And, surprisingly, these threads of light are much more than just light. The light beams provide many, many different things. But in the case of Amie's sky fleet, the beams of light provide a steady form of energy to each sky ship."

"Huh?" grunted Kai.

"Another way of saying this is that the sky fleet doesn't operate using *fuel*. The sky fleet harnesses the natural energy of the Luminaries. This is why they move on tracks determined by beams of light. As each sky ship moves it continues to draw energy for its flight."

"I think this is brilliant . . . and beautiful, Boggles," Amie answered. Turning to Kai, Amie expounded, "When constructing the sky ships, Boggles assisted our engineers with developing *energy harnessing equipment* so they could run off the energy of the Luminaries."

"Oh, I see," Kai nodded as he once again pressed his face on the viewing apparatus.

Genesis placed his hand upon his chin, "It is amazing to think how it is *all connected*—all of Creation moving in concert with itself." He looked down at the jewel of the Earth—with the Luminary Systems in the background each dancing like precious stones upon a blackened sheet, moving up and down.

"Yes! Yes!" answered Boggles, "It is *all connected*. And, I can show this in *many, many* different ways," she said as she once again motioned to her goggles. "Here, I will get you set up with another viewing."

Boggles gently pushed Kai aside. As Boggles swapped out the lenses, she gave Kai the first viewing opportunity.

Genesis felt awkward as he stood waiting with arms-crossed, so he distracted himself with an attempted conversation...

"I must say, Boggles, you sure are a *Nut*," Genesis laughed. The irony was too much, and he could not resist connecting his memories of mythology with his present experience. Here Boggles was detailing an immense web she designed to *hold up the Earth's sky*—providing the practical means of Amie to cleanse the sky from impurity, returning it to its original state established in Creation.

The group was silent—with Genesis' reference falling flat. Alas, Genesis remained standing with arms crossed, patiently waiting. Of course, Boggles may have never heard of such things—like *Nut* or *Atlas*. And, maybe during her lifetime upon Earth, Amie might not have given attention to such things. Last, most certainly, during his brief tenure on Earth, Kai was much too busied upon battlefields to muse upon the myths of the ancients.

Thousands of years after his previous life, however, Genesis' mind was still captured by such thoughts. His mind constantly stirred on such things as he attempted to somehow connect his past experiences on Earth with his present reality. Perhaps it was his constant research into Earth's history which entranced his mind.

Desiring to anchor himself by unburdening his past, Genesis turned to Amie as Kai's face remained buried in the viewing apparatus…

"Amie, can I ask you a question?"

"Sure."

"Well, you and I both have Earth in common. We *both* lived there. And we both lived in similar situations. Seeing the Earth as it is, do you ever wonder at how upside down everything was during our lifetime?"

"What do you mean?"

"We were taught Earth was a ball—floating through an endless air vacuum." Motioning at the domed jewel beneath them, Genesis continued, "Certainly it was not—and is not—*a ball*. And, certainly there is no *outer space* vacuum." The pilgrim took a deep breath—illustrating his point.

"Yes, it is *different* than described," Amie agreed. She scoffed playfully at her subtle underestimation. Indeed, she recognized the Earth was *nothing* like described in the Earth's 21st Century.

For a moment, Amie strained to remember her thoughts during her lifetime.

"I guess I never gave it much thought when I was there," Amie said as she pointed at the jewel of the Earth, "I was always very busy…work and all."

"I get it," Genesis conceded, "On Earth it was so easy for us to get caught up in *stuff*. Yet, now, people like Boggles tell us that the most basic thing is cosmology…understanding Creation around us."

Boggles briefly glanced up, as she snapped a *third* lens into the apparatus—now resolving herself to a Luminary menagerie for Kai, simply sliding random lens as if handing a kaleidoscope to a child.

"I agree, Genesis," joined Boggles, "The most important thing—or at least the most important thing for orientation—is to know *where you are*. So, for people on Earth, they should begin by understanding the stars above them. And, by figuring out the Sun, Moon and stars, a person has a shot of understanding where they are standing."

"Exactly!" answered Genesis as Boggles placed a fourth lens in the viewer for Kai.

"Ouch!" blurted Kai.

"Oh, too much?" Boggles answered as she quickly swapped the lens for another. "Try this one instead, Kai."

"A n y w a y," drawled Genesis.
Seeking a *more engaging* conversation, the pilgrim chose to poke the bear: "Boggles, I might not have told you this before, but people on Earth thought the Earth was *spinning*."

"Ridiculous... The Sun and Moon are the ones that move. The Earth's ground is *not spinning*," Boggles interjected.

"Yes, but many thought otherwise," Genesis smirked.

Boggles scoffed, "How would it be possible for the Earth's ground to be *moving!*?" Boggles paused, then continued: "If the Earth were moving or spinning, then *anything* which left the ground would immediately enter a different *reference frame*. That clearly is not true, therefore, the Earth is not spinning."

"What do you mean, Boggles?" asked Amie.

"Simple, as soon as an aircraft left the ground, the Earth would move *underneath* it. So, there would be no need for aircraft to propel themselves forward. They could simply hover as the Earth spun underneath— waiting for their destinations to arrive underneath them."

"Yes, Boggles, but during my time people would say the Earth's atmosphere rotated *with* the ground. So, they would say aircraft were not entering a different reference frame, because the air moved in concert with the ground," answered Genesis.

"Earthlings are incorrect, Genesis. Air is made of gas. And gas moves rapidly in *all directions*. Therefore, gas would not stick to the ground. Gas disperses. It always moves to fill available space," Boggles replied as she snapped another lens for Kai.

Boggles moved to expound further, "And, Genesis, if the Earth were a ball floating in a vacuum, all

129

the gas of its atmosphere would immediately disperse in the vacuum. So, you guys *should* have known you were being lied to. It is impossible for gas to stick to a ball inside an *outer space* vacuum." Boggles concluded, "The people on Earth are ridiculous—which is why we need to fix the Earth for them in the first place."

"Deception on Earth is profound, Boggles. Imagine living in a world where you are told from the beginning that there is *nothing spiritual*—that *only physical things* exist. Earthlings are taught of billions of years of evolution and about an outer space which extends incomprehensibly in all directions—pushing the Creator so far away that people stop spiritual ventures. So, people on Earth are thoroughly conditioned to accept *The Deception*. They are so indoctrinated by it that they become incapable of seeing anything beyond it."

Boggles stepped back, "If that is the case, Genesis, then I shouldn't be mad at them. They broke the Earth because they do not understand. Since they don't understand, we can help those who are willing to learn."

"Yes, we can," smiled Genesis. "I long for the day when Earthlings will be capable of breaking free from the physical shackles of their minds. When Earthlings look at the stars their minds should be drawn to thoughts of *spiritual transcendence*—how to step into the reality *beyond* the physical world. However, as it is, whenever an

Earthling looks at the stars, his mind is captured only by *physical thoughts*—like the *distance* to stars and absurd notions of physical stuff." Genesis paused, then continued, "The pathway to all those places require supernatural transcendence—most specifically 4th Dimension capability via the Luminary Watchhand. And *physical* thoughts will never get a person there."

The conversation fell silent as the moment passed. To Kai's chagrin, Genesis and Amie resumed their turns at the viewing apparatus.

"Check out this one!" said Boggles as she snapped a new lens in place.

"Ah, *creepy!*" exclaimed Amie. The lens imparted a view of the Outer Darkness plane surrounding the Earth's Luminary System.

"What's *creepy*?" asked Boggles.

"I don't know. The Outer Darkness chills my spine. I don't like looking at it," said Amie ironically as she continued to look at the Outer Darkness through the viewer. Somehow, she was drawn to it, even though she desired to turn away.

Boggles slipped her hand in front of Amie, "Sometimes these things are just too much." As she slid another lens in place, Boggles offered, "Try this one instead."

A moment passed as Amie relinquished the viewer to Genesis, then Genesis to Kai...opening opportunity for further discussion.

"Genesis, I guess I have never thought much about the Outer Darkness. What is it?"

"Beats me. To our knowledge, no one has ever been out there. *Boggles?*"

"Don't ask me," Boggles laughed, "I have plenty of observations *of* the Outer Darkness—and I can tell you much about *some* things. But, concerning its *composition*—I have no clue. And, in my business, I don't offer speculations."

"Oh," Amie said in dejection.

Genesis jumped, "Fortunately for you, Amie, I *can* offer some *speculations* based on *my* studies."

"Sure!" Amie replied.

"Well, in the Bible, Creation begins with *water*. And when the Creator made the Earth, He did so by separating the *water* of the Earth from the *water outside of it*."

"You mean the Outer Darkness is *water*?"

"It certainly *appears* to be water," Genesis said as he motioned to the Darkness beneath the Watchhand. A deep black rippled throughout—only revealing itself when momentarily dispelled by the beams of light from the Luminaries.

"But it might not be water like we think of water."

"Or it might just be really yucky water," Boggles hiccupped, then placed her hand over her mouth—halting it from offering any further speculation in defiance of her previous statement.

"Yeah, it might be *super* yucky water," Kai whispered into the apparatus—suddenly feeling sick to his stomach.

Amie proceeded further, "So, what are the domes of the Luminary Systems made of?"

Boggles shrugged, "Something apparently capable of separating the Outer Darkness *stuff* from the things *within* the Luminary Systems. What I can tell you is that the *domes*—if that is what you want to call them—also provide a level of refraction to the light. So, the light moving into the Luminary Systems is displaced."

"Interesting," Amie shifted to look at the pilgrim, "Genesis?"

"To add to what Boggles said—now and earlier—we can know for certain whatever the *domes* are made of, the material is sufficient to *hold in* the gas of each atmosphere."

Boggles perked up, "Yeah, earlier we were talking about gas. The Earth's sky is made of gas. And, in order to have gas pressure, you *must* have a container. Therefore, since the Earth has gas pressure, it *must* have a container. To form gas pressure, gas must have something to press upon. If there were no container, and if the Earth were simply a ball floating in a vacuum, the gas of its atmosphere would rapidly move in all directions—dispersing in the vacuum."

"And, since the Earth must have a *container* to maintain *gas pressure*, this means the Earth could not have spaceships, satellites and other stuff moving *into and out of* its atmosphere. To have anything leave the Earth's atmosphere, would mean that gas could also escape—and it would escape! On Earth, gas is produced at ground-level, then disperses the higher you go into the atmosphere because you get further from the source…kind of like how it the air is hottest and wettest near the boiling teapot spout, and colder and less dense the further you place your hand from it. This is why there is a gas pressure gradient on Earth, in addition to the different cycles which exchange and transfer gas," Genesis added.

He paused, then continued, "What I find most remarkable is that the more I see, the more I understand about Creation. In fact, Creation occurred *exactly* as described in the Bible." Motioning at the Earth beneath them, Genesis continued, "The Earth was created in six days. In regard to our conversation, on one of the days, the Creator formed the *dome*—if that is what you call it—providing separation from what is *within* from the Outer Darkness. And, that same dome provides the *container* necessary to *hold in* the Earth's atmosphere. That dome also prevents those *within* from *physically leaving* through it. Therefore, to transfer *through* that boundary is a spiritual process *beyond the physical*. Hence, spirituality—that is 4th Dimension ability—is required to move in or out of a Luminary System."

"Interesting," mused Amie, "Can you touch it?"

"The dome?"

"Yeah."

"From the inside of a Luminary System—*maybe*. But we are not sure if the composition of all domes would be similar. Perhaps they are somehow illusionary and impossible to reach, and then *beyond the illusion*, there is some physical nature which forms the actual boundary—capable of *holding in* gas pressure and *holding out* the Outer Darkness." Genesis appeared puzzled.

"Hmm," Amie reflected as she drew her hand to her chin. "What about touching the dome *from the outside*?"

"Well, that would require traversing the Outer Darkness to reach it."

"Oh, yeah—true." Responding in unison with Genesis, Amie said, "*And no one has done that.*"

"But—" Amie began.

"*Don't, Amie!*" Kai exclaimed as he waved his hands. "If you are about to say you *want to touch the dome from the outside*, Genesis might actually send you to do it!"

Kai offered the comment in jest, with a smile on his face, yet held captive by the realization of his last musing to the pilgrim as he reflected on the Earth. A much more naïve Kai was suddenly ushered to a distant mission—transporting him far from his native Mahanaim.

Genesis smirked as he raised his hands—touching his fingertips. He rubbed his hands as if plotting—toying with Kai.

Kai shook his head as he looked at the pilgrim—doing his best to feign a sinister motive.

Recoiling from his playful gesture, Genesis answered plainly, "We *are* working on a plan to *chart* the Outer Darkness."

"Yuck. Why in the world would anyone want to do that?" asked Amie as she shook her shoulders.

"A couple reasons: *First*, if we ever need to rescue someone who falls into it. *Second*, for discovery. Frankly, we do not know *what* is out there. Certainly, the Outer Darkness will be one of our Frontiers."

"*What* do you think is out there?"

"Who knows?" Genesis offered, "Do you want my speculations?"

"Sure—" Amie replied as she placed her hands on her hips. Her mind ached from all the new sights and discussion—so surely, she could find room for *another* thought.

"Based on the Creation account of the Bible, I think of the Outer Darkness as *waters of chaos and void*. Whereas the things *inside* the Earth follow natural laws; the Outer Darkness might be *beyond* those natural laws."

"What do you mean?"

"Well, an easy way to put it would be to say the Outer Darkness could be like an ethereal dream land— where an explorer could encounter impossible, imaginary things amid a pseudo-physical world which lacks definite physical substance."

Amie shuddered.

Kai piped up: "Sounds more like a *nightmare* than a *dream*."

"It certainly *could* be a nightmare. So, an explorer would need to be grounded psychologically and spiritually. This would add another dimension to its exploration. Whereas Luminary Systems can be explored in the first three-dimensions; the Outer Darkness would absolutely require some 4th Dimension capability. Otherwise the person might be blind-sided by shifts in their physical surroundings out there."

"Wow."

"Yeah, I know it is a lot to take in. Beyond this, I think we might even encounter Wanderers out there. So, there are many layers to the Outer Darkness plane as a Frontier."

<u>9</u>:
Farmlands

In a secluded area of the Luminary Watchhand camp, a large dark figure glided his way to a table.

At the table sat Kai, currently serving as the assistant to Genesis Pilgrim—the commander of the Mahanaim task force.

Although it was remarkable for Mahanaim to undergo activities to repair the Earth's Luminary System, this certainly *would not* be the last time Mahanaim would dare such a daunting task. Thus, Kai busied himself by making all activities into a *matter of record*—to the end that future Mahanaim citizens could assemble more efficient task forces for future endeavors.

As the dark figure approached, Kai anxiously reviewed the pages of notes on the table before him. In his role he held the responsibility of compiling records of events for progeny.

Kai's anxious review of his notes came to an abrupt halt—seeing the intimidating figure now standing before him. Kai dropped his pencil as his knee jumped from the table beneath him—as if attempting to catch the pencil and being hindered by the table.

"*BUMP!*" said Kai's knee.
Kai winced, then choked out the muffled words: "Good morning, Ketu."

"Good morning, Kai," answered Ketu with a chuckle, "You okay, bud?"

Kai rubbed his knee—kneading it like a ball of dough...
"Yeah, I'm okay," Kai laughed dismissively, removing his hand from his knee and regrasping his notes. Kai knocked the sheets of paper against the table to align them:
"Ketu, are you ready to begin our interview?"

"I am. I have been looking forward to speaking with you, Kai. I think it is important to get all this information on record as best we can. The Earth certainly is a challenge."

"Yes, it is," Kai agreed, "But with us making the effort to create records of our activity, it certainly will be easier for Mahanaim to repair *other* Luminary Systems in the future."

Ketu nodded. Kai's statement left him somewhat puzzled—being uncertain whether or not he would be capable of explaining his contributions in a way which others *could* understand. Ketu was a Visionary of incredible power—unequaled in many ways. Nevertheless, he desired to do his best to provide all the information he could.

Ketu distanced his chair from the table. He lowered his body into the chair *sideways*—crossing his legs and immediately removing what appeared to be a slender pipe from his cloak.

"Comfortable?" Kai laughed.

"Yes, I'm *quite* cozy," Ketu spoke with an air of satisfaction—directing his voice to the side of the table while avoiding eye contact. Ketu removed the pipe from his mouth—pointing it toward Kai. As he spoke, the pipe bobbed up and down as his words moved past it...

"What questions do you have for me, Kai?"

The comfortable manner of Ketu set Kai at ease: "Well, Ketu, can you please begin by telling us about yourself—where you come from and what you do?"

"Certainly. I will do my best," Ketu paused, mouthing his pipe, then continuing—trying to begin at a place which *could* be understood by Kai and future readers…

"In my first life, I was on the Earth."

"What's it like—coming back to Earth again?" Kai interrupted.

Ketu shifted his body, resting his hand on the tabletop momentarily, "It is great being back on Earth! In my first life, I often struggled with many of the problems which afflicted the Earth. It feels fantastic to be in a position where I can be a *part* of the solution—bringing Earth back to what it was intended to be at the beginning of Creation."

Ketu's enthusiasm transferred across the table. Although Kai did not share a similar past with "Earthlings" like Ketu, Genesis, Amie and others, his heart was warmed by such intense feelings of love expressed by people like Ketu.

"Please continue, Ketu," Kai offered as he gestured his hand.

Ketu resumed, "In my first life, I had *difficulties*. Certainly, all of us on Earth had difficulties in one way or another—such as it was. Earth was a broken place, and in one way or another, the brokenness of Earth transferred upon all who lived there. Of course, I do not want to speak for *everyone* on Earth, but suffice it to say, conditions have not been optimal. Thus, the lives of those upon the Earth were lessened in many ways."

"I think I understand," Kai offered. "Genesis spoke to me about many of those things—and after I achieved 4th Dimension capability, I was sent to experience some of those things for myself...*unfortunately*," Kai completed with a sigh—reflecting on the pain he experienced and witnessed in the eyes of others.

"So, you get it!" Ketu replied—looking off into the distance, "Lots of pain—in different ways—but pain nonetheless...all shared in different measures—but nonetheless shared."

BOOM!

Ketu slapped the table *hard*—as if in violent defiance of the pain caused within the Earth...

"It is about time we did something to fix this place!" He held out his arm—gesturing toward the distant Luminary System of the Earth. His voice *echoed* with profound authority—peppering down upon the dome before him.

As if to answer his powerful proclamation, the Sun suddenly grew *brighter* then faded to *normal*.

I reckon the Sun may have opened a portal of sorts to allow Ketu's words to move within the Earth's system beneath it. But who knows for sure?

Kai smiled. He could feel Ketu's unbridled concern—no longer restrained, but unleashed, like a dam releasing a mighty surge. His motivation was contagious.

Indeed, over the duration of their mission, the *entire* task force grew increasingly bolder as they heard for themselves the death throes of the Earth. Ketu was focused with righteous indignation—serving as an advocate for the depleted and unkempt Earth.

"Please explain your first life upon the Earth, Ketu."

Ketu sighed—moving his mind to remember things now only a distant shadow.

"Kai, for me, physical things were *difficult*—many would say *impossible*, but for a much larger purpose. I see that now. I spent much life in confinement—being *incapable* of movement. And there was *much* doubt and *much* grief. I was long mourned with many who stood nearby, then forgotten as my body lingered," Ketu paused to greet once again his grief paired with this now ancient memory.

Ketu looked down at his hands...unveiled by his cloak. His hands radiated with ethereal pulses from *within and without*—sensed and felt only by himself, save when he chose to unleash the incredible power from them. His mind and body—which were once set at naught—now capable of serving as a most mysterious gateway of Dimensions. And, from this grounding in his *new reality*, Ketu's grief was immediately assuaged. The ancient grief was traded for his humble veiling—where he was a barrier of sorts, holding back and controlling unimaginable waves of strength from the ether...both beyond and below.

Ketu smirked—a most subtle sign to Kai and the visible world, yet inwardly he reveled and rejoiced. With his free hand, Ketu made a crackling, tightly-clenched fist before his face—drawing ethereal power back within his body.

Kai—*on the other hand*, was oblivious, seeing only the quivering hands of his companion. It is unlikely he would ever fathom what Ketu held *within and without*.

And, indeed, who could?

Dropping his free hand and mouthing his pipe, Ketu continued, "As I have said, life on Earth was difficult for everyone—and for me, it was a bit *more difficult* than most. *But*," Ketu boomed, "It is our past which shapes our present. And suffering always opens a portal to something *greater*—if only we ask for the strength to see it through *to the end*."

"I see," offered Kai encouragingly—working to understand Ketu's words.

Ketu continued, "Many on Earth shrunk back *too early*, falling short of the gift which *could* be obtained. *I, however*—"

Ketu faced the table, outstretching his arms. The table beneath Kai's arms rattled—as if brought to its breaking point and held steady to maintain its form. Emanating forth from the table, the ground of the Luminary Watchhand quaked as waves of energy flowed outward from Ketu's form.

In the distance, Kai watched with subdued amusement as some fellows in the camp steadied themselves amid the quaking power—kneeling to prevent themselves from toppling amid each passing surge.

Ketu receded from his demonstration—returning to his previous side-sitting, pipe-holding posture. He paused, reflecting deeply on the difficult path he once tread. Behind the smoke of the pipe, Ketu hid small tears…welling in his eyes, yet remaining in place—being met with immediate rejoicing at his form achieved through the supernatural.

Ketu spoke deeply through the puffs of smoke:

"But I am re-made, Kai."

"Just as we will *re-make* the Earth—restoring her vitality," Kai added.

"Exactly!" Ketu puffed.

Kai noticed in the distance the stirrings of fellows in the camp—as each lifted himself back to his feet, brushing himself off. Although he was too intimidated to say so, Kai thought it hilarious: Ketu caused all that mess, yet now sat comfortably smoking his pipe.

"*Whatcha looking at?*" Ketu asked, snapping his head to the right to Kai, then to the left to trace out the object of his vision.

"*Them!?*" Ketu gestured toward the frazzled fellows. Calling out with a loud voice, he exclaimed, "*Their lives are too easy as it is! They should have to deal with a quake from time to time. Make you tougher it will!*"

Recognizing Ketu's voice and immediately tracing him as the cause of the disturbance, the fellows answered in dulled unison:

"Thanks, Ketu."

"You're welcome!" Ketu answered as he returned to his posture, taking a drag from his pipe. Speaking further to the fellows, Ketu continued:

"When the ground is shaking, why do you grab onto it!? Next time you are in danger of falling, reach up and hold the unshakable grounding *above* your heads!"

The fellows were nonetheless *lost* concerning Ketu's advice. And Kai sat puzzled by his words.

But, like I said, it is unlikely *anyone* could really understand Ketu.

Ketu moved his attention back to the interview: "Concerning what I was saying, Kai…In my first life, my name was Chuck. Some would call me Chuck the Crusher."

"Why?"

"It was just a funny thing. People giving nicknames to people they like. That was my name *and* my nickname."

"So, what's the deal with 'Ketu?' Why don't you go by Chuck? Heck—" Kai said gesturing at the frazzled fellows, "It seems like 'Crusher' is still a fitting nickname!"

"*Eh . . . maybe*," Ketu offered reluctantly, "But calling me 'Ketu' makes sense—especially when we consider how 'Ketu' is what makes me different from *everyone*," he paused, "At least everyone you know."

"Please explain."

"Well, as I said, my first life on Earth was tough— where I had many *physical* limitations. But those limitations helped me to see beyond the physical—*well-beyond* in fact. I saw so far that I achieved something which is quite *unachievable* from a physical perspective."

"Huh?"

"Kai, I read your interview with Genesis—just to brush up on a *different* perspective. In his interview, he mentioned what he called 'Wanderers'—people in his estimation who are physically limited, yet somehow able to achieve what you call 6th Dimension ability through *Inversely Proportional Dimensional Consciousness* theory." Ketu reflected further: "I reckon this was the case for me. My soul's vitality was elsewhere and opened a means for me to move into a *higher dimension* because of its limitations in the *3rd Dimension*."

Kai nodded. He understood.

Ketu continued, "So, although I wasn't a *Wanderer*—that is, I wasn't found by anyone on the Luminary Watchhand or anything like that—*I found myself* moving within what you 'might' call two Luminary Systems."

Kai's head was spinning, "So many questions," he blurted.

"Well, I guarantee you have never heard of these things—so it makes sense for you to have questions. Anyway," Ketu continued, "The *two* Luminary Systems are really *one*—at least how I experience them: One is Ketu and the other is Rahu. And they are *one* Luminary System."

"Oh!" Kai exclaimed as his mind struck realization. He smacked his knee, then immediately regretted it. Rubbing his knee, Kai asked, "Don't *Ketu and Rahu* have something to do with Sun eclipses in the Earth's Luminary System?"

"Yes, they do!" Ketu was surprised, "Where did you hear that?"

"Boggles."

"Okay, got it. No further explanation required," Ketu laughed. As the star expert, Boggles was notorious for being *thorough* in her explanation of the stars. Ketu didn't doubt Boggles likely talked to Kai about *everything* dealing with Earth's Luminary System—including seemingly obscure topics like '*Ketu and Rahu.*'

"Just to clarify, you have been to the '*shadow planets*?'"

"Yes, Kai. But you must understand they are quite different than many of the ideas which have been attached to them. Some people stick various myths to each place— so many of those myths are not really accurate. Overall, Ketu and Rahu are shrouded in mystery—especially to those entrapped within the Earth's Luminary System. So, there is much speculation among them."

"You are right. I have never heard this before."

"Well, Ketu and Rahu certainly are a special Luminary System. Perhaps the best way to explain it is that it is veiled—and moving there would be about as difficult for someone who isn't 6th Dimensional as it would be for you to be in two places at once."

"That does sound confusing."

"Yeah, but no worries," said Ketu smacking on his pipe, "I am sure there are far more difficult things on the Outer Darkness plane."

"No kidding," Kai scoffed, "So how are you helping the task force's mission in regard to repairing the Earth."

Ketu leaned over the table, "It is quite interesting actually, Kai. This is how I do it…"

Ketu grabbed a sheet of paper—separating it into parts, placing them in different areas of the table. Then continued his explanation.

"…To move into Ketu and Rahu, I left my physical body in the Earth's Luminary System. I shifted my 'soul,' *if you will*, into my body and within the Luminary System of Ketu and Rahu. Then I transferred *between* until I moved into the new system."

The papers placed by Ketu on the table puzzled Kai. His eyes traced out their positions—attempting to discern a pattern, but to no avail. At the end, although the position of the papers appeared to be conveying an archaic message to Ketu; to Kai the paper scraps appeared only a mess of rubbish strewn randomly atop his table.

Kai scratched his head, resolving to re-read his recording later to re-attempt understanding. Kai had no idea how to continue, so his mind babbled words into a sentence...

"Okay, how do you use this?"

"Well, Kai, I am able to transfer between the Luminary Systems of Earth and Ketu and Rahu. Sort of like a bus driver."

"Ah, I see," offered Kai. Although he could faintly follow his explanations, Kai was entertained by the thought of Ketu driving a 6th Dimension *bus*.

Ketu continued, "And, since I can move between Earth and Ketu and Rahu *at will*—very quickly in fact—I am able to open portals of exchange, where I can drop what is needed in one Luminary System and not needed in another."

"So, what do you transfer?"

"It is genius actually," Ketu placed his hand on his chin, then pointed toward Kai with his pipe, "I have been placed in charge of agricultural farmlands on the Earth. So, I transfer all the man-made nonsense out of farmlands—pesticides and whatnot. For me this is quite easy."

"Please explain how it is done."

"Well, I don't do it on my own—you must understand. I work along with microscopic machines designed to find all the tiny particles of bad stuff."

"What are the *microscopic machines*?"

"Kai, I think Goat might be better to ask that question. But I can tell you as I best understand."

"Yes, that would be good," Kai gestured with his hand, "Please continue."

"Okay, the microscopic machines are *biological*— somewhat similar to bacteria. They have been designed to 'feed' on pollutant particles—being set in each location to seek after the chief contaminants in that area of farmland."

"What if they run out of 'contaminants' to eat?" asked Kai.

"Then they stop replication and their movements slow to the point that they go dormant. It is brilliant actually because as they complete their purpose, they slow and halt. So, they don't starve or die off."

"I remember hearing Earthlings attempted similar things—that is *biological means* to counter-balance their industrial pollution."

"Yes, they did. But they got things wrong. And it was disastrous."

"So, what makes *us* think *our* attempt to fix Earth's farmlands will go differently?"

"Well, for a start, *we* actually understand what *we* are trying to fix!" Ketu replied with a pointed finger, "We don't just go tromping into things. We have designers who make things that *actually fit* what we are trying to do with *zero trickledown effects*."

"Ketu, have you heard of *chemtrails*?"

"Oh my gosh—no kidding!" Ketu exclaimed, "As if that isn't the most foolish example of Earthling nonsense of all time." Imitating an Earthling, Ketu held out his hand as if holding a lantern—feigning himself a blind man lost in the woods: "Well, golly! The Sun is too hot, so let's spray a bunch of aluminum, barium and strontium in the sky to keep the sunlight out. Nonsense!"

Kai scoffed, "I know! Boggles has been having an awful time trying to figure out how to un-do the damage done to the Sun, Moon and the Earth's sky."

"Yes, and there wouldn't be such large problems if Earthlings were smart enough to understand what they were doing *before* they did it. They have no regard for trickledown effects. They are reckless children."

"Why do you think they did it?"

"What?"

"Chemtrails."

"Well, Kai, they did it—like I said—to try to keep the Sun's heat out. But ultimately what led them to this conclusion was their faulty understanding of the Earth itself."

"Huh?"

"Kai, I know Genesis explained this to you before, but the people on Earth are so entrapped by the 3rd Dimension it is *impossible* for them to see anything beyond the physical. They just *can't*. In fact, for them the 3rd Dimension is a prison—which leads them to view all things as 'physical.' It is absurd, but people on Earth are so trapped by their perception of the 'physical' that they imagine physical space stretching infinitely in all directions. They just don't understand *anything spiritual*—let alone the true structure of their Luminary System from the Watchhand. After all, you need the 4th Dimension to move out of a Luminary System, so the people on Earth are utterly trapped within their own *physical* brains."

"Earth is such a bizarre place. Every time I hear about such things it is mystifying."

"No kidding, Kai! Imagine growing up in such a place—bereft of spiritual understanding…being placed in a cage, yet incapable of *seeing the cage*."

Ketu digressed, returning to the original question with an exasperated breath:

"Kai, the people on Earth decided to start spraying metals in the sky because they thought the Sun was a giant physical ball millions of miles away, sending radioactive light onto the Earth."

"I see," said Kai—scratching his head. Although completing an earlier mission upon the Earth, Kai had little opportunity to learn such things firsthand during his brief stay.

"Yeah, the people on Earth thought the giant Sun ball was going to *scorch everything*."

"Ridiculous!" Kai blurted.

"It is. But you don't understand how difficult it is to be imprisoned by 3rd Dimension thinking. In fact, the people on Earth are so trapped, they think of the Earth as stretching out in all directions, then *folding back onto itself* as a globe ball. The whole idea formed by the prison-masters was to design a concept from which the minds of those they deemed lesser could *never escape*. And, a ball surrounded by *endless* physical space did exactly that! No one can think of anything beyond the physical because that is all they know."

"*This* Earth?" Kai asked aghast, gesturing down at the domed jewel beneath them—where the Sun and Moon were moving in circuits.

"Yes, *this* Earth," answered Ketu, mirroring Kai's gesture.

"It makes no sense to think the Sun would hurt the Earth—after all the Sun was *made* for the Earth, Ketu!" Kai looked upon the Earth's Luminary System ponderously—carefully considering how it was designed to work, appearing as a most magnificent watch-piece, with two grand invisible arms containing a Greater Light and a Lesser Light, respectively.

"I agree, Kai. But you must understand, the people on Earth could *never* see what you see. Therefore, they felt vulnerable. After all, since *all* they could see was *physical*, then life *beyond the physical* was something they could not grasp. So, Earthlings fear *everything*—constantly *imagining* danger everywhere. This is why they even imagined the very lights in the firmament as being their enemies."

As he spoke the words, they made Ketu's head ache. It was tiresome to think of such things. And, by his reflection, he wondered at how he was ever *lifted to transcendence* from such an *utterly* impossible place. Truly, Ketu's escape was a miracle! And, with that thought, Ketu leaned back in his chair with a profound sense of satisfaction—drawing a deep breath from his pipe.

Kai's head bobbed up and down from the waves of information breaking upon his mind. Pondering the depths of Earth's *Deception* was staggering.

The previous discussion of *microscopic machines* was now distant. Ketu rested a moment, then wrangled Kai's mind…

"Kai, to answer the question about the *microscopic machines* which are used to clean the farmlands, Goat has all the maps containing the soil samples and whatnot recorded by Lewis and Mage. Goat sends out teams to deposit the microscopic machines in the correct locations. Then they feed. Easy."

"Isn't there danger of the Earthlings capturing some of the *microscopic machines* and damaging them? Or—worse—attempting to dissect them?"

"Not really, Kai," answered Ketu, "I don't know all the specific inner workings of the *microscopic machines*, but they are equipped with what I believe is called *Quantum Eraser technology*."

"What's that?"

"Goat would be better to explain this for sure, but the gist of it is that *Quantum Eraser technology* causes an automatic shut-off in a microscopic machine if it is *viewed by a human*."

"How?"

"It mirrors the base function of photons to behave differently *based on human knowledge*. In other words, if a microscopic machine 'knows' it is being tracked or observed, it halts."

"Very cool," answered Kai with enthusiasm.

"Yeah, it is!" Ketu winked, adding further, "But I wasn't involved in making them. I almost got to name them though."

"You almost got to name the microscopic machines?" Kai scoffed—amused by Ketu's childlike wonder for such simple things. To Kai it seemed 'naming machines' would be something *far beneath* Ketu—due to his greatness. However, Ketu held a nostalgia for simple things, enjoying comfort and relaxation—just as his pipe would indicate.

A moment passed as Ketu shifted his posture—looking directly at Kai in anticipation. His pipe fell idle before him—refusing to take another puff until Kai progressed the conversation.

Ketu's gaze made Kai uncomfortable…
"Alright, Ketu: I'll bite," said Kai, "What did you want to name the microscopic machines?"

Ketu smacked his lips on his pipe, swinging his chair sideways to fall back into his normal, comfortable, side-sitting posture—
"I wanted to name them *roly-polies*—of course."

"*Of course!*" Kai chuckled, amused to play along with Ketu's jovial nature, "And what, *pray tell*, is a '*roly-poly*?'"

"You know…the little beetles who scamper about, but if you touch them or get too close, them clamber up into chambered balls."
Ketu outstretched his non-pipe arm—shaking it free from the sleeve of his cloak. He held up his hand toward Kai, forming a small, roly-poly sized hole with his

index finger and thumb—holding it at eye level for Kai, awaiting his inspection.

"I get it: They are little bugs," Kai laughed as he waved away Ketu's demonstration, "What do *roly-polies* have to do with the microscopic machines that clean Earth's farmlands?"

"Well, they both *clamber up* when pesky humans come too close, of course!" Ketu crossed his arms defiantly, "No matter what anyone else says, that is what *I* am calling the microscopic machines!" He poked himself in the chest with his thumb: "To me, they are *roly-polies*!"

Kai smiled, then changed the subject: "So, how do you do *your* thing, Ketu? How do you help the *roly-polies* clean the farmlands?"

"My job is easy," replied Ketu leisurely as he reclined back in his chair—balancing upon its legs, "From time to time, I swoop in and pull *everything* from *all* the roly-polies, leaving behind the machines and taking what you call 'pollutants' to the Ketu and Rahu Luminary System. Then I return equal, yet harmless mass back to the Earth's Luminary System to maintain its balance."

"So, Ketu and Rahu's Luminary System is a *junk yard*!?"

"No, *certainly not!*" Ketu objected, "I wouldn't be named after it if it was! Rather, Ketu and Rahu's Luminary System can *make use* of many things which Earth cannot. And, when certain things are taken there, they are separated into harmless particles which become quite useful in fact," Ketu mouthed his pipe.

Then he concluded, "Call it an equal trade: *Earth* lets go of things it doesn't need and *Ketu and Rahu* do the same. And in the exchange, both are better off. The exchange happens so quickly that balance is maintained in *both* Luminary Systems."

"So, you are like a middleman for both Luminary Systems?"

"Yes," answered Ketu, "It would be very difficult for you to understand, but perhaps the best way I could explain would be to say I have a similar agreement with Ketu and Rahu as I do with Genesis Pilgrim."

Ketu grit his pipe betwixt his teeth, freeing his hand from its grasp. In a final, hilarious display, Ketu held up both his hands as if to represent both Luminary Systems. Then, through clenched teeth he mustered these words through the balanced stem of the pipe: "*I am working for the benefit of both the Earth* and *Ketu and Rahu.*"

Kai choked in laughter at the ridiculous display—watching the pipe nearly bob free of Ketu's lips as they twisted with the words.

Kai settled—thinking this a good place to conclude his interview…

"Well, I am sure I have ample information for my report, Ketu."

"Kai, I am certain it is enough information to put our future generations on the right path if ever they must venture to *repair a Luminary System*. I am sure once they reach their Frontier, all the things I described will seem like mere child's play—so advanced will they be in the Dimensions Beyond."

Ketu paused. Recognizing Kai had no further questions, Ketu offered him a final nod as Kai bowed in respect.

"I must bid you farewell until next time. I have matters to attend," said Ketu as he stowed his pipe—perking up in his chair.

"Farewell, Ketu!" called Kai to the transforming form of his companion as he shifted in a brilliant display of colors—rapidly withdrawing from sight.

Thus, Kai's interview with the 6th Dimension Visionary was concluded. And, as his name suggests, Ketu was left to his ethereal work—far beyond the perception of both Earthlings and the Mahanaim task force.

<u>10</u>:
Regions & Lifeforms

The early morning light cascaded on the Luminary Watchhand camp. The Earth's Sun radiated light—like a train approaching in a long tunnel.

Although it was "morning" within the Earth's Luminary System nearby, this held no relevance to those on the Watchhand. Nonetheless, Kai took the increased light as cue to begin his day's activities. And, *like any other day*, Kai moved *first* to Genesis to conduct their morning brief.

Kai groggily stirred from rest, being beckoned forth from the light of the Earth's Sun. He quickly gathered his belongings—which were stowed near his sleeping position. He lifted himself to his feet, meandering his way to the pilgrim's tent. Kai slowed peeled back the curtain, careful to avoid spilling *too much* light into the tent.

However, to his surprise, his eyes found Genesis in the *same* position he left him *many* hours earlier. The pilgrim sat hunched over stacks of paper, hastily capturing words under the flickering of a single candle.

Genesis looked up, "Good morning, Kai."

"Morning!" Kai echoed, "Just checking in on you. How's it going?"

"It's going," Genesis offered reluctantly—looking down as if holding within himself a conflicting balance of accomplishment, weariness and…disappointment.

Kai picked up Genesis' confliction, so he asked for further clarification…

"Did you finish *the list*?"

"I did," Genesis offered with a sigh untypical of his usual radiance of completion. Kai often noted when Genesis completed a project, he would clap his hands, shout and make all types of boisterous celebration to usher himself *out* of a phase of diligent study. Yet today, Genesis was reserved and quiet in his supposed completion.

"What's wrong?" fished Kai.

"Well, it is very complicated, Kai. Frankly I did my best, but I am afraid all I have is a detailed '*example*' of how it *could* be. I am not sure if it will be enough to do the job."

Kai smiled nervously—not sure what to say. He reflected for a moment, allowing Genesis to compose his thoughts. The moment passed, and Kai moved to gently ease Genesis into *whatever* the next step *might* be...
"Genesis, look on the bright side! We have a full day ahead of us—and nearly an endless amount of ways we could attempt to solve the problem."

The wind passed the tent—causing the unsecured curtain to wave open and fall. The ground seemed to hold it in place, beckoning a radiant wave of sunlight into the tent. The humble candle immediately succumbed to its radiance—being extinguished by the wind with the arrival of the sunbeam.
Genesis shielded his eyes—as the light rushed upon him. He laughed as he covered his entire face with the cloth of his cloak. The blazing light was almost

comical—as if to compel Genesis to immediately set aside self-pity, to embrace the day. Although his project was not yet complete, Genesis chose to greet that moment with enthusiasm.

"*Hooo*!" Genesis shouted, as he clapped his hands and jumped from his seat.

"That's the spirit!" said Kai, "We'll figure it out, boss. Where are we off to?"

"Good question. I *guess* we have lots of good minds around here—let's *maybe* rustle up some advice from *someone*?"

Kai nodded in agreement.

With that, Genesis bolted out of the tent—stretching outside its entrance. As he lifted his hands upward, the papers in his hands flopped in the wind.

"Let me carry those for you, Genesis," Kai stated as he plucked the papers from the pilgrim's outstretched hands.

"Thank you. Let's go see, Boggles. I was thinking she *might* be able to help."

"Where is she?"

"She will be in her mobile observatory on Earth. Unfortunately, to go to her we will need to leave behind the sunlight," Genesis chuckled—meaning they would need to venture to the *other side* of the Earth where it was still evening, out of reach from the Sun's radiance.

As the team's Luminary expert, Boggles preferred to do most of her work in darkness—so she could "see" all the stars.

Mind you, Boggles didn't need to "*see*" the stars to "*see*" the stars—holding in her mind all the complicated calculations of the positions of *all* Luminaries on the Outer Darkness plane. Nevertheless, being able to "see" the stars in the darkness held a certain nostalgia for Boggles. So, to find her, one simply needed to go to the place where the skies were clearest—and her observatory would be resting comfortably under the blanket of the peppered evening firmament.

Without warning, Genesis placed his hand on Kai's shoulder. In a flash, the sunlight receded behind them as their feet came to rest on the soft ground under them.

"We're here!" said Genesis, as he took a deep breath of the fresh evening air.

"Geez! Warn me next time!" exclaimed Kai in a gasp.

Genesis laughed heartily as the darkness dispersed—enabling their eyes to adjust to the diminished light. Kai closed his eyes tightly, then re-opened them—allowing himself to reorient in the new surroundings. The observatory slowed emerged from the veil before them—as if materializing from beyond the void of shadow.

Satisfied, Genesis whispered to Kai: "Let's go."

With Kai in trail, Genesis approached the large dome of the darkened observatory. A small dot of light appeared on the narrow path. Under the dot of light was a large sign—which read…

"No lights. No electronics. Silence."

Genesis chuckled to himself—thinking the sign reminiscent of old gas station signs, which would read: *"No shirt, no shoes, no service."*

But as he reached out to grasp the staircase railing before him, the pilgrim was fully aware this was no place of *convenience*—for within this observatory worked the great Boggles, star-gazer extraordinaire!

As Genesis began his labored trudging to the heights of the observatory, he mused on his past interactions with Boggles—who was a passionate professional with exceptional skill.

In their past meetings, Genesis recalled his swirling thoughts as Boggles showed him exhaustive star charts—not only from the perspective of Mahanaim, but also from the perspective of many other Luminary Systems. She spoke of *many* things. Most notably she could pinpoint and triangulate the movement of just about *everything*.

Certainly, there is no one like her, thought Genesis.

The pilgrim had a knack for *thinking in pictures*—working to draw connections in his mind to relate his *present* experiences with his *past* knowledge. And, in the case of Boggles, Genesis thought of her as a Spirit-empowered conductor of a grand symphony—knowing *every* rise and fall of *every* note within the Grand Composition.

But, although this thought was helpful for Genesis, it merely scratched the surface of the great gift within the mind of Boggles. In fact, she was so in-tune with the Outer Darkness plane that she could *feel* the movement of *all* the Luminaries upon it.

Most notably, Boggles could *predict* the location of new Luminary Systems before exploration teams could reach them! She would even prepare charts to show *ahead of time* what they would encounter upon their arrival.

Now, this may not make much sense to you—if you are not familiar with the Luminary Systems of the 4th Dimension. To predict such things was not only *prophetic* on about the highest order of *prophecy*, but also *lifesaving*. Indeed, many exploration teams were saved from much loss—simply by following the charts provided by Boggles.

So, how did Boggles do this?

Who knows?

One can merely reflect with his own limited capacity. From the perspective of 3rd Dimension humans, they would say Boggles is *thorough and intelligent*—merely calculating star positions using mathematics. However, from a 4th Dimension perspective, one could more rightly declare Boggles was entrusted with the spiritual gift of vision—holding within herself an empathy for all the movements of Creation.

And, we are left to only muse how Boggles' powers would appear within still *higher dimensions*, like the 5th and 6th. If you are interested in such things, maybe you should ask Ketu for his evaluation of Boggles' work.

Or one could be so bold to say Boggles was even a *personification* of the Luminaries in some form?

Indeed, such reflections were always common when attempting to define the abilities of *Visionaries*. After significant thought, one would grow weary or enraptured in the pursuit. And, then, individuals would relegate themselves to simply sit and listen.

Who knows? Perhaps the Creator so gifted *Visionaries* for this purpose—to completely overwhelm others so they might choose to draw near and silently learn in their presence. After all, the Creator seldom speaks *directly* and instead sends speakers to bring life to His people.

Thus, in his trudging to the top of the observatory, Genesis' thoughts occupied his mind. His thoughts eased the normal aching of his legs associated with climbing steps. In this way, Genesis slowly rounded the staircase one step at a time—*up...and up.*

Kai was at the pilgrim's heels—kindly bearing with the pilgrim ahead of him. Many times, Kai thought he would need to *reach out his hand* to stay Genesis' frequent loss of balance. While climbing the steps, Kai wrestled with his thoughts. He imagined what might happen *if* the time-traveling pilgrim ahead of him were to lose his balance.

Kai thought, *If I touch Genesis—even to prevent him from falling—I might be injured, or worse— accidently blasted forward or backward in time!*

Of course, this thought was ridiculous— *or was it?*

Notwithstanding, such is an example of how Visionaries are perceived, *even* among their close associates and other Visionaries. When in the presence of a Visionary, citizens of Mahanaim were cautious—stepping aside to listen, watch and follow. They were certainly cautious to avoid stepping *out of bounds* in *any* regard.

Finally, the pair reached the top of the staircase—moving silently into the clear dome of the observatory.

The air was clean and moist. Genesis looked up to see the Moon in her brilliance—drawing radiance from the Earth below, increasing her light.

Greetings, old friend, Genesis thought with a smile. He quietly reflected tomorrow would mark the beginning of the Moon's waning—as it shifts its monthly cycle to pushing, rather than pulling.

Genesis' eyes traced the dome above, searching to locate Boggles, as his feet followed the path before him. As he moved, Genesis stepped off the path—placing his body under a large line of shadow, shading himself from the radiance of the full Moon.

Boggles, deep in thought, suddenly felt the energy in the observatory shift. Seeing Genesis and Kai below, she set aside her present occupation with the messy charts displayed before her. Looking down from atop her crow's nest, Boggles quickly lowered herself on a zipline.

The pilgrim looked up to see a form descending from the beams above. Genesis stopped suddenly, causing Kai to bump into him.

Kai immediately gasped and winced—unsure what would happen: *Didn't I just warn myself about this!?* Kai thought.

Kai looked himself over rapidly—first his hands, then each limb in order. Satisfied with his self-assessment, Kai was convinced he was still *here*—that the inadvertent bump didn't send him *elsewhere*.

"You okay, Kai?" Genesis whispered.

Kai nodded, "Sorry, Genesis."

"*Look out!*" yelled the pilgrim as he darted from the path of the descending shadow!

Kai lost his balance, spilling himself onto the ground.

"Howdy!" Boggles blurted—zipping herself within *inches* of the pair. She quickly landed on her feet, and—with a tug—removed tension from the zipline.

"*Oopsie!* Let me help you up," Boggles offered. Before Kai could object—having had his fill of *bumping into* Visionaries—Boggles swooped in gingerly, lifting him to his feet.

Now back on his feet, Kai mused on the irony—now having another pick *him* up.

"Well, I'll be—" said Boggles with a feigned Southern accent, "If it isn't the great Genesis Pilgrim and Kai Anthropos! To what do I owe the pleasure?" Boggles gestured upward at the grandeur of her dome under the deep, speckled majesty of the heavens above: "What brings you to my humble abode?"

Genesis removed his hood—as if to show respect before the unveiling of Creation above him. He allowed the moment to pass as he gazed at the sky in thankful reflection.

Several moments passed in silence as the three gazed upward—each falling under the spell of the lights above. Some lights flickered. Some raced. And some held steady—as if holding places for their partners as they each traced out their course.

That simple sign of respect for what she honored most greatly impressed Boggles. She could sense the sincerity of the pilgrim. There was much he did not know—and *could not know* of the heavens, nor of Boggles' observations. But she reasoned anyone who held such reverence for this grandest part of Creation was certainly her friend.

If the Luminaries call you 'friend,' then you are my friend as well, Boggles thought. Boggles raised a hand to her heart as a sign of empathy. Leaning forward, she spoke…

"Genesis, you seem troubled. Why is your heart heavy?"

"Boggles, I am stuck," Genesis stated—motioning with his hand toward the stack of papers held by Kai. The pilgrim took a lunging step toward Kai, unburdening him from the weight of the documents. Then, in a sweeping move, Genesis positioned himself to the side of astronomer. Flipping through the pages, he began his explanation…

"Boggles, I know it is outside your realm of expertise, but I wanted to get a fresh perspective on my *Eden List*."

"What, *pray tell*, is an *Eden List*!?" the expert astronomer inquired with a smirk. Her dark eyes gleamed under the glow of the starlight above. She was intrigued by the name—*Eden List*—which seemed to point with reverence to the foundation of Creation through the name "Eden." Although Boggles generally disliked conversation and preferred the silent company of the Luminaries, she always greeted Genesis' ideas with enthusiasm.

181

Boggles moved closer to the pilgrim to view the document. She moved her hand quickly to her glasses, flipping a switch. Her glasses illuminated, causing a steady flow of light to pour onto the papers. And, with the arrival of the new light, the pair pored over what was written.

Genesis continued…

"Boggles, let's start where the Earth is *currently* and work our way *back in time*. As it is *currently* in the broken Earth, many of the geographical regions have collapsed. Environments have shifted for many different reasons."

"Got it," Boggles signaled with a finger pressed upon her head.

Kai thought the gesture reminiscent of Earth *sign language*, but wasn't sure. He shook his head.

The pilgrim further explained his *Eden List*: "Since the Earth's regions are so messed up, I am certain from my studies it will not be 'good enough' to simply *remove pollution* and fix just a *couple* things. In order to *truly repair the Earth*, we will need to chart *every* geographical region—considering the specific dynamics in *each region*."

"What do you mean?"

182

Genesis continued, "We need to do this by making a chart for each region, determining the exact environment. Then we need to make sure each region is stable. In other words, a 'desert' region must remain a 'desert,' a 'jungle' must remain a 'jungle' and so on."

"Makes sense."

"Yes, this is important to make sure Earth is balanced based in her different environments—that there is a spot for all the different wildlife."

"So, what will you do with that information?"

"Well, I already have the geographical region information prepared—and it makes sense because our data shows the regions recorded *here* will remain as we re-structure them," Genesis flips to a certain page with a large graph, tracing his finger down the margin to direct the vision of the astronomer to his side.

"That's great! So, your *Eden List* is done?" Boggles retorted.

"No," Genesis chuckled in exasperation, "This chart isn't the *Eden List*." Genesis paused, buzzing through the remaining pages with his thumb—
"*This* is the Eden List," laughed the pilgrim.

Boggles glasses bobbed up and down in astonishment.

"What is written on *those* pages, Genesis?"

"Alright," Genesis sighed—as if mustering his entire mind to assist him in forming a sufficient explanation. "These pages contain the lists of all the microscopic life, plants, sea creatures, land creatures and everything for *each* region."

"So, that's the Eden List?"

"It was my best shot at it anyway," Genesis appeared downcast. "Frankly, Boggles, there is just *too much* information. Earth is so messed up. So many creatures are gone that I fear it might not be possible to stabilize each geographical region with life. And, although we have a complete plan to balance the environment in each region, I am certain each will eventually collapse if they do not have appropriate plants and animals to fill the necessary niches."

"Huh?"

Genesis reformed his thought—shaping and tailoring it for Boggles' mind: "To relate it to the Luminaries: It would be like saying each Luminary

System needs a Greater Light, a Lesser Light and other Luminaries to complete the Sky Clock of its system."

Genesis paused—surveying Boggles' eyes as he waited for a sign of understanding.

Boggles nodded. She understood the simple concept that each system has specific niches which need to be occupied. And it made sense that each region would need its niches to be occupied by appropriate plants and animal life.

"I get it, Genesis. So, you don't think your Eden List is *good enough*? What are you going to do?"

"I'm not sure. And frankly I don't know if anyone in the Mahanaim task force has the expertise to evaluate the remaining lifeforms on Earth—let alone develop a *master plan* to use the existing lifeforms to stabilize each region."

Genesis' shoulders dropped—as if the energy was sapped from his body by the ground under his feet.

He was discouraged.

Boggles stood motionless as the starlight reflected from her eyes and glasses. Her head drifted slightly up and down in the evening breeze—sending shards of brilliance upon the ground near Genesis and Kai.

The moment passed as Boggles searched her mind for a solution. She felt for the predicament which faced her leader. She sensed his sincerity and his heart's connection to the Earth. She wanted to help.

Boggles suddenly broke the silence…

"I do have an idea. *But*—"

Genesis bit: "*But* what?"

"I am not sure if it would work. But I can certainly do *my* best."

"What are you thinking?"

"I am thinking I can *find* you an expert."

Genesis was surprised, "How?"

"Well, if you need a person who has the knowledge of *all* Earth lifeforms…who can arrange a list to balance each region, I know of one such Visionary who *might* be capable."

"Where did you meet him?" Genesis never heard of a Visionary who had such a deep connection to *all* lifeforms.

"*First*, I never met the person, *Genesis*," said Boggles with crossed arms. "*Second*, it is a *her*, not a *him*," Boggles sassed with hands on her hips. Then she playfully waved a finger in Genesis and Kai's faces—taunting them.

Genesis laughed. He caught Boggles' point: He and the other *men* on the team were starting to get outnumbered by *women*. That was fine with him—having no concern either way. He just thought it funny to see the serious Boggles having a good time with the idea.

"It doesn't matter to me at all," Genesis said with a waved finger directed back at Boggles. His imitation of Southern sass, however, was less adept and *far less* graceful.

Kai let loose a choking laugh—taken aback by Genesis' ridiculous attempt to shake his hips.

"*You okay!?*" Boggles quipped at Kai.

"You *boys* are ridiculous! … But I will help you anyway," Boggles said with a wink.

"This is what I'm thinking—" said Boggles as she snatched the papers out of Genesis' hand. "I will find *her* for you if *you* make *me* a promise."

"Sure!" Genesis agreed, happy to receive Boggles' help: "What's the promise?"

"Her name is 'Red.' If I find her, you have to *promise* to leave me alone—at least for one night! I can't get any work done around here!" Boggles said motioning with flapping papers to the observatory above her.

"Agreed!" Genesis nodded.

Kai smirked, "Fine with me!"

Boggles picked up Kai's sarcasm...
"Watch it, buddy. I got my *eyes* on you!" Boggles lurched toward Kai—drawing his attention to the complex vision apparatus on her face.

Kai gulped and swallowed hard.

With a tug on her zipline, Boggles made a dramatic withdrawal back into the heights of the observatory from which she emerged. As she ascended on her cord to her crow's nest, she shouted down—

"Give me a couple minutes. I will tell you where you can find 'Red.'"

Genesis was hesitant to holler back to Boggles. Having read the sign which commanded 'silence' moments earlier, he decided it best to refrain from calling out. After all—for all he knew—Boggles might have had other workers diligently preparing data in the ceilings of the observatory.

Genesis looked at Kai, then whispered…

"Kai, this matter of the *Eden List* is *very* important. We will need to resolve this as early as possible. To make sure we have all the information we need—if in fact we are leaving to find '*Red*'—we will want to bring Mage with us."

"Got it. I'll signal the warning order now, Genesis."

"Also, Kai, we will want a security team. I am sure Boggles will be sending us off to some distant, *perhaps uncharted*, Luminary System. Signal to have Mage and a security team prepared *before* our arrival back to the Watchhand. And, most importantly, Kai, get *The Goat* to assemble the team. Send him a report now so he can assemble and brief the team for our arrival."

"*The* Goat?" Kai gulped and swallowed hard.

"Yes."

Kai nodded, removing a device from his cloak. After a series of muffled beeps and a flash of light, Kai answered:

"It's done."

The next moments passed as Genesis and Kai busied themselves viewing the gentle flickering of the deep firmament above them. It glistened like a jewel—most priceless and ponderous beyond measure.

Boggles descended again—with papers in hand...

"Here you go, Genesis. I found '*Red*.' She is located in an *uncharted* Luminary System. I cannot tell you exactly what to expect upon your arrival, nor can I tell you anything about her...*disposition*," Boggles searched as if unsure how to describe a person such as 'Red.'

Genesis took the papers from Boggles. He quickly glanced at them before handing them to Kai.

"*Disposition?* What is it about her '*disposition*' which concerns you, Boggles?"

"Nothing exactly—" Boggles answered, "But I think it wise to exercise caution when moving into the presence of a *being* who is detectable through the movement of the Luminaries."

"What do you mean?" Genesis scratched his head. Although he had limited time to complete his Eden List, he realized it was vital to glean all possible knowledge from Boggles.

"Do you want to know how I found 'Red?'"

"Yes."

Boggles took a deep breath: "On the Outer Darkness plane the Luminaries move in a predictable pattern. However, I can detect 'imbalances' in Luminary Systems. So, to find 'Red'—a being who intuitively balances the Luminary System in which she is connected—I just needed to find a Luminary System with a nearly perfect balance.," Boggles continued, "And fortunately for you, Genesis, I found such a *perfectly balanced* Luminary System."

"You found *the perfect* Luminary System!?" Genesis teased.

"No, not *perfect*," Boggles clarified, "But with a *high amount of balance*. The amount of balance there is so high compared to other Luminary Systems that I am 100% certain she *must* be there."

"Could you be wrong?" Genesis asked, adding humor, "You know if you *are wrong*, Kai and I will be right back here bugging you again!"

Boggles poked Genesis: "No way! I am *100% certain*."

Boggles continued with a smirk, "If '*Red*' isn't there, then there must be a giant magical rainbow unicorn with a thousand pots of gold! That Luminary System's resonance is nearly perfect—and that doesn't just happen on its own."

Boggles motioned to the papers in Kai's hands, pointing to the sheet she prepared:

"Genesis, if you go to the Luminary System *listed here*, you *will* find 'Red.' No doubt about it. And *if you are nice*, she *might* help you with the Eden List."

****

Genesis and Kai opened their eyes—finding themselves back within the Luminary Watchhand camp. With the *partial* Eden List and Boggles' instructions in hand, the pair needed only perform final checks before stepping off to their next mission:

Locating Red

Genesis held many doubts within his mind. Sure, he was convinced by Boggles' advice. *Certainly*, he could trust her council. And, *certainly*, the pilgrim trusted the accuracy of Boggles' report: That the Visionary, Red, must *certainly* be located in the *uncharted* Luminary System recorded on the papers in his hand.

But the pilgrim's doubts centered upon that word...*uncharted*.

Indeed, it was one thing to venture into a *charted* Luminary System—which was previously explored and determined "secure" by a trustworthy explorer.

It was a different thing, however, to venture into an *uncharted* Luminary System—stepping blindly into a new world, full of surprises. Although this was a thought which invigorated explorers like Lewis Clark and Mage Paige, Genesis held no fondness for such dangerous ventures. His dangers were all faced in the ancient deserts of his first lifetime. And, he had no desire to return to such places.

"Greetings, Genesis!" shouted Goat—with a smile brimming from ear-to-ear. The shout was so boisterous it not only disrupted the entire camp, but also shattered Genesis' inner conflictions.

The Goat was an old man—with a large goatee, bright eyes and an absolutely brilliant disposition. He lunged toward Genesis and Kai—greeting them with a hug, lifting them off their feet.

Kai burst out in laughter—being held as a child, embraced in a hug with legs dangling. He felt every eye within the camp fixed upon him. He felt embarrassed, yet thankful to know he was appreciated and loved by his people.

"Let me down!" shouted Kai with a laugh. Once again on his feet, Kai straightened the folds from his cloak—as if recomposing himself from the intrusion of the kind embrace.

"It is good to see you too, Goat," Genesis and Kai spoke in unison.

Goat's joy was infectious—brightening the spirits of all who came into contact with him. Indeed, this was one of the reasons why *The Goat* was assigned as the supervisor of the Luminary Watchhand camp. It was Goat's job to track the movement of all teams through each day. To do this, he used a large board—where he would record the names of each person assigned to each team, the team's location and massive amounts of other data. Before teams would move, they would check-in and check-out with *The Goat*. He was always faithful to send them out with the proper supplies—and, more importantly, he would send them forth with council, blessings and words of encouragement.

So, why was *The Goat* in this position?

Well, since he was a seasoned explorer, Genesis thought it best to assign him as the camp supervisor. That way, The Goat could use his many years of experience to teach and provide council to younger team leaders as he sent them on their missions. Moreover, since he would receive reports from team leaders on the ground, Goat was the first person to provide guidance *in a pinch*.

So, why the name…*The Goat*?

Simple: In a flock of sheep, you only need one good, strong goat to *protect the fold* (or at least this is the case with Mahanaim sheep and goats). The Goat certainly was that person—caring for each person within the Mahanaim task force as a dear member of his fold.

Many years earlier, The Goat picked up his nickname by chance. But in the many years since, his fondness for the nickname grew to full acceptance. To cement his deep connection with his nickname, a long time hence The Goat began clothing himself with only wool and goat hair garments—making him instantly recognizable to anyone unsure of his identity. Around his neck dangled a chain with a large ram's horn—which he would use to rouse and summon the camp.

Sure, *sheep's wool* and *ram's horns* aren't from *goats*. But the Goat thought, *Eh, close enough*…simply choosing to go for the pastoralist vibe with his appearance.

"Boss, Kai messaged me the details on the upcoming mission," Goat said to Genesis, "Can you explain it more so I can make sure you have everything you need?"

Genesis nodded.

Goat motioned with his hand toward his attendants—who moved forward with papers in hand to capture Genesis' words.

"Alright, here is the order, Goat," began Genesis...

"*Situation*: Earth's geographical regions need to be balanced with appropriate lifeforms for each region—including plants, animals and microscopic life."

Genesis paused to ensure his words were captured by Goat's attendants. He continued:

"*Mission*: To accomplish this, we must locate a Visionary, named 'Red,' who possesses the remarkable ability to internally balance entire Luminary Systems in which she places herself."

Genesis motioned to the document in his hand which contained details on the Luminary System where Red was located...

"*Execution*: An exploration and security team must be led to this Luminary System to conduct hasty exploration and set conditions to compel confrontation with Red. Our success depends on our ability to convince Red to abandon her current situation so she can travel to Earth to assist with the execution of the Eden List."

Genesis concluded: "*Administration, Logistics and Command*: Goat, I need you to ensure we have adequate provisions for the duration of the mission. As usual, all movements within the target Luminary System will remain Anchored at all times on the Luminary Watchhand. Kai and I will lead this mission. I want Mage to lead exploration—perhaps she will be capable of forming a connection with Red. And, we need strong security teams with strong leaders."

Goat eyed over the papers held by his assistants. Satisfied with their furious scribblings, he turned to Genesis—motioning toward the papers held in Genesis' hand...

"Can I borrow *those* papers, Genesis?"

Genesis raised a cloaked hand—bringing with it an ethereal floating orb. He placed the documents within the orb—which immediately changed in hue from white to pink. It vanished, then two orbs reappeared. Genesis reached into the two orbs simultaneously—removing two stacks of paper, handing one to The Goat.

"*Uh, thanks.*" Goat said with an astonished laugh, "You didn't have to make me a copy!"

The astonishment passed with the gravity of the upcoming mission. The Goat pointed to his assistants—who ran in different directions, moving with urgency to accomplish the necessary preparations.

"We will make all the preparations, Genesis. The mission brief will take place shortly at the sound of the ram's horn."

The pilgrim nodded, "One last thing, Goat."

"What?"

"To locate Red . . . we will need dogs on our security teams," Genesis paused, "*Many* dogs."

The Goat's eyebrows dropped—being puzzled by the additional instruction.

Clarifying, Genesis concluded: "Since *Red* thrives with the creation and maintenance of lifeform harmony within a Luminary System, my goal will be to disrupt that harmony temporarily by moving *dogs* into set locations along certain geographic lines within that Luminary System. I think this may bait Red into moving to *figure out* the source of the change. Then, we will make contact at one of those points."

"Oh, I see," Goat said with an upraised finger tapping his temple, "That's a smart idea!" In his humor, Goat added, "I am sure Red will think, *'What's the deal with all these dogs!? Where'd they come from!?'*"

"Exactly!" jumped Genesis, "Besides—who doesn't like doggies!? Red will probably show up just to see them."

Goat laughed.

The Mahanaim *dogs* were certainly not gentle *doggies* in any regard. In fact, as discussed in detail elsewhere, the dogs of the Mahanaim army were something *different* indeed! Nevertheless, Goat—being a funny guy—enjoyed the humor in the thought: An outstanding *Visionary* like Red being humbly entertained with Man's Best Friend.

"Got it, Genesis! You and Kai should take a break in the meantime. Let the Goat put this together for you, and I'll call you when it's time for final mission brief."

****

As would be expected, *The Goat* and his attendants made all required preparations. And, at the appointed time, Genesis, Kai and Mage were standing by for transport on their mission to locate *Red*.

"I'm on it, Genesis…Like white on rice!" joked Mage Paige, the explorer. "I'm at the top of my game," Mage said as she gently patted her backpack—which was doubtlessly full of many trinkets and gadgets used by an expert charter like herself.

Usually, Mage was accustomed to working alongside her partner, Lewis. But on their current mission, Genesis thought it best to take Mage as the *solo* explorer.

After all, the pilgrim reasoned, *Mage's expertise is with measurements, data and she possess mountains of exploration knowledge. Certainly,* Genesis thought, *Mage's ability to tinker and think outside the box to arrive at solutions might be most helpful as they ventured into this uncharted Luminary System.*

"Confidence check," Mage queried as she eyed over the team members who stood in a circle with her.

"I'm at 100%," responded Genesis playfully. His reply was enthusiastic—but spoken as if guessing, merely positing the right answer, his shaking knees concealed under his heavy cloak.

When in doubt, Genesis found it always best to *feign confidence*—if only to inspire others to greater courage. He mused on an old saying: *Fake it 'til you make it.*

Mage cut a glance at Kai…

"I'm at 70%," joked Kai. On this day perhaps Kai held the *most* confidence of the three. He merely wanted to razz Mage.

"*Only* seventy percent!?" Mage was disgusted, "Kai, I need you to bring that back up to one-hundred percent!"

"Got it," answered Kai, "I'm back at 100% now."

"That's more like it. No need to fear *boys*, you have the great *Mage Paige* on your side!" exclaimed Mage as she modeled herself with leg raised and hands on her hips in a majestic pose, reminiscent of royal sculptures.

The three smiled and clasped hands.

"Okay, are we sure we know what we are doing?" Genesis continued, "…As soon as we are on ground, Mage—you need to use your equipment to get the required data. Then we will immediately transport the additional security elements. After that, we will put together next steps. Good?"

"Good," Kai and Mage responded in unison.

"If anything is awry or fishy, let me know instantly and we will be *outta* there."

"Got it," Mage said as she squeezed the hands of the two guys, "Let's go."

Genesis nodded at the security teams standing near them on the Watchhand, then the three vanished.

...

Mage, Kai and Genesis opened their eyes.

Mage quickly sprung to action—removing her backpack, then in order placing different items and gadgets upon the ground.

Genesis and Kai squatted on the ground near Mage—with both looking in opposite directions as Mage busied herself with preparations. In those quick moments, sweat already formed on the brow of Mage—as she worked feverishly to coax numbers, beeps, tones and various buzzes from items she placed on the ground.

To Genesis, Mage appeared like a child playing with a vast train set—working diligently to set the track, engine and cars in order. Distracted by Mage's tinkering, Genesis momentarily drifted from his purpose:
Watching.
He pushed aside thoughts of Mage's work—focusing intently on the air around them. The area around

them was truly *unknown*—being completely *uncharted*. In fact, it was silly for Genesis and Kai to watch anyway. After all, *anything* could spring from the air around them at any moment. *Any* danger could be present—and if a dangerous form were to approach, it would be most unlikely Genesis or Kai would even "perceive" it—since human senses operate within a very narrow range of the light and sound spectrums. For all they knew, a giant creature could be *breathing on* them—and they would be none the wiser!

Nevertheless, Genesis and Kai continued to look—peering into the milky fog which surrounded them, being incapable of perceiving any shape within it. Kai shuffled backward, until his back came into physical contact with Genesis' back. Then, they both scooched closer to Mage—a handbreadth away from her. The fog was indeed *eerie*.

"Just another minute," Mage whispered as she waited for several more muffled beeps and tones.

The moment passed.

"A l r i g h t…" drawled Mage cautiously—as if attempting to convince herself. After a pause she continued, "We are good now. Switching to Resonance setting one."

Mage flipped a switch, causing the milky fog to cascade downward, with green grass rising up to meet it. The fog dissipated into the trees behind it.

Genesis' eyes darted back and forth, reorienting himself with the new surroundings. A peaceful forest appeared around them as Genesis carefully replayed Mage's words in his mind. Then he spoke…
"Mage, did you say 'Resonance setting *one*!?"

"Yeah—*believe it or not* . . . we are in '*one*' now," answered the explorer reluctantly as she scratched her head.

"Wow! I guess Boggles was right—this must be the land of rainbow unicorns with pots of gold," Genesis laughed, "I never thought it possible for a Luminary System to be that balanced. It's no wonder Boggles could *feel* this was the right one."

"No kidding," agreed Mage. She continued, "The rest of the measurements are good. What you see is what you get. Nothing will be sneaking up on us."
Mage quickly stowed her gear, "Unfortunately, I can't tell you anything about rainbow unicorns or pots of gold though, Genesis. You have the wrong girl for that."

"Notwithstanding on the unicorns and gold, good job, Mage," answered the pilgrim in jest, "Let's move in security team, Kai."

Kai—whose finger was already hovering over the buttons on his wrist device—quickly pressed them. A moment later a circle of dogs and soldiers appeared around the trio. The security force sprang into action—moving outboard and forming a perimeter.

"I'm *oscar-mike*, Genesis," Mage whispered as she shouldered her backpack and tapped the security leader, Centurion, on his shoulder. The pair hustled off in the distance in a jogging pace—with a large pack of surprisingly silent dogs and soldiers in trail.

Genesis and Kai held their position with a small security team remaining with them as their personal guard. The mission depended on them *remaining in place*—waiting to be signaled to the appropriate location where *Red* would *hopefully* appear.

Kai removed his backpack—placing several items on the ground. After a series of unfolding and snapping sounds, Kai found himself within a set of poles with dangling wires. From this position, it was Kai's job to remain in place—using these now unusual, and ancient, wiring tools to relay communications from the security team positions being established by Mage and Centurion.

Being uncertain what to expect in this uncharted Luminary System, it was preferred to use very basic, wire transmissions in preference to the usual *ethereal* methods. In fact, Goat insisted—much to Kai's chagrin. After all, they were uncertain whether conditions in this Luminary System might preclude other methods of ethereal communication. And, certainly, with a Resonance setting of *one*, it is likely Goat was right!

Several moments passed as Mage radioed various transmissions to Kai—who in turn, echoed those positions to the Anchor on the Luminary Watchhand.

Meanwhile, at the Anchor position, Goat organized insertion of the "dog elements." Since the goal was to move dogs into set positions around the Luminary System's latitude lines at set points, Goat had each "dog element" standing by.

A departure queue was formed. And, as the Anchor received map coordinates from Kai—being received from Mage—the next "dog element" was immediately deployed to the received map coordinate.

Thus, the whole mission progressed rapidly in this leap-frog pattern. Mage and the forward security team quickly moved to a coordinate—Centurion ensured it was secure, then radioed coordinates to Kai. Then, in turn, Kai relayed the map coordinate to Anchor—which rapidly deployed the next "dog element" to the location, followed by a short confirmation message back to Kai.

From time to time, the embattled Kai momentarily looked up from his devices—wiping beads of sweat from his face—passing on confirmation messages to Genesis…

"Dog element at Point 1."
"Dog element at Point 2."
"Dog element at Point 3"
…And so on.

Time passed as Genesis watched the Greater Light on its daily circuit. As he received more reports, Genesis grew increasingly more confident of their mission—at least in its present phase. It seemed as if things were developing *without a hitch*—as Mage zipped around the Luminary System at incredible speed, quickly securing areas with Centurion and emplacing "dog elements."

And, then there was a pause.

The regular rhythm was halted. Having passed the day with reports at regular intervals, suddenly there were no more reports.

Mage was silent.

"When was the last time you received a coordinate from Mage?" Genesis asked Kai while peering over his shoulder at the electronic devices.

"Longer than expected," answered Kai with a look of concern. "Let me message her now," said Kai as he raised the transmitter.

"Did you boys miss me?" Mage shouted as she suddenly tapped Genesis and Kai on their shoulders. Kai was startled—and seizing its opportunity, the transmitter wriggled itself free of his grasp.

The pilgrim spun around—finding before him Mage, Centurion and the security element which departed with them. Immediately, Centurion and the other soldiers moved outboard to join the guard surrounding the central position.

Brushing off the transmitter, Kai sighed— "Glad to have you back, Mage!"

Genesis patted Mage on the shoulder, "Congratulations to you and your security team, Mage! You are certified explorers—having circumnavigated the entire Luminary System!"

Mage laughed dismissively—being a serious, cerebral professional, she was focused on the next step of the mission.

"Alright, Genesis. Once we are back safe on the Watchhand I'll let you know what I want to name this new place. Perhaps we will name it in my honor," Mage once again struck a regal pose—imagining the silly statues which would be erected in her honor in this new system.

"Good job, everyone," stated Kai as he thumbed a report confirmation to the Anchor. Then, he shot a glance at the pilgrim...
"What's next, boss?"

"Exactly as we planned in the mission brief," answered Genesis, "We monitor Resonance setting and wait for the disruption to compel Red to reveal herself at a map coordinate point where we have a 'dog element.'"

Kai and Mage nodded.

Genesis continued, "Kai, message the dog elements—instructing them to immediately report *Red* if she appears. Have them stall until our arrival."
Turning his attention to the security element around them, Genesis spoke further: "Ladies and gentlemen, stow gear and be prepared to relocate all on-site personnel as soon as we receive a report of *Red* from a dog element."

In the next moments, the security team around the trio reappeared from beyond the trees. They consolidated close to the central position—near to Kai's odd radio relay center.

"All dog elements confirmed receipt of the order, Genesis. They will notify 'Red' if she appears and will stall until our arrival."

"Good," said Genesis. "One last thing, Kai."

"Sure, what do you need?"

"Kai, as soon as we relocate to Red's location, I need you to immediately signal Anchor. Have Goat recall every other dog element back to the Watchhand. Have Anchor report each dog element as it arrives back at their position. And I need you to tally the reports while I speak with Red. Before *we* leave, we need to make sure *everyone* made their way back first."

"Got it. I'll coordinate with The Goat."

****

Many moments passed as the trio waited— surrounded by their security team. The peaceful setting in which they waited was *most serene*. In fact, it seemed like paradise. The air itself was borne aloft with gentle harmony.

Yet, as they waited, the electricity of the ether surrounding them seemed to drift—as if overtaken with a fog. The sensation of gentleness subsided as the area around them shifted—moving from an otherworldly white to a reddish hue.

The trio—Genesis, Kai and Mage—all noticed the shift. Clearly *something* was happening.

"Standby," said Genesis, "Kai, report to Anchor we are experiencing environmental shift. Verify if 'dog elements' are experiencing any changes."

"On it," answered Kai.

Just then, there was a *CRACK!*

From the woods near the team, a loud bending and squeaking sound rose from the silence—as if an oak tree were being bent like a grand bow, preparing to let loose a volley of arrows. The sounds were indeed *terrifying*, leaving the trio with a shared sense of impending doom.

"*Who approaches?*" called Genesis into the red-hued forest, "*Show yourself!*"

The color of the forest swirled and pulled in upon itself—drawing to a single point of red in the distance. It was as if the *essence* of the forest was gathering—lending *form* to the *being* appearing before them.

Slowly, a short figure stepped forth from the point, draping her hand upon the bark of a distant tree—as if to draw strength from her connection with it.

"*Who are you to call out to me?*" a voice answered. The ethereal voice rushed upon the trio from *all directions* as the lifeforms in this strange Luminary System seemed to be imbued with speech governed by the will of the short figure next to the tree.

The disconcerted Genesis shook himself free from the fantastic vision, being reminded of the urgency of his mission.

He answered, "We mean no harm, *Red*—in truth we are friends of all that is good within Creation. We care for the same things as you—the wellbeing of lifeforms within Luminary Systems. We are pilgrims who seek council in our mission to save such a Luminary System— called Earth."

Red slowly drifted forward from the tree, releasing her hold from its rigid bark. She drew nearer to the trio— beckoned forth by Genesis' kind words. Having a connection with *all* living things, Red sensed the heart of the pilgrim who spoke.

Truthfully, Red had no need for *words*—feeling for herself the intentions of the trio through the pulsing movements of their bodies as they touched the ground beneath them. In other words, Red communicated with the feet and blood of Genesis more than she communicated with his words.

Red glided ever nearer in graceful form. Her hands breezed upon the tall blades of grass near her—as if they were rising up to greet her, ushering her a path to her mind's intention. Her power was found in this connection with all living things—granting her the ability to materialize and dematerialize through her connection with lifeforms near her.

Over many centuries, Red desired connection with humans, yet was ever deterred from drawing near—ever sensing humanity's inclination to break and bend Creation.

However, in this moment, Red could sense the broken heart of the pilgrim. She could feel how Genesis mourned for *the Earth*. Although unfamiliar with Earth, Red's heart broke for Genesis' pain. *Through the pilgrim*, Red could feel the cries of Earth—mourning for relief under the heavy hand of her oppressors.

In this moment of silent reflection, as the words of Genesis hung in the air unanswered, Red was already convinced within her spirit of the necessity of her calling.

I will meet this 'Earth' and I will heal her life, thought Red.

Red spoke from her intuition…

"Genesis, Kai and Mage—I understand your mission. I understand your goal to help Earth. I feel your sincerity. I will help."

Genesis swallowed hard, then smiled. He bowed—thankful to meet a new 'person' who actually understood. Inwardly the pilgrim was convinced of Red's intuition. Red already *felt* his heart—capturing for herself a vision of the Earth's desire.

Red spoke further to the pilgrim, "Two things I require."

"Yes, Red. What is the first?"

"The first thing I require is for you to ensure all your dogs, humans and all their things are withdrawn from this Luminary System."

"Yes, Red. As soon as we are done speaking, this Luminary System will be left in the perfection we found it. We will take *all* things we brought with us."

Red smiled. Although she was a Visionary possessing unequalled abilities, she still maintained a humble human form—feminine and graceful. Her long red hair dangled gracefully, flowing down across her body to meet the rising grass at her sides.

Genesis broke the silence...
"What is the second thing you require, Red?"

"Show me Earth—her location and her lifeforms. Then I will go and begin healing her."

"Okay," answered Genesis, unsure how he might *show* Earth to Red. Before he could answer, Kai plucked the Eden List from his backpack—handing it to Genesis.

"Red, this is a copy of what I call Earth's *Eden List*. When the Earth was created it was populated by the Creator through Heavenly pattern animals contained in the Garden of Eden. So, in its perfection, each geographical region on Earth had *exactly* the correct animals and plants necessary to stabilize each region."

Red nodded.

"But," Genesis continued, "Over countless years, Earth fell into chaos—eventually leading to its present condition of disarray. This *Eden List* I compiled is my *best attempt* to explain which animals and plants *should* be located in each Earth region—" Genesis trailed off.
"Unfortunately, this Eden List is incomplete and I am totally lost on this matter," Genesis said with tears welling in his eyes. His throat was dry as he concluded: "There are too many animals and plants which have been lost—and I cannot put it back together."

Genesis broke eye contact with the red-haired Visionary before him. As tears fell from his face, Genesis directed his voice toward the ground...

"I fear the Earth is too broken to be fixed."

Red sighed deeply as tears welled in her eyes.

Kai removed the hood of his cloak in reverence and Mage bowed her head.

Somehow—in a most miraculous way—the brokenness of the trio joined them to the empathetic spirit standing before them. Although they were ever many worlds apart, they were joined in their love for the Earth which was broken beyond all hope.

Genesis' grief weighed heavy upon him—as if pulling his shoulders downward. His body ached under his cloak—feeling doomed to shoulder such an impossible burden.

Suddenly, in Genesis' vision—distorted by tears— the ground around him burst forth in radiant bands of colors, each rising up to embrace him and his partners in their grief. The colors transformed into petals, pistils, leaves and stems. In a moment, the ground blossomed around them in a beautiful symphony. The new flowers danced about—gently brushing the feet and legs of the trio, as if sapping away their sorrow. The sensations of grief—held only a moment earlier—were absorbed by the brilliant colors of the flowers in their waxing.

"*Fear not*," Red spoke to the three standing before her. "Hand me your *Eden List* and leave it to me."

With his grief melted away, Genesis reached forward, gently pushing aside the new flowers—handing the documents to Red.

"Now for the final matter," said Red, "You must *show* me Earth."

The words danced within Mage's mind. Mage was convinced *she* was the one to accomplish this task. After all, Mage held within herself the fullest *visions* of the Earth—having explored it with Lewis Clark. In Mage's mind she held all the data needed by the Visionary *Red*.

Mage weaved herself between the flowers, positioning herself before Red.

"Be still," Red spoke gently, "I must touch you."

Although just meeting this outstanding Visionary, Mage held within herself an empathetic connection to the person standing before her. She stood prepared to grant Red all the information she required.

In a flash, Red's form swirled about in hues of red, pink and white. The colors blazed outward—each settling in turn upon their new positions, completely transforming Red's appearance.

A grand avian form now stood aloft before Mage—with majestic wings outstretched and a long, slender beak. The form retained the gentle disposition of the human form as it continued to send surges of peace and comfort toward the spirits of the trio.

Mage stood relaxed and at peace before Red— ready to pass her knowledge to the Visionary who was gifted for this exact purpose. Mage knew her interaction now would be the direct cause of restoration for the entire Earth.

Red flapped her wings—rejoicing in the showering of sunlight from above, as if recharging herself through the power of Creation itself. Red was called to give agency for the created orders of life—guiding and blessing their continuance through her presence among them.

Red looked up, extending her slender beak, then causing the tip to gently rest upon Mage's forehead. Upon the connection, a brilliant burst of white light shone forth—fleeing in every direction.

A moment passed and Red withdrew herself from Mage. Completing the information transfer, Mage stepped away—rejoining Genesis and Kai.

With that, the brief meeting with Red was concluded. The form of Red swirled and faded as she entered her portal to Earth. Then, a whisper moved upon the trio…

"It will be done. Farewell, my friends."

With the departure of the apparition, the trio's surroundings faded back to the gentle, serene forest setting. Genesis, Kai and Mage found themselves once again standing in the midst of Centurion's security force.

So, what can be further said of this tale?

As promised, the trio ensured all Mahanaim task force personnel were removed from this newly charted Luminary System.

And, upon return to the Luminary Watchhand camp, Genesis carried with himself a sense of profound satisfaction—knowing the *Eden List* would finally be completed through the gifting of one created for the task.

In the cool of evening, Genesis lifted his face— setting aside the thoughts which held his mind captive. The wind of the Watchhand breezed across his body, cleansing and drawing away the burdens he carried. A surge of fresh energy passed throughout his body— preparing him for the path ahead.

<u>11</u>:
Seas

Now, I know what you are thinking. . . .

At some point or another, while reading this book, you have said to yourself—

"Hey, what's Genesis going to do about the oceans?"

Well, pipe down a bit and I'll tell you how the oceans were repaired!

But I must admit, the repair of the oceans contains a much more *mundane* tale.

One could say it is *entirely* mundane…and that is perhaps the entire point.

The story of how the Earth's waters were fixed began with a simple man. His name was "Steve." And, on this particular day, we find "Steve" standing quietly on the Luminary Watchhand—where he was serving as an assistant to *The Goat*.

Now, of course, you remember *The Goat* from our discussion of the castle in Chapter 2.

Who could forget *The Goat*!?

After all, he was the only guy strolling around with a *goat hair* cloak and a ram's horn hung from his neck. In the Luminary Watchhand camp, The Goat still tinkered on different inventions. But mostly he was in charge of all the *comings and goings* for the Mahanaim task force.

So, who the heck is "Steve?"

Well, Steve was a guy who *worked for* The Goat. Whenever the Goat went *anywhere,* he was followed by *at least* a couple young fellows—each working as an

apprentice of sorts. The Goat would train them up, and—
when they were ready—he would send them forth,
entrusting them with various tasks and missions.

Steve was *one* of these fellows. And, as such, he
was at first *most unremarkable*.

This is how it happened…

On this particular day, we find Steve—an
altogether *normal, ordinary* young man—standing idle on
the Luminary Watchhand. During that day he was busy
with the *usual, normal* tasks—writing down this and that,
recording information on the tracking board and so on.

The day was *ordinary*.
Steve was *ordinary*.

Just then, The Goat burst onto the scene!

"Steve, put these on!" muffled a voice
under a stack of equipment on a massive cart.

Steve wheeled around to face the sound of the
voice. Suddenly, Goat's head emerged from behind the
cart—bobbing back and forth amid a dangled mess of
gadgets in his arms, dragging on the ground beneath him.

A lump stuck in Steve's throat as his temperature
rose…

"Whaat!?"

Steve was puzzled—being so *thoroughly ordinary* and *thoroughly unfamiliar* with the machinery being pushed into his chest by The Goat. Steve refused to hold up his arms to receive the gear—certain he could somehow return to the *comfortable* embrace of the *ordinary* day if only he could *keep away* from those items. Steve turned up his nose—refusing to cast another glance at Goat or the equipment.

Under the stack of gear, Goat kneed Steve's hands—forcing them to rest underneath the large stack of machinery. And, before Steve could realize he was holding the gear, Goat quickly distanced himself. *"You got it, Steve! I have faith in you!"* shouted Goat as he sprinted off—leaving behind an anxious Steve, buried under a pile of archaic devices.

For a moment Steve listened to the mechanical whirring of Goat's legs as he sprinted further away.

He collected his thoughts. *Goat is a good boss, but I know he is always short on time*, Steve thought.

In the past, Steve and the other apprentices learned quickly to simply *do as the Goat said*. In many cases they would not realize *the purpose* of being assigned a critical task—only to learn *much later* that their quick obedience to an order resulted in the saving of another's life.

Steve reflected further: *Perhaps this is one of those times—where Goat can't explain now, but I just need to find a way to be obedient?*

Steve stood motionless—his back tightening from the weight in his arms. Of course, there were many things which made Steve feel uncertain. He was just an *ordinary* man after all. But one thing he knew *for certain*…he needed to set down the *heavy* pile of machinery!

Steve bent over, unburdening himself from the metal disks, orbs, cords and dangled mess which were forced into his arms a moment earlier. He did so carefully—mindful of his lack of knowledge and the potentially vital importance of the items.

This could be some sort of test, reasoned Steve, *And, if it is a test, I will figure it out by the time Goat returns.*

Steve swallowed hard. A bead of sweat ran down his brow—falling onto his lips. He blew a boisterous blast of air—pushing the bead of sweat aside.

That's what I'll do, thought Steve, *I'll un-dangle this dangled mess of electronics and arrange it in piles. Then Goat will be impressed!*

Steve wiped his face with the arm of his cloak. He knew this was the responsibility of everyone in the Luminary Watchhand camp: They were called to solve problems. These electronics certainly were *a problem*—so the *ordinary* Steve set about to make them into something other than "a problem."

Many moments passed as Steve hunched and lunged atop the gadgets on the ground beneath him…

One moment, another apprentice arrived to take Steve's *old* documents—officially leaving him to the gadgets as his *only* responsibility.

Another moment, a group of fellows walked by— bewildered by Steve's anxious, dangled arrangement on the ground. To them it appeared Steve was a disheveled man—pointlessly striving with the pieces of an immense jigsaw puzzle.

Nevertheless, the ordinary Steve persisted. He bumbled and strove with each piece of gear—considering *every aspect* of each piece…what made it *similar and dissimilar* to other pieces. And, thus he continued to place the items in a new ordering upon the ground—one by one—going back to each one with great care, moving them over and over again.

The Sun of the nearby Earth faded from the Luminary Watchhand, exchanging its position with the Moon. Several exchanges took place, as the light waned and waxed from the nearby Luminary System.

Nevertheless, Steve persisted.

From time to time he would doze off, then awaken—as if with a renewed understanding of the pieces. Under the waning of the Moon, Steve would view the pieces and they would appear *different*—as if he could somehow sense aspects of them which were ethereally inhibited by the brighter sunlight. So, over the cycles of time, Steve began viewing his placement choices under sunlight, then under moonlight—ensuring his ordering of the pieces remained true under *both* circumstances.

Steve began pacing about the pieces—ensuring *from every angle* they were arranged in the proper order based on their attributes.

Thus, through such painstaking effort, the ordinary Steve moved upon something quite extraordinary.

"I got it!" exclaimed Steve.

In some miraculous revelation, Steve suddenly *knew* the pieces! In a flash, Steve's *ordinary* mind received a most *extraordinary* vision—capturing for itself a stunning picture of the purpose of the pieces.

Although at first, The Goat told Steve to *put on* these items—a most absurd demand. Now arranged properly, however, Steve visualized exactly *how to put them on*.

In fact, the ordinary Steve was *so familiar* and *in tune* with the pieces, he could don them *from memory*—seeing *in his mind* each piece, and visualizing *exactly* how to place each upon himself.

Now that was *extraordinary*! An *ordinary* person—through sheer determination working his way to something *beyond his comprehension.*

Was that Goat's original plan? To somehow compel Steve to figure it out?

Perhaps.

But who knows?

The Goat is *The Goat.* I am sure there are many things he *plans*, but who knows how they fit into the grander scheme. Maybe there were *ten* apprentices—each with a tangled set of gear and Steve was the only one to figure it out. Or, maybe there was only *one* set of gear and only *one* Steve.

Tell yourself whatever you need to tell yourself.

Nevertheless, on that day Steve was ushered into a new purpose—finding for himself the ability to don a powerful mechanical suit. And, depending on how you like to think about the situation, perhaps this makes Steve *unique* among everyone.

He was the guy who figured it out! And, if you think that's exciting, just wait 'til you hear what Steve did with the suit!

Some could say—quite correctly in fact—that we would have never guessed where Steve would have travelled with that fancy outfit.

But, don't worry, I'll tell ya!

****

The Goat—as we have told before—was an explorer extraordinaire, having charted many Luminary Systems. He was a trailblazer—setting forth by his example the "gold standard" followed by all later explorers, who followed in his footsteps.

However, in the Goat's more recent years, he instead gave himself to leadership—training the next generations of explorers. And, in our present circumstances—repairing the Earth and all—Goat is the *aide de camp*, in charge of the Luminary Watchhand camp while Genesis is off doing this and that. So, while Genesis was busy smacking down politicians and making sure all the pieces were put in place, Goat ran the show at base camp—planning, assembling teams, handing out lunches, and caring for the *whither-to's and the why-for's*.

A n y w a y...

Let's get back to Steve. I'll tell you how the ordinary *Steve* became *Aqua Steve*!

...

"*GOAT! GOAT!*" Steve yelled across the camp. His eyes surveyed the gear laid out on the ground before him. To onlookers it would appear an absolute junkpile, neatly spread yet nonetheless worthless. Yet to Steve, it was a complete *masterpiece*—evidence of his diligence.

At this moment, however, Steve was neither boastful nor haughty—having mastered the puzzle which he presumed on the pile handed to him by Goat. Steve instead looked at the arranged pieces with gratitude and a strong sense of responsibility—somehow knowing he was the only one with the ability to wield their power. As Steve looked down at the pieces, his head swirled…reflecting on the absurdity of trying to *explain* the pieces to another person—one who did not strive to understand them for himself.

Sure, Steve reasoned, *there are many more people who are far braver and smarter than me, but none of those people know these pieces.*

As the shout of Steve still hung in the air, Steve's mind raced through all these thoughts. Goat heard the call of Steve amid the normal ramblings of the Luminary Watchhand camp. And, upon hearing Steve's shout, Goat set out quickly—racing toward Steve.

ZIP-WHIZ-ZIP-WHIZ-ZIP-WHIZ-ZIP-WHIZ

The large mechanical legs of the Goat glided him across the vast space.

As the Goat lurched nearer, Steve looked down with fondness for the arranged pieces before him. A sadness arose to meet his fondness—as Steve realized these pieces did not "belong" to him. The pieces *belonged* to the Goat.

Would the Goat demand them back from me? Steve wondered. Steve's body was weary from his great effort. He lifted his hand to support his chin—standing as if drawn into thought.

Goat arrived, "Hello, Steve."

"Greetings, Goat."

"W e l l…what have you got here?" answered Goat—looking at the pile of electronics now spread like a vast picnic blanket on the ground.

"I figured it out," responded Steve from the midst of his thought—still holding hand to chin, eyes locked in a trance *to the pieces* as if speaking to them.

"*What* did you figure out?" asked Goat. Realizing the importance of discovery, Goat was reluctant to hand out answers to his apprentices. He ever insisted at youngsters arriving at their own conclusions.

"The pieces, Goat!" Steve gestured downward as he swung his body toward his boss.

"I see," Goat drawled, veiling his inner confliction.

However—*between you and me*—Goat didn't see *anything*. To him, the pieces were just as unremarkable as when he dropped them in the hands of Steve.

Goat mirrored the earlier posture of Steve, moving his hand to his own chin. Careful to avoid revealing his own lack of knowledge, Goat slowly delivered his words...

"So, what are we going to do with the pieces, Steve?"

"Goat, *I can use them!* I can put them on—just like you told me to," Steve exclaimed. In his mind he held captive a vision of how the parts were to be used. And Steve assumed—quite wrongly—that Goat also knew the purpose of the parts.

Goat donned his best poker face, "And, what will you use the pieces for, Steve?"

Steve eyed Goat suspiciously.

Goat withdrew a step backward and swallowed.

"You don't know what they are...*do you!*?"

"Me!?" Goat responded with a scoff—doing his best to feign insult, trying to maintain his bluff. Unable to absorb the piercing stare of Steve, Goat crossed his arms—shielding himself. Then he laughed nervously, looking down at the parts.

The moment was shattered by a shift of moonlight from the nearby Earth, bringing an end to the brief, laughable exchange between the pair. The moonlight reflected upon the faces of Steve and Goat most ponderously—bouncing off the motionless parts. Their eyes gleamed as the parts sparkled—as if gazing upon the most mysterious jewels secluded from the foundation of time.

Suddenly, Goat—although he could not perceive it *fully*—could see a *pattern* within the parts. His mind was overtaken with wonder. His arms dropped and were followed by his jaw.

"You okay, Goat?" Steve said—expecting Goat to start drooling on himself at any moment.

Goat snapped himself free with a subdued whisper, "Yeah I am okay, Steve."

In a daze, Goat spun around, stammering to himself, "*We need to get Genesis.*"

"What!?" said Steve—as he split his attention between *The Goat* and *The Parts*.

"I am going to get Genesis!" Goat repeated, "Stay here and *guard the parts*, Steve."

The Goat sped off—lunging with a whir into the distance.

Steve receded back into his thoughts—being beckoned singularly upon the pieces before him...

"*Am I guarding the parts . . . or are they guarding me?*"

****

"*CRACK!*"

Steve nearly jumped out of his boots as a whir of electricity zapped and collapsed upon itself. A radiance of white and pink flickered with waves of ethereal power.

Genesis and Goat emerged as the ethereal passageway closed behind them.

"Howdy, Steve," offered Genesis playfully in an attempt to assuage Steve's startling.

"Howdy," echoed Steve as he glanced down at his cloak, brushing himself—casually glancing to make sure all his body was left intact by the arrival of the pilgrim.

"You're okay—I assure you, Steve," offered Goat with a smile.

"Yeah, as soon as I heard of your breakthrough Steve, I wanted to get here as soon as possible—hence the dramatic entrance. Sorry if we were a little 'danger close,'" chuckled Genesis. At times, Genesis had a tendency to be *careless*…at least a little. And, also forgetful. Genesis withdrew into his mind—jotting down a note to consider making entrances which are more considerate to others…especially people who are not accustomed to throwing themselves at will through spiritual veils as the primary means of transportation.

Maybe next time I can consider walking, Genesis thought to himself. Immediately, however, his mind shrugged away the thought: *What's the point of being 4th and 5th Dimensional if I just walk everywhere?*

"*Boring!*" whispered Genesis aloud—his thoughts escaping his mind through his voice. Genesis emerged from his mind to find a bewildered Goat and Steve staring at him—trying to snap him back to his surroundings.

"You okay, boss?" asked Goat with a jesting look, patting Genesis on the shoulder as if to shake him back to his body.

"Yeah, no worries," Genesis dismissingly smiled. "Sometimes after I move, I think it takes a minute for my body to *catch up* and my brain re-boot," said Genesis.

"Old age and all," Goat teased—imitating the pilgrim grasping his back as if to feign pain with a cracked smile.

Genesis waved his hand to dismiss Goat's joke. Of course, Genesis' *mental stalling* had nothing to do with *old age*. In fact, it wasn't a bad thing at all. But in the company of others who might not understand, Genesis often permitted the shortcut—jestingly allowing others to attribute his bizarre inner workings to *aging*.

Steve looked puzzled; Goat broke the ice . . .
"Don't worry, Steve. One day you will be like us *old guys*, and you'll understand what its like to have a body and mind that doesn't work right."
Goat put his arm around Genesis' shoulders—embracing him as a dear friend, letting him know he was in the company of friends who would look after him in

the midst of *any* physical affliction. As Goat jostled Genesis back and forth—holding onto his buddy as a kind gesture of encouragement—he called out to Steve in an unnecessarily loud, motivated voice…

"So, what do we have here, Steve?" Goat gestured down at the arranged mechanical pieces. "Can you please explain what you discovered?"

Genesis interrupted as he slipped free from Goat's grasp—

"Steve, we are very proud of what you have accomplished." Genesis could immediately sense the profound attachment Steve had forged with the pieces. Although unseen and unperceived by the untrained eye, ethereal cords of intent connected Steve to the pieces before him. Genesis could not *quite understand*, but nonetheless sensed the greatness upon which Steve stumbled.

In his own eyes, Steve was an ordinary 3rd Dimension man. In his mind he was no Visionary, nor a person destined for greatness. However, there was something far greater at work—far beyond his vision.

"Thank you, Genesis," said Steve as he looked down upon the pieces. He edged his way casually between the two men and the pieces—as if to subtly guard them. Of course, Genesis and Goat did not *want the pieces*, yet Steve—having worked so diligently to *know* the pieces could not bear the thought of another tromping upon them, nor taking them in hand.

"I get it," offered Genesis with a kind look of assurance directed at the thoughts within Steve's mind. "We are here to help, Steve. I am here to give you a *gift* to use as you are called to do so."

Steve nodded. He was unsure of Genesis' words—but was eager to receive a *gift*, especially if it would help him in his new responsibility to steward the pieces. He was drawn to them as a part of himself. And, you must understand, to be drawn to such an impossibly large number of things without the ability to truly care for *all of them* is quite a conflicted state. Having grown into his connection with the pieces, Steve was now at a standstill—being incapable of carrying *all* the pieces and bearing them hence. And, surely, he could not spend a lifetime huddled atop a blanket of pieces on the Luminary Watchhand. So, somehow, Steve would need to gain a *new ability*—which enabled him to *maintain his connection* and also *move to other places*.

Hopefully, you feel the contention—the impossible predicament of our previously *ordinary* Steve. So, with the arrival of Genesis on this day, Steve held uncertainty for his future—yet was hopeful that the cloaked pilgrim before him would somehow help him in his newfound mission . . . whatever mission it might be.

With that, Genesis extended a veiled arm, shaking his hand free from the sleeve of his cloak. He placed his hand upon Steve's shoulder. A flash closed in upon the three—causing The Goat to stumble back from Genesis and Steve.

Steve's vision tightened as the pieces rose up into a walled structure—collapsing in upon him. The pilgrim vanished with a blast of ethereal energy. In a moment, Steve was transported to Earth in the wake of the pilgrim's departure.

Steve opened his eyes—peering through a mechanical veil. He shook his arms, jostling them with a whirring quake. Steve shifted his weight left and right upon his feet—sending pulses of energy rippling beyond his body. At once, Steve's eyes cycled through a cascade of visions—each enhancing his surroundings with remarkable acuity.

Steve breathed deeply—drawing in the power of the air surrounding him, then letting it go with a rush which rattled nearby trees to their roots. A fire blazed within Steve's heart as his mind danced through thoughts of what would come to pass. As if to clearly separate himself from his previous life and usher himself into his new state of being, Steve brought together his fists with a

CRASH!

Steve's mind was now fixed upon *a vision*—and he was drawn to it. He embraced his path forward as the pieces embraced him.

Steve was re-born.

****

Waves of bubbles rose past Steve's face as the mechanical shell around him plummeted in the waters. The metallic material was solid—yet somehow malleable, *and even comfortable* against Steve's skin. His body rapidly pushed aside sheets of sea water beneath him as he descended in a flurry—leaving behind him a wake of escaping air.

"Bzzt… Bzzt, Steve this Goat— Can you hear me?"

"Loud and clear, Goat," spoke Steve into his headset, "Send your traffic."

"Request report."

"Goat, I completed a good patch on Seal 6—following the diagram you displayed for me."

"Excellent!" exclaimed Goat, "I will send the diagram for Seal 7—and that should complete your present mission. Upon completion, I will arrange a transport for your return to the Luminary Watchhand—to be followed by brief for *follow-on mission*. How copy?"

"Got it, Goat," answered Steve, "I am ready for the diagrams now—please display."

"Sending."

Amid the ascending bubbles, the visor before Steve traced upon itself the translucent shapes of lines with various mathematical measurements, distances and detailed descriptions. Steve double-clicked his radio— offering a non-verbal signal to Goat he received the transmission.

Steve immediately began poring over the data displayed before him with the same meticulous attention-to-detail granted to the mechanical pieces thrust into his arms many days earlier.

"THUD!"

As Steve studied his display, his mechanical shell came to rest on the seafloor. In the background of the display the bubbles slowed to a predictable pace—moving outward with each exhale of Steve's lungs.

Several moments passed as Steve sank into the muck beneath him—so focused was he upon the diagram. Satisfied with his knowledge of the map display, Steve toggled his visor back to its normal vision. With a *whirring*, Steve lifted his legs with ease—propelling himself forward in the water.

He gently glided through the sheets before him— carefully following the blue illuminated path.

A couple minutes until I am there, Steve thought— resolving to make use with the time by speaking more with Goat. To Steve, the ocean floor seemed *eerie* at times, so it helped him to hear a friendly voice.

"Goat, you still there?"

"Yes, absolutely. I won't leave you, Steve, until you are mission complete and we have you safely back at the Watchhand. What's up?"

Steve proceeded with some small talk…

"Goat, I want to let you know I am impressed with the *clarity* of the radio transmissions here on the ocean floor," Steve paused, "I think the use of the floating relay station and the wire was a great choice."

"*Definitely*, Steve," Goat mused, "Nothing wrong with *old-fashioned* technology. Sometimes the older stuff is the best stuff."

Steve caught Goat's humor—
"I get it, *Old Guy*."

Goat double-clicked the transmission.

"Goat, do you *really* think we can fix these oceans after the Seals are restored?"

Steve's mind was puzzled as to the next steps for the overall mission. As he moved through the Earth's seas over the last couple days, Steve noticed the dire conditions and vast amounts of pollution. Frankly, he was unsure where he fit in the process of restoring the oceans after the last Seal. To him, the seas felt *toxic*—as if they were corrupting even his mechanical suit. Steve shivered.

"Steve, we have a plan once the Seals are restored. No worries, mate. Focus on getting to that last Seal, clearing it as per the diagram. Don't worry about anything else, Steve."

"Wilco," responded Steve—encouraged by Goat's singular focus on the mission at hand.

"Don't worry, I'll have plenty for you to do when you get back here, Steve."

Steve smiled. His many days of being an *ordinary person* seemed a lifetime ago. Now, here he was rocketing along the seafloor—well on his way to completing a vital reset for the *entire* Earth.

"Goat, you never fully explained these *Seals*. What are they?"

"Short version, Steve—" replied Goat, "The Seals are the connections of the Earth's Luminary System on the Outer Darkness plane. The waters from outside and inside move through the Seals—allowing the Earth to level itself."

"In other words, you probably don't want me to get sucked out by the Seals," joked Steve.

"Yes, remain away from the Seal if unstable!" Goat's voice was stern and forceful—nearly knocking Steve away from his headset. "If the Sea is unstable and you get pulled out of the Earth's Luminary System, we have *no way to retrieve you* from the Outer Darkness plane, Steve. So be cautious and follow the instructions in the diagram. *Do you copy?*"

"I copy," replied Steve, followed by a hard gulp. His throat was dry. His vision waned and waxed. His palms became wet and a bead of sweat fell from his brow. With Goat's last exchange, Steve convinced himself to re-open the diagram on his visor…just to take *another* look.

As Steve's eyes darted along the diagram, Goat continued to speak:

"Steve, the Seals are the source of the rising tides on Earth. So, the Seals are the entry points where water is cycled *in and out* of the Luminary System. They are *very important*—but dangerous if not treated with the utmost respect. Another way of putting it: The Seals are kind of like the *foundations* of the Earth, but the water points."

A moment passed.

"Okay, I got it," said Steve confidently as he once again toggled out of the diagram, "I won't let you down, Goat."

"Easy day, Steve. You just have this last one to go, then we'll get you back here." Goat continued, "Who knows? If you do a good job down there, I might have a plate of cookies and some hot cocoa waiting for you."

"No raisins on those cookies, Goat!" replied Steve with a chuckle as he came to an abrupt halt at his destination.

"On location, Seal 7," reported Steve as he toggled his visor to reveal the vortex waves near the Seal before him. Using the surrounding features, Steve carefully traced out his path to the Seal. Taking his set of mechanical anchors in hand, Steve began the trek forward—leaving behind a maze of cord. He took a deep breath with his first step—treading on the *very edge* of all that is *known* from all that *is not*.

Steve looked with curiosity upon the focal point of the vortex—attempting to perceive that which has been evermore beyond the vision of all humanity. His mind wandered—thinking perhaps he has now ventured the closest to the Outer Darkness than any man in human history.

And, in that moment, Steve reckoned: *That ain't too bad for just an ordinary person.*

****

Upon completion of his mission and successful transport, Steve opened his eyes to see the entire Luminary Watchhand camp assembled before him.

"*Steve!*" shouted the camp with roaring applause, "You did it!"

Steve felt dizzy—immediately taking a knee to re-center himself, feeling the weight of every eye upon him. With that, Steve's mechanical suit collapsed inward, condensing itself into a blue gem on a necklace suspended from the hero's neck. Kneeling on the ground was no longer a towering mechanical behemoth, but a *simple man* wearing his simple cloak.

Steve stood up. Immediately Goat seized him by his shoulders, hoisting him upon a cart—which began without interruption carrying Steve hence to his next appointment.

"Nice to have you back, Steve!" said Goat—as the camp *whizzed* past them upon the cart. "*No time now for applauses, parties and chit chat in the camp.*"

"Nice to be back, Goat! *Umm*…Where are we off to?"

"Well, you are being taken to your tent so you can rest. And, while you rest, *The Goat* will make the final preparations for your *follow-on mission.*"

"Sounds good," answered Steve. The thought of getting to *shut his eyes* was most inviting.

"You did a great job, Steve. The data we received indicates a *successful restoration* of all seven Seals," Goat playfully slapped Steve on the shoulder, then jostled him in a side-hug, "We are proud of you. So, for now, be happy in your accomplishments, friend."

****

Time passed as Steve regained his strength in seclusion. Meanwhile, Goat busied himself with preparations—culminating once again in the re-gathering of the Luminary Watchhand camp.

Eyeing the crowd before him, the Goat began: "Alright, let's begin the mission brief."

In turn, beginning with the apprentice on Goat's left, several people each spoke—offering various bits of information concerning the mission, including administrative and logistic considerations, Earth conditions and so on.

As each apprentice completed his brief report, *The Goat* nodded. Finally, the circle of apprentices worked its way back to Goat's position—signaling it was *his* turn to provide the operation instructions for the mission.

Goat cleared his throat, then took a breath…

"Ladies and gentlemen, the Seals of the Earth have been restored to 100% function—thanks to our friend, Steve," Goat offered with a kind gesture toward Steve.

After a pause, Goat continued:

"Now we enter our *next phase* for the repair of Earth's waters. Everyone *ready to copy*?"

Goat surveyed the eager attendants standing around him and his apprentices—looking into the eyes of those who would accomplish this grand mission.

Goat pressed forward as his cadre scribbled notes…

"*Situation*: Earth's Seals have been restored. Now we must remove contaminants from Earth's waters and implement the Eden List in the water environments.

"*Mission*: Deploy clean-up vessels and their crews from the Luminary Watchhand to the Earth to travel in diagrammed circuits in Earth's waters. Steve conducts liaison with Red to obtain Eden List support.

"*Execution*: Transfers in and out of the Earth Luminary System will take place via coordinated transports. Each clean-up vessel will follow predetermined, charted courses."

"*Administration*: As per Genesis' political agreement, Earth leaders have de-conflicted its waters along the clean-up routes."

"*Logistics*: Clean-up vessels have been inspected and found to have all required supplies on board."

"*Command*: During this operation, Steve will be on-ground command on Earth. Steve is the immediate point-of-contact, and he has all the diagrams and mission information. I, Goat, will remain on communication support here at the Luminary Watchhand camp. Upon completion of this brief, all mission personnel will move to staging areas and standby for transport. Commencement of transports will be announced."

Goat paused—allowing the people circled around him to complete their notetaking. Satisfied, The Goat loudly clapped his hands—

"You can do it, everyone! I believe in you! . . . Let's move!"

As the personnel scattered in a flurry, Steve remained next to Goat. Steve's blue gem waved on his necklace, reflecting the light of the nearby Sun.

Goat placed his hand on Steve's shoulder.
"Steve, once you are on the ground, I will need you to locate Red."

"Who's that?"

"Red is the Visionary who Genesis recruited to repair Earth's environments using the Eden List. Simply put, we will need you to catch up with her. She might not be able to go into the waters right away, but it would be good if you worked out a timeline with her for when she is available. That way you can see if she will need us to move the clean-up vessels or coordinate with the Earthlings."

"How will I do that!?" Steve scoffed.

"Good question. Right now, I have Boggles crunching numbers on the Earth Luminary System— triangulating Red's suspected location."

"Will that work?" asked Steve.

"Well, Boggles was able to locate Red in a far-off *uncharted* Luminary System—leading Genesis to her. So, we can be confident Boggles can use the Luminaries to track her again."

Steve nodded.

"Once you get to her, you might need to tell her about the Earth's Seals."

"Why?"

"Well, this is why I am putting you in command, Steve. Frankly, there is much we do not understand about Red's power. Although we need her help to re-spawn and ensure the seas thrive with wildlife once again, you will need to caution her about venturing too near the Seals. You might even need to *escort* her to the Seals if she requests."

"So, you basically want me to hold her hand down there?" Steve laughed.

"No—but yes," answered Goat. He smiled, "Here's the thing, Steve: There are many things which could get messed up down there. And, if you like, I can list all the potential problems: *First*, Steve, Red might not be able to *see* the vortex near Seals—which might suck her out into the Outer Darkness. *Second*, Red might be *unfamiliar with water*. After all, Boggles found her *on land*, so we don't know if she even has the power to repair life populations in seas. *Third*, if we lose Red, then the plan for the Eden List on the rest of Earth is a loss. *Fourth*—"

"Alright! Alright!" interrupted Steve with a

smirk—bringing a halt to Goat's explanation. Steve was amused, yet doing his best to maintain a poker face. He was convinced and looking forward to this mission, but he was enjoying razzing Goat—*especially* after all the times Goat razzed him…dropping giant piles of mechanical equipment in his arms and whatnot. Although he attempted to maintain a grim demeanor, Steve cracked a smile. He covered his face to hide his amusement— feigning reflection as he drew his hand to his chin.

"I know you are getting a kick out of this, *Steeeve!*" said Goat as he kicked Steve's boot, "But we are in this *together* now!" Goat wrapped his arm around Steve's shoulders as a sign of brotherly endearment…

"Me an' you, Steve, are like peas an' carrits."

Steve laughed—shattering his ill attempt at a poker face.

Goat jostled Steve, "That's more like it, Steve! We're gonna be okay, buddy. Look on the bright side," said Goat—holding up his hand, outstretching his fingers in turn to correspond with his words, "You are gonna get plenty of sunshine…you're gonna get to see new places today…you're gonna get to be *in charge* of an *entire* fleet for the first time…and, best of all, you get to meet a new lady! Cheer up!"

Steve laughed as Goat shook him vigorously. His jowls flapped like a bulldog. His brain rattled—making it impossible for him to respond, so intense was Goat's encouraging embrace.

Goat immediately halted, jerking Steve to a stop. Holding his hand out, Goat carefully delivered his words—as if dragged to a mighty revelation. Thus compelled, Goat spoke further…

"But I must warn you, Steve—"

Steve leaned it, waiting on Goat with anticipation.

"Warn me about what!?"

"Red—the lady you are seeking, whom you must protect with your life…" Goat paused.

Goat's words hung in the air—being suspended next to their motionless bodies.

"Yes, Goat, what about *her!*?"

"Steve . . . the lady you are seeking…she's a *red-head*!"

"*Noooo!*" called out Steve in a dramatic jest—taking full advantage of Goat's weak attempt at humor.

. . .

Now, did it matter that Red was a *red-head*?
Of course not.
Obviously, she was a red-head—certainly the name implies so.

What would we expect…a woman named "Red" to be a blonde or brunette!?

Get real.

Notwithstanding, as you would expect from our newfound hero, Steve—an *ordinary* man who became *most extraordinary*—his final mission in the Mahanaim task force upon Earth was performed successfully.

And, wouldn't you guess it, Steve and Red became buddies. Sure enough, Red was able to somehow muster the ability to re-balance the lifeforms in the Earth's oceans.

And, finally, in a grand effort of the Mahanaim sea fleet, the plastics and other garbage were *schoonered* from the Earth's waters. Moreover, as Genesis directed the Earth politicians, the Earthlings made the required preparations to stop the production of industrial garbage—thereby cutting off future ocean pollution at its sources. Even Ketu—the 6th Dimension Visionary—chipped in with a helping hand!

So, what can be said further of this tale?

If ever you are inclined to think yourself *ordinary*, remember Steve. Find your own pieces—and through extraordinary effort, find your extraordinary quality.

Since Steve could do it, you can do it!

I believe in you.

<u>12</u>:
Landfills

The political auditorium on Earth was abuzz with chatter. Dulcet tones rang out in the ether of that large room—each seeking to overtake another.

In a flash, a large pink orb appeared: A shadowy, cloaked figure balanced within—*scraping* a walking staff across the floor. The shrill scraping sound felt as if it were amplified from underneath, like blaring white noise from a television. As the figure moved, the eyes of all the politicians were drawn to him in anticipation.

The figure halted—pressing the tip of the staff upon the floor and kneeling beside it. As with an invisible mallet, the staff was struck—driving it deep into the boards of the flooring.

At once the pink orb pushed outward, forming a wall stretching the length of the auditorium. The dispersion of the pink wall was followed by a quick series of blue flashes across the breadth of the entire wall. Within each flash there was a brief materialization of a second cloaked figure which passed away with its respective flashing.

The flashes subsided and the pink wall slowly faded until it disappeared. In its disappearance, the pink wall left behind only two cloaked figures and a single embedded staff.

"Genesis!? Is that you!?" demanded Mr. Sly.

"Yes," answered the second figure through the cloth covering his mouth. The voice reverberated throughout the room from underneath, vibrating the feet of the politicians as they sat in their chairs.

Different than their previous appearances, Genesis and Kai were covered *entirely*. Even their faces were covered by their cloaks. Their hands were gloved and their eyes hidden behind what appeared blackened glass.

The politicians were stuck to their chairs—pressing their bodies to them, seeking physical security amid the supernatural apparitions before them.

For the first time that morning, the auditorium was silent. However, the display continued beyond the perception of the political council. For—at this moment—a silent succession of appearances continued to occur throughout the heights of the building as a *third* figure danced through the shadows above. As Genesis and Kai carried out their interactions below, the third figure busied herself—rapidly sending data on each position to The Goat on the Luminary Watchhand.

In the silence of the auditorium, the voice of Genesis rang out—

"Ladies and gentlemen, as scheduled, today we are here to discuss details concerning the Earth's manufacturing processes, landfills and garbage."

Genesis shook his covered hand free of his sleeve. He removed a stack of papers from his cloak, placing upon them a single gold coin. Extending his arm, a pink orb appeared around the papers and coin. With the withdrawal of his hand, the orb quickly travelled across the room to Mr. Sly's desk—neatly depositing the items before him.

"What's this?" asked Sly.

"The papers are an outline of our previously agreed plan for Earth's garbage reduction and landfills. The coin is to cover the repair of the floor," Genesis said as he gestured to the ground beneath his staff.

"Yes," Sly agreed. His hand grasped the coin—holding it in the light before his face. Sly's eyes strained upon the coin as he flipped it. The coin was certainly ancient—appearing as if it were pressed similar to an old wax seal upon a letter. The coin bore arcane markings—unknown to Sly.

The pilgrim continued, "In regard to this phase of the plan, the biggest thing Mahanaim needs from Earth is for the manufacturing guidelines to be followed and the landfills sorted for transport—*exactly* as specified."

"It has been arranged," said Mr. Sly with an air of aloof pomp—seated amid his council at the highest position. In a sweeping motion, the politician placed the coin in his pocket.

"Excellent," responded Genesis. "Since everything is in order, transports will be sent as detailed. For the safety of all involved in the work, ensure they *do not* deviate from the plan. If a deviation is expected, the supervisors must *immediately* contact our camp via the outlined procedures."

Sensing the moment was fleeting—as if Genesis was preparing to vanish, another politician, Mr. Overcompensate, moved to stall. He stammered upon his words, unsure *what* to say. During their previous meetings, Mr. Overcompensate enjoyed the privilege of hearing the words of the cloaked pilgrim. Therefore, not content to allow the opportunity to pass, Overcompensate moved quickly to draw the cloaked pilgrim into conversation...

"Genesis, if you don't mind," began Mr. Overcompensate, "Previously we have not had opportunity to discuss this matter with you—although we have read the instructions. I was hoping you could perhaps discuss this matter further before you leave."

"Certainly! What do you want to discuss?"

In previous meetings, Genesis was at first suspicious of Mr. Overcompensate, but he slowly grew fonder of him. He saw in Overcompensate a genuine desire to understand. Genesis saw Overcompensate as a politician who truly strove to do his best to represent the interests of the people he represented.

"Genesis, for the benefit of the assembled council, can you give us a brief overview of the plan?"

"Sure," answered Genesis, "Earth needs to stop making things which just end up in landfills. Items and packaging need to be made *as detailed* to reduce this plague upon Earth's lands. Everywhere your lands are covered with *hills* made of garbage—with pipes spewing up from them. Your stores sell things which are all *destined* for such landfills. Your manufacturers make items which are *deliberately designed to fail*—having no concern for the Earth. This needs to stop."

Viewing the politicians to his right, Mr. Overcompensate nodded.

Sly interrupted—
"Genesis, I don't understand how *what you call* the *transfers* will occur—nor what you mean by *transfers*," poked Mr. Sly as he thumbed the papers. "You are from outer space, right? Why not just put the garbage on another planet?"

Genesis was taken aback by the absurdity:
"Mr. Sly, as I previously discussed: *There is no such thing as outer space.* This is important for you to understand. There is no empty physical space separating floating *globes*. The Earth is not a *floating globe*—and to access anything beyond it requires a *supernatural* process."

Kai blurted in laughter behind the veil of his cloak. Catching himself a second before Genesis' glance, Kai quickly covered his mouth in embarrassment.

Genesis, however, gazed at Kai—appearing like a welder prepared for his task. The pilgrim shook his head…equally at the blurting of Kai's unrestrained laughter and the ponderous imprisonment of Earthling minds. Such Earthling absurdities were *painstakingly* understood by *anyone* who held a *mere glimpse* of what lay beyond the 3rd Dimension. But, alas, to those thus imprisoned in the lower dimensions like Sly, the perception of *even* the *basest* things of the Created order were grievously flawed.

As he eyed Kai, sharing a *veiled* smile bordering upon laughter, Genesis added: "Mr. Sly, we can't take a dump truck, load it up and drive all this crap somewhere else. Leaving the Earth is a *supernatural* activity—so you can't just take mountains of physical stuff out of the Earth."

Kai buried his face in his hand to restrain himself.

"That's not what I mean!" retorted Sly, "Send a spaceship with all the garbage. It certainly would be easier than all the sorting required for the *transfers* you are asking us to prepare. Just send a spaceship and have them scoop up the *entire* landfill and take it to another planet!"

"Okay, *Sly*," began Genesis, "Earth is a closed system—which means spaceships *cannot* physically pass *into* the Earth and *out* of it."

"Huh?"

Genesis shook his head, "*What* are you breathing, Mr. Sly?"

"*Air*," scoffed Mr. Sly.

"If spaceships or rockets could leave the Earth, this would mean *air* would also leave it. And, since Earth has *air* to breathe, this means Earth is *not open* at the top. A rocket could not pass through a barrier which holds in air," Genesis concluded, "Therefore, there is no such thing as outer space. No proof required. Just think about it."

Sly shook his head, "Not true! We send rockets to the Moon. And we have satellites in space!"

"Uh, *no* you didn't and *no* you don't," whispered Kai.

Genesis amplified, "*Nope. Never happened.* But let's leave that point aside, Sly. It is impossible to fly Earth's garbage somewhere else. And, *second*, even if it *were* possible to send all your garbage *elsewhere, who* would want it?"

At this point, Genesis was beginning to enjoy toying with Sly. The politician's demeanor—declaring with certainty *untruths*—was amusing. The irony of the two positions within Sly was absurd—declaring things *beyond his perception* as true, yet possessing no *actual* knowledge of them.

Kai caught the irony as well, thinking to himself: *No one in all Mahanaim would talk to Genesis like this, and yet he suffers this Earthling's banter?* Kai crossed his arms impatiently.

Mr. Overcompensate began to speak, but was interrupted by Sly.

"Take all the garbage to Venus or Mars," demanded Sly, "Venus is hot so all the garbage would just burn away there anyway."

"Venus doesn't want Earth's garbage. And, Venus isn't what you think it is." Stretching his point further, Genesis attempted to move Sly to retrospection:

"How 'bout I bring all Venus' garbage *to Earth*? Actually, why don't I just bring all the garbage from Mars to Earth as well? What is your address, Mr. Sly? I'll drop it all off at your house."

At this, the political council erupted. Some politicians laughed. Others to the left of Sly missed the point *entirely*—responding in anger, being unsure of what Genesis meant but guessing he offered some type of insult to the chief politician.

Sly slammed his gavel. Normally the sounding of the gavel would be followed by words, but at this moment Sly could muster nothing further. It felt as if his words were held fast within his mind—unwilling to manifest themselves further.

The room fell silent.

Genesis spoke, "The *transfers* of the sorted materials is the *proper* method—as detailed in the plan provided. The Earth must maintain its materials. The transfers will allow for a quick swapping of Earth's inorganic material with organic material from a place called *Ketu*. In the long term this means the landfills of Earth will quickly recede as organic material can reduce itself. The changes in manufacturing will control garbage production at its source. And, last, it will empower your citizens. By controlling this process on the highest level—regulating manufacturers, your countries can fix this problem. Your political council will need to ensure these measures are kept in place for all future generations."

"What is *Ketu*?" blurted another politician.

"It would be hard to explain," offered Genesis reluctantly, "If a person is stuck on concepts like outer space, planets, floating globes, rockets and spaceships, concepts like Ketu would challenge you to change everything." Genesis surveyed the faces of the politicians—finding in some a spark of *something* he desired.

"For those of you interested in learning more about Ketu and how your Earth relates to what is *beyond* it, I will have my Luminary expert prepare some reading material. Then you can slowly review that information at your own pace."

Some of the politicians nodded heartily— capturing Genesis' offer. Others raised their hands, as if to ask for a copy. Sensing their eagerness, Genesis spoke further…

"It is a *very* interesting topic—considering Earth, Ketu and other places. Keep in mind, we do not understand *everything*. But we can pass on the knowledge we have for those of you who are interested. Earth and what you call *stars* are all what we refer to as *Luminary Systems*. Concerning the Earth—the Sun and Moon are actually a part of its own Luminary System. Outside each Luminary System is a vast expanse called the *Outer Darkness plane*. And stretching between the Luminary Systems is a connector called the *Luminary Watchhand*. The Luminary Watchhand is somewhat similar to

Rainbow Road on Mario Kart—for those of you who are familiar. But it is different in the sense that it is a 4th Dimension place—which means you absolutely *cannot* get there *physically*. Getting there is a 4th Dimension process."

"So, the Earth is *completely closed*?" inquired another politician, clarifying further, "Nothing can enter it or leave it?"

"Yes, the Earth is a closed system in regard to its air. But even for us, the boundaries of Luminary Systems are very difficult to describe."

"What do you mean?"

"Like I said, this is all difficult to understand. Perhaps a good way of explaining would be to say the boundaries of Luminary Systems seem to be *warded* from the inside. In other words, those physical beings within the Earth might be completely incapable of *physically* approaching the barrier on land or air. And, even if the barrier were approached, *physical* beings—like humans— might be precluded from its perception. This might be why it appears impossible to reach it from within. Interestingly, however, it appears the seas are directly connected to the Outer Darkness plane via Seals—which control the passage of water into and out of the Luminary System."

"So…we cannot leave the Earth through the atmosphere, but we could leave the Earth through the oceans!? That doesn't make any sense!"

"Like I said," repeated Genesis, "This is difficult to understand."

"How would we find our way out through the Seals?"

"Well, you would need the technology to make that physically possible. And you don't have it. And, even if you *had* the technology, you would need to be capable of locating the Seals—which I am convinced no one on Earth would be capable of doing. Last, even if you could do those things, I would not recommend anyone attempt leaving through the Seals."

"Why?"

"Because leaving the Earth through a Seal would likely place you within the Outer Darkness plane—an area which is entirely uncharted, and in theory a supernatural dream land of endless spiritual waters. And, somehow, those waters of the Outer Darkness plane may flow in part along the outer boundary atop the Earth's sky—meaning that Earth's sky is held within by spiritual waters. But I digress. I will have my Luminary expert provide those interested with some materials on these topics," Genesis concluded with a smile.

"Wait— Since no one can leave the Earth, how do the *transfers* happen?" asked another politician.

"The *transfers* are what you would call a *supernatural process*. To do the transfers we rely on a person named Ketu—who transfers material using a spiritual exchange," Genesis scratched his head as he approached this topic which was beyond even himself, "Suffice it to say, we each have *our* part in the process of repairing the Earth. You guys are doing *your* part by regulating manufacturing and overseeing the sorting process. Be thankful you have good friends who are also doing *their* part to help you."

****

"No problem, Genesis. Consider it done—just like the roly-polies," answered Ketu with a smile, followed by a solemn bow.

Genesis, Goat and Kai returned a bow of courtesy in unison. And, with that, Ketu's form collapsed in upon itself in a brilliant display of light. The light retreated—vanishing out of sight.

"Well, *there you have it*," belched Goat.

"Yep, *there we have it*," echoed Genesis, shifting his shoulders with a crack.

With that, the three turned around—beginning their walk back to the Watchhand camp.

"So, Genesis—"

"Yes, Goat?"

"That *Ketu* certainly is a *different* character," said Goat reluctantly—as if he could not find the proper description for the 6th Dimension being who just vanished from sight.

"He certainly is."

"Where'd you meet him?"

"It's hard to explain. I haven't met him *yet*—*but* I have," Genesis answered, also showing within himself a great deal of uncertainty. Looking at the puzzled look on Goat's face, Genesis walked back his explanation to make it more palatable...

"Maybe it would be best to just consider he is on our side," Genesis smacked.

"Okay," conceded Goat—thankful to set aside his uncertainty. His forehead was starting to ache. He raised his hand to his brow—as if to push the sensation aside.

"Besides," Genesis continued, "Ketu has taught me quite a bit about myself." Genesis was not sure what that point was *beside*—so his words hung awkwardly in the air, as if baiting one of his companions to scoop it with his hand.

Kai bit:

"How did Ketu help *you!?*"

Kai had mixed thoughts about this concept. At times he tended to *look up* to the pilgrim so greatly—to the abolition of the concept of Genesis' own *journey*.

However, Genesis was far from perfect. He had *much* left to discover—and he patiently allowed himself to learn, humbly bowing to others who were endowed with abilities more advanced in some regard. Thus, the pilgrim bore a humble sensibility...allowing himself to wade through his experiences—carefully assessing others, searching their minds for enhancements not yet realized in his own form.

Genesis snapped free of his thought—repeating the question...

"How did Ketu help me?"

Kai nodded. Behind him Goat mirrored the nod—as if to second the motion.

"Well, Ketu taught me about *refraction*."

"Refraction?"

"Yeah…The ability to redirect thoughts, emotions, physical things. It is similar to *Tai Kwon Do*—where a person uses the energy of an attacker against him. So, the person being attacked merely maneuvers himself to *redirect* the power of an attacker back upon himself."

"That is *Tai Kwon Do*?" asked Goat, appearing lost within the term.

"Yeah, to my knowledge—but I might not be explaining it right," Genesis said as he surveyed the faces of his companions. Realizing he led them into a quagmire with the term, Genesis retreated from it…

"Er…Never mind the *Tai Kwon Do* part," Genesis began anew: "Ketu taught me how to repel negativity."

"How?"

"Ooo…" exclaimed Genesis, as they drew nearer to the camp, "That is an interesting topic—but we might need to walk slower to have time."

Goat was happy at the prospect of remaining away from camp a little longer:

"Why not? I need to let my assistants have a chance to run things every once in a while."

Genesis nodded, "Well, Ketu is from the *shadow planets*—or what is referred to as the *shadow planets*, Ketu and Rahu."

"Hence, his name is Ketu," offered Kai.

"Hence *Ketu* is from *Ketu*," Genesis repeated, then continued: "He has a different name, however, but he goes simply by Ketu because it is likely he is the only one anyone has met from there."

Goat poked, "You know other people from Ketu, Kai?"

Kai shook his head left and right.

"A n y w a y," continued Genesis, "When you think about these *shadow planets* you can make sense of the dome of light atop each Luminary System. In other words, when you are standing on Earth—looking up at the sky—you must understand *everything* is seen through *refraction*."

"Like seeing fish in a pond?" summarized Goat to the nod of Genesis. Encouraged by the nod, Goat continued: "Because of the water the fish are not *exactly* where you see them. The light is bent by the water."

"Yup," agreed Genesis, "And when you apply that same concept to the Earth's sky, that means the air above the Earth causes *refraction* as well. So, all the things in the Earth's sky—the Sun, Moon and light of the Luminaries—are *all refracted* from the observer's perspective on the ground."

"Why does that matter?" inquired Kai.

"Well, just as Ketu and Rahu—the shadow planets—are in locations beyond the refraction, so also the Sun and Moon are actually in ethereal locations beyond the refraction."

"Oh, I think I heard of this before!" interjected Goat, "They say there are two Suns—one physical and one spiritual."

"Pretty much," conceded Genesis, "But calling one Sun *physical* and the other Sun *spiritual* might not be the right terms."

"I am sure Boggles can tell us *a lot* more about it," sighed Kai.

275

"She could," agreed Genesis, "And she would also tell us about how to use refraction of the Luminaries to produce energy in the ether. In fact, this is one of the sources used by Amie's sky fleet."

"Very cool."

"It is cool."

"So, what did all that stuff teach you about yourself, Genesis?"

"Refraction teaches me that there is much *beyond our sight*. Even in the case of the sky, the Creator has embedded the concept of spirituality—beckoning us to consider spiritual things…the reality beyond the reality. Even beyond the Sun, there is the unseen *source* of the Sun from beyond the firmament."

"How do you use that information, Genesis?"

"Simple: Whenever negativity is directed at me, I take that negativity and place it in a box within my mind. Then, just like how the person Ketu does, I push that box to transfer it off of me. In other words, it is like me putting the negativity back on its source, or setting it aside where I can process it later."

"I see. So, it isn't with the shadow planets themselves, but just following the basic idea."

"Pretty much," answered Genesis, "Whenever negativity is placed upon me, my mind contains it—transferring the negativity back to its source or parrying it away. Now I cannot do it perfectly—and certainly at times negativity can get the best of me. But I do my best to follow the pattern of Ketu in this regard."

"Interesting."

"Yeah it is a cool idea. Glad you find it interesting, Goat. But I have found this has further reaching implications that just how to deal with 'negativity.' In fact, since within the entire created order there exists a reality *beyond the physical* which imprints upon the lower dimensions, then the spiritual man cannot be held captive by anything in the lower dimensions. Just as a fish in a pond can elude an arrow through refraction, the spiritual man can offset himself from the lower dimensions through refraction. And, even if such a man is targeted within the lower dimensions, would it be possible to truly strike the *core* of his being? Arrows may be loosed, but the spiritual man uses the *veil beyond* to gently remove himself from harm. The arrows zip past the fish in the water, being veiled by refraction. And those who remain on the shore are oblivious to the true power of the fish. Although possessing no weapons, the fish's reliance in the order of the Creator protects his true form from harm. Such is also the case of humans…if we desire to have it: Refraction."

<u>13</u>:
Deserts

So, at this point you may be wondering about the Earth's deserts. Because, since the goal of Genesis was to *repair the Earth*, certainly he should start with the places which needed the *most* repair. Right?

This is true. However, before Genesis' task force could tackle the problems of the desert, they needed the tools to do so.

Thus, nearing the end of entire mission, conditions were finally ripe for attention to be focused upon the deserts. And, even more interestingly, we find the deserts were the most *enjoyable* aspect of the entire mission for the members of the Mahanaim task force.

Why?

Well, let me start by explaining some things about Mahanaim…

On Mahanaim, there is this strategy game called *Bumble*. And *Bumble* is a huge deal! So, whereas Earthlings have games like *chess*, *checkers* and the Chinese game *Go*, *Bumble* is the popular game of strategy on Mahanaim.

So, how do you play *Bumble*?

This might be complicated to explain, but let me begin by saying *Bumble* has a gameboard—somewhat similar to the boards of other games. The gameboard, however, is stretchable—being pulled across a tabletop. Depending on the size of the table, the *zones* on the gameboard can be bigger or smaller. Think of the zones like the squares on a chessboard.

Like other games, *Bumble* has game pieces which are moved on the board. The pieces look like stones which fit in the palm of one's hand. The game pieces are interactive—because the game involves *feeling* the pieces.

So, each stone piece can change—in color, texture, temperature, shape, smell and so on—as they are manipulated on the gameboard. Generally, however, it is taboo for the pieces to be programmed for *taste*—as that would require players to slosh the pieces around in their mouths. Yuck!

Bumble is a strategy game of *sensation and variable harmony*.

How can I explain this?

Think about a lightning bolt.

Before a lightning bolt strikes, it *plans* its path—tracing out where it will go. So, a lightning bolt moves in *harmony* with its surroundings—zapping itself through the ether along a pathway where harmony exists for its transfer.

Likewise, the game *Bumble* is about the player moving pieces to discover the *harmony* on the board. Bumble is about balancing the variables of each piece through the senses—as the player toggles each game piece through its different attributes (texture, temperature, color, weight, variances in shape, and so on). But by altering one attribute of a game piece, it may cause alterations in other attributes within itself and nearby pieces. So, there truly is a strategy in the game—as the player must rapidly shift through attributes to determine changes, constantly checking nearby pieces to detect *new* variations.

The pieces in *Bumble* hover above the gameboard. To interact with a piece, the player grabs it and takes it off the board. Then the player can touch, feel, smell or do whatever to the piece. When complete with assessment or adjustment, the player can either put the piece on the border of the gameboard or put the piece in a specific place. If the piece is set near the border of the gameboard, the piece will float back to its previous *zone*—if that zone is empty. If the *zone* is occupied, the piece will float above the border of the gameboard.

So, how can you win in *Bumble*?

When the entire board has achieved "*harmony*"— with all the pieces and zones achieving balance—the player has completed the game. (Daring to complicate things further, games can also be designed where the objective is to reach specific *discord* conditions. In other words, a person may design a story objective for their game which requires the player to manipulate the pieces until they reach a certain color pattern. This would mean the player would be attempting to pull the pieces *out of harmony* to achieve that objective. In those games, the game is completed when the person achieves "*discord*.")

So, how do these games work?

Well, each *Bumble* game comes with pre-set scenarios that are adequate for *novice* players.

But for *master* players, however, Bumble games can be designed which require incredible precision. The *Bumble* pieces can even be set with 4th Dimension variables—which can dramatically increase the difficulty of the game. And, it is assumed it will one day become possible to set pieces for 5th Dimension variables—which would require the player to achieve harmony in layers. Of course, for you this might not make a whole lot of sense. But for *Bumble* fanatics, the prospect of such intense gameplay is intriguing.

Indeed, with the high esteem held for this game in Mahanaim, there was much anticipation at the arrival of Genesis Pilgrim. Many *Bumble* fanatics wondered if they might now be upon the cusp of gaining a new dimension of gameplay with the arrival of the first time-traveler. I know it sounds silly…the idea of many people hearing of *time-travel* and how it might enhance their *game*. But if you do not understand such fervor for this game, then you clearly do not understand Mahanaim. They love *Bumble*!

How is a *Bumble* game set up?

A player can design a Bumble scenario in an attempt to stump his opponent. The player who sets up the game might pit himself against the other player. For example, if I am setting up the game, I might work to set up the pieces in a way that is very difficult for you to achieve "harmony."

A designed scenario often involves pre-reading material for the player before beginning the game. Often it is common for Mahanaim citizens to design a story for each game—where pieces and gameboard zones may be named. Additionally, the variables used in the game may represent something within the story to give the player a logical framework for the game.

However, in advanced games set up for master players, they may be expected to go into the game "blind"—being provided with no previous reading material on the scenario. This means a master player often must begin by *diagnosing* the board—which involves a rapid sequence of steps to ascertain all the variables present on the board. From there, in order to facilitate his gameplay process, it is common for master players to utilize the technique of *memory palace*, also known as *memory journey*, to improvise their own stories for the board.

Why is this important?

Well, based on the structure of the human mind, few can accomplish such Bumble games without the use of story.

Think of *Bumble* like a *Rubik's Cube*—but with many more dimensions than color. It is played on a gameboard and enhanced with an underlying story to guide the mind of the player to the game's completion.

So, why is *Bumble* important in this story?

And, what in the world does *a game* have to do with "repairing the Earth?"

Simple...

Have you ever read <u>Ender's Game</u>?

Genesis did. And, surely his use of the game *Bumble* in this regard borrowed from the same concept. For in the Luminary Watchhand camp, Genesis directed the set up of a large *Bumble* tent. In the outer court of the tent, there were many tables where task force members would spend much of their free time designing and playing leisurely games.

However, in the furthest room of the tent, one *Bumble* gameboard was designed for a much more productive purpose. As Genesis waited for Amie's sky fleet to clean the Earth's skies, The Goat tinkered diligently. Goat designed drone ships—which he endearingly called *bumblebee drones*. And, each *bumblebee drone* was linked to a different piece on that special *Bumble* board.

Once Amie's sky fleet completed its work, Boggles was able to re-set the Earth's *Ether Grid*. Similar to the Ether Grid on Mahanaim, the new Ether Grid on Earth allowed for the direct transfer of electricity and physical material through the sky itself. This meant the bumblebee drones gained the ability to instantly transfer water and material from one drone to another—including the transfer of various animals, plants, insects and microscopic lifeforms as specified in the Eden List.

Furthermore, Genesis used his Eden List to develop a story for that special *Bumble* game. The various physical aspects of the pieces were each assigned "names"—linking them to physical things which needed to be increased or decreased in the Earth's desert environments.

As Red worked diligently to balance the Earth's ecosystems, the *Bumble* game was designed to control the drones who would provide for the gradual build up of these desert regions.

How?

Well, unlike Ender's Game, Genesis was forthcoming with his team—notifying them that each *Bumble* piece on that special gameboard was really a drone. And that special gameboard was the means to repair the deserts of the Earth. The zones of the vast gameboard were each programmed with the coordinates of the desert locations throughout the Earth. So, moving a piece on that gameboard would cause an instantaneous movement of the corresponding drone to the *exact* zone location on Earth.

Thus, in most remarkable fashion, the Mahanaim task force provided for the leisurely repair of Earth's deserts through the use of a game! Indeed, the task force members were all overjoyed to play the game—each taking turns moving the pieces all morning and night. By doing so, they effectively terraformed the deserts back to life remotely. Some drones were used for farming resources—while other drones deposited. And all the transfers between drones were made possible through the Ether Grid of Boggles.

When seeing the drones, some Earthlings called them UFOs—for they would instantly zap in and out of sight. The drones were large, lacking typical characteristics of planes or helicopters. After all, since the Ether Grid was made operational, it was no longer necessary to use "fuel" to remain airborne. Rather, each drone kept itself suspended in the air through its connection with the Luminaries through the Ether Grid. So, the appearances and disappearances of the bumblebee drones were indeed bizarre occurrences in the eyes of Earthlings. Nevertheless, with the continued appearances and disappearances, the Earthlings also noticed the quick transformation of their harsh deserts into lush oases.

Thus, the Earthlings began to relate to these "UFOs" just as bumblebees. For, when we see bumblebees in our garden, we do not swat them away.

Nor do we consider them threats. Rather we silently leave them to their good work of pollination—as they tend to each flower in succession. In this way, the Earthlings left the bumblebee drones to their work. And this is how Earth's deserts once again bloomed with life.

It was all accomplished with a game.

<u>14</u>:
Earth Shepherds

"Hey, Amie. How's it going?"

"It's going well, Genesis," Amie said as she took a breath—preparing herself to offer a hasty report on the progress of her sky fleet.

"The sky ships have been carrying out the plan we developed with Boggles. A large portion of the plan is complete, and the fleet continues to move along its assigned tracks to mop up the aluminum, barium, strontium and other contaminants."

289

"Excellent," answered Genesis as his eyes surveyed the large video display in the air command center.

"Would you like coffee, Genesis?" asked Kai—standing in the shadows behind him.

"Of course, I want coffee!" sassed Genesis. "Everyone knows I drink coffee while watching radar!" Genesis laughed to himself—unsure whether Kai would catch the pop culture reference.

He didn't. Instead Kai quickly poured several cups—handing the first one to the pilgrim.

Genesis drank slowly—guarding his mouth from the scorching beverage. He lowered the cup, holding it in his hands—drawing warmth from it. The cup quivered as a small amount of the liquid ran upon his wrist.

"Amie, I was curious if you would be willing to lead *another* project?"

"Sure!"

Although she would *never* admit it, lately Amie had grown restless amid the *monotony* of her daily tasks.

Since everything in the sky fleet was already in progress, her supervisory role morphed into *mere tasks*—recording data from pilots: Just *lots* of numbers and *not enough* personal interaction.

"Good, Amie. Thank you," responded Genesis as he took another drink from his cup. "I drafted a plan for the *4th Dimension training program*. As outlined, *you* will be responsible for interviewing Earthling applicants."

Genesis handed Amie a stack of papers.

"In these documents I lay out my 4th Dimension training program. I want to gain new task force members through the program. I think you would be a good fit to oversee the implementation of the program, Amie," Genesis smiled.

In remarkable irony, the pilgrim desired *Amie*—who was only 3rd Dimensional—to lead the 4th Dimension training program. Kai immediately sensed this irony and a gentle wince betrayed his mind. He was uncertain *how* Genesis could expect Amie to do this great thing. The wince quickly passed and left Kai to wonder *why* the pilgrim would choose to do this.

Wouldn't Ketu or another Visionary be a better choice to lead the program? thought Kai.

Amie, however, held no such reservations. She was an adept planner and had within her a genuine heart. In the moment she was enraptured with the thought of meeting new, interesting people like Zeg-E. And, in the enrapturing of *that thought*, Amie moved quickly to seize the opportunity presented.

"Ooo…that does sound interesting!"

Amie danced with enthusiasm as she snatched the remaining papers from Genesis' hand. She immediately offset her body—putting distance between the pilgrim and all the papers. Now that they were in her hands, she viewed the program as *her own*. She didn't want Genesis to *take it back* from her.

Genesis always admired this about Amie. She took tasks personally—developing empathy for her assignments. Seeing her enthusiasm, Genesis was convinced the program would be successful through her leadership.

Genesis continued, "Amie, if you look on page—"

Amie offset herself *further* to guard the papers from Genesis' outstretched finger—smiling playfully. She needed no further explanation and relished in the opportunity to read something *new* this morning. She didn't want Genesis to spoil the surprise by blurting out further *explanations*.

"Is everything written *in here*, Genesis?" Amie asked curtly as she smiled—balancing her abruptness with pleasantry. Her hands shuffled to bring all the papers together in a neat stack.

"Yes," Genesis laughed.

"Then just leave me to it!" said Amie as she tucked the papers under her arm and grabbed a cup of coffee from Kai.

"I can read! And I am sure you have better things to do!"

With a chuckle, Amie used her free hand to guide Genesis to the door.

"Thank you for selecting me, Genesis. I will read the document carefully and prepare notes to discuss with you. Then the plan will be carried out diligently."

She concluded, "Before Kai can shake his tail twice, you will see plenty of new Earthlings here on our task force!"

Genesis was quite amused by the enthusiasm of Amie—playfully conceding to her bold undertaking. He allowed himself to be jestingly *pushed* to the door—sloshing coffee from his cup as Kai was pushed in trail.

"See you l a t e r, A m i e!" Genesis and Kai drawled together in unison—as if echoing down a long hallway.

"L a t e r!" Amie echoed as she now used her free hand to wave. She stretched her arm over her head in a dramatic display—imagining herself a homemaker living on a prairie of old, sending off *her boys* for their daily chores before the evening meal.

"Y'all come back now, ya hear?"

Now several steps removed, Genesis was quick to grasp the hilarious development within the situation. He cupped his free hand to the side of his mouth—as if calling out across a field...

"Alright, we'll be back soon! Love ya, Ma!"

****

"So, Genesis...What's the deal with the program you were discussing with Amie? Why bother offering to teach 3-D Earthlings to become 4th Dimensional?"

"You never know, Kai. There might be some who could benefit our future missions. Besides, it is always best to offer opportunities to the next generation," Genesis paused, "We certainly aren't getting any younger, Kai!"

"True, but it seems like we have everything under control. Maybe we should just focus on recruiting another person like Ketu or Red. Why bother with Earthlings?"

"Well, for all we know, Kai, there might be *another* Red or Ketu hidden amongst the Earthlings. Either way, we can leave Amie to sort it out," offered Genesis in mediation for Kai and himself. "If there are good candidates out there, Amie will find them."

Kai rubbed his chin, then scratched his arm as he nodded in agreement. *Best to leave this to Amie*, he thought.

"I do, *however*, share some of your reservations, Kai—perhaps for different reasons than you," Genesis added.

"What do you mean?"

"In the back of my mind I have considered what *might* happen if 3-D Earthlings developed *another* way to gain 4th or 5th Dimension ability."

"*Eck-hem…*" grunted Kai as he gestured back at the pilgrim.

"Not what I mean, Kai. I know I am a human who was previously 3-D, who gained 4th and 5th Dimension ability. But what I mean is what would happen if a *non-spiritual* person did this. In other words, a person with no regard for the supernatural—who merely *found another way* to push himself onto the Luminary Watchhand, or even seize the ability to do time-travel for merely *physical* reasons."

"Whoa!" Kai halted, holding out his hand as if to object to the pilgrim's point. "I didn't know that would be possible. You think a 3-D Earthling could do that!?"

"I'm not sure, Kai. Granted, I am happy we were given this opportunity to *repair the Earth*, but I am concerned our arrival may somehow set in motion something far more nefarious," Genesis added, "During our mission this threat has been growing as a shadow in my mind. Although I have fasted and moved to break contact from it, I fear something is happening *behind the scenes* on Earth."

Kai scratched his head—as he searched his mind to understand the pilgrim.

Genesis broke the silence: "Maybe if we offer 4th Dimension training to *some* Earthlings, we can get ahead of this. If there is a more nefarious plot in motion on Earth, *maybe* some of our new recruits from Earth could help us find and squash it."

"It does make sense, Genesis" offered Kai as he passed his hand across his face. "If there are Earthlings who are up to some sort of devilish plot, who better than an Earthling to sniff it out?"

"Exactly. And frankly, I want to be ready *when and if* these things happen. My study of ancient prophecy has taught me that there will be a *Great Tribulation* upon the Earth. And, what better time would there be for an *anti-Christ* to seize power?"

"That is scary."

"It is. If a plot is in motion on Earth, it would be easy for an *anti-Christ* to seize upon our withdrawal from Earth—claiming he was also appointed by Mahanaim, or that he is from our own company, or that he was appointed from *Beyond*. Then he *could* direct Earthlings to do *whatever* based on their deception. And, if we are gone, there would be no one to check his deception. He could do simple 4th and 5th Dimension actions and all the 3rd Dimension humans would believe he was doing miracles. He could make himself out to be a 'god'—and spiritually-imprisoned humans would be convinced by his *supposed* miracles."

Genesis paused, then continued: "*But* if we train a company of Earthlings, they could shepherd the Earth— ensuring all things we repaired *remained repaired*. And, if an anti-Christ *were* to arise, he would have his 4th Dimension and 5th Dimension abilities countered by other Earthlings who have been trained *by us*."

"Now that you mention it, Genesis, when we first arrived at the political council, Mr. Sly and some of the others sure were persistent in trying to call us *outer space aliens*," Kai recalled.

"You see, Kai! That is exactly what I am talking about! It is like some of the Earthlings in power *want* to twist us to fit into their grander scheme in some way…like we are a piece in *their* puzzle."

Kai felt a chill down his spine, "I don't like this at all."

"Me either, Kai," Genesis exhaled, wiping his forehead. "Hopefully we can sort it out. Regardless, it is a good step to train some Earthlings so we have a *chance* of holding everything together. Sure, the Earth *needed* to be repaired by us. But now that the repairs are almost complete, I am concerned about the next Frontier which will break out upon the Earth. We cannot forsake the Earth to *fallen* humanity. We must prepare Earthlings to shepherd the Earth."

<u>15</u>:
Party

As in all cases, it is important to celebrate when celebration is warranted. And, certainly, when the *Mahanaim task force* was nearing the completion of Earth's repair, celebration was warranted.

So, Genesis appointed a party committee within the task force. The grand event was scheduled. All things were put in order, and invitations were sent. Many Earthlings were also invited—especially those politicians who were instrumental in coordinating Earth's efforts during the repair.

Of course, the opportunity for an Earthling to venture to the Luminary Watchhand was a great honor indeed! Transports were scheduled to bear them hence and back on the appointed day.

As it has been discussed elsewhere, Genesis has a knack for pointing out the *blessings* in the mundane—drawing attention to those things most neglected within Creation. So, it was no wonder this magnificent party would incorporate this theme. After all, Genesis sought most to leave Earthlings with a profound appreciation for the Earth herself. For, by giving proper honor to *Creation*, Earthlings would gain respect for the *Creator*. Therefore, the party was designed to honor the creation of the Earth.

So, what was the way Genesis chose to *honor* Earth?

Well, Genesis chose to do this by employing the vast skills of two people—Lewis Clark and Mage Paige. Specifically, due to their roles as explorers, Lewis and Mage were often left to fend for themselves in the wildernesses of various Luminary Systems. And, to fend for themselves, Lewis and Mage developed an *incredible* knowledge of plants. In other words, whereas you or I might be inclined to see only *weeds*; these explorers knew *nearly everything* there was to know of plants—what portions could be eaten or used for various purposes. Truly, the explorers' hearts were drawn to the *bounty* contained within *nature*—which Earthlings now sadly held in little regard, preferring the artificial and plastic over the breathtaking wonders of the lower dimensions.

So, what does this have to do with the party?

Well, the program of the party was set and preparations were made for Lewis and Mage to share their knowledge with both the Mahanaim task force and the Earthlings in attendance.

On the appointed day, the transports bore hence the Earthlings. The Mahanaim task force was in full attendance. Some leaders maintained devices in order to monitor the activity of various things still a-buzz on Earth and elsewhere—including some of the meandering ships in the skies and seas.

And, after the requisite *cocktail hour* allowed for the arrival of stragglers, all found their ways to the *seating chart* and their assigned seats.

The program began—as many do—with a brief overview of the task force's *recent accomplishments*. In this case, the overview included a large video display which summarized the completion of the various missions over the last several moons.

Then, there was an *orientation presentation*— where foundational concepts like cosmology were introduced, helping the Earthlings in attendance to understand *where* they were located on the Luminary Watchhand respective to the Earth.

Then, the people were dismissed from their seats as music swirled throughout the camp during *intermission*. The band played various tunes from *many* different Luminary Systems. Some tunes were most bizarre in instrument and composition. Nevertheless, for the discerning ear, one could decipher the harmony present within each.

Throughout the evening, the music would stop at appointed intervals. Mage and Lewis would kindly interrupt the jovial conversation with a brief discussion of a *specific plant* from the Earth's wilderness. Mahanaim volunteers distributed small dishes which were prepared from each respective plant discussed. In parade fashion as the evening progressed, Mage and Lewis introduced and discussed *many* different plants from Earth. And, during the discussion of each plant, all the attendees were invited to taste the adeptly prepared food.

Many Earthlings in attendance were held in fascination by the presented plants. As each round came to an end and the music began anew, the minds of Earthlings were enraptured by the great blessing contained within these plants—aghast how they could escape the notice of *all* humanity for *all* history.

Perhaps that was Genesis' goal. After all, one would think the highest calling of *Earthlings* would be to understand *Earth*. And, after *thousands and thousands of years*, one could be so bold to say that *Earthlings* should *know Earth*—being wholly connected to her in every regard. Alas, the inhabitants of Earth during their tabernacle had become detached from the Earth in heart. They fell prey to deep magic which enticed them from the very order which was created to sustain them. So, it was most apropos for the one who bore the name of Creation, who was called to repair what was lost, to lead humanity out from that spell through a renewing of their minds. Thus, the *parade of plants* was strikingly reminiscent to the *parade of animals* at the Earth's founding—with both intended to move humanity to reverent appreciation of the gift granted.

But I digress. That is another tale for another day.

During the musical intermission, *gifts* were also distributed. Mahanaim volunteers brought forth various trinkets and cultural articles from different peoples located throughout charted Luminary Systems. So, by the evening's conclusion, each attendee had upon himself wreaths, jewelry, clothing articles and several goods carefully stowed within his pockets.

Earthlings were invited to offer something *in return* for each gift—whether small or great—which would be kept for use as gifts during the Mahanaim task force's future travels to *other* Luminary Systems.

Finally, the evening ended with *dinner*—consisting of a parade of prepared plant dishes using the *unknown* plants of Earth. At that time, attendees were dismissed to their casual conversations and musings throughout the camp—being free to leave when necessary.

Why did I tell you these things?

Perhaps you are interested in parties. Or, perhaps you are fascinated by the celebratory habits of other Luminary Systems. Either way, you are wiser—having been informed on the cultural practices of the Mahanaim task force. And, perchance you ever find yourself in their company, you will be prepared to celebrate in the *proper* way.

Notwithstanding, as the dulcet tones of jovial conversation moved to the melody of music throughout *this* evening, there were several conversations which bore relevance to the scope of this book. To find *one* such conversation, let's listen as Genesis and Ketu are approached by Mr. Overcompensate…

"Greetings. Genesis."

"Greetings, Mr. Overcompensate. I'd like to introduce you to my friend, Ketu."

"Greetings, Ketu."
Mr. Overcompensate shifted his attention to the darkened figure who reclined atop a wall, feet suspended before him. He held in his hand a long, slender pipe—

which bellowed sweet smoke. Ketu was a *side-sitter*, seldom facing others head-on. For Mr. Overcompensate, he made no exceptions.

"Greetings," echoed Ketu as he continued to stare off into the distance.

Overcompensate held curiosity for the topic of discussion between the two cloaked men. However, his arrival signaled the conversation's end. His curiosity would not be assuaged.

Tipping his pipe toward the pilgrim, Ketu mouthed, "*Later, Genesis*," with a pointed finger tracing the brim of his hat.
In a flash, Ketu blazed into the distance.

Overcompensate and the pilgrim stared in unison at Ketu's departure—venturing to trace his path with their eyes.

"Interesting—" offered Overcompensate with an open mouth.

"Yes," agreed Genesis with a hand wave and a racing explanation, bored of explaining Ketu's backstory to inquisitive Earthlings:

"That guy is from a shadow planet. He does stuff in a higher dimension that no one understands. *Yada yada*."

"R i g h t," Mr. Overcompensate drawled with a gulp, "Sorry if I interrupted your conversation, Genesis."

The pilgrim shook his head, "What's up?"

"I know this might not be the right time for us to talk—since this is a party and all."

"No problem," answered Genesis, "What's on your mind?"

"Sly."

Sly…Genesis knew him well from their previous meetings. *Mr. Sly*—as the chief politician—always held contempt for Genesis. And, the feeling was mutual! At first, Sly seemed to Genesis a normal, slippery individual—intent on the pursuit of self-interests. Now, however, Overcompensate was poised to shatter that illusion. Whereas Genesis was inclined to view Sly as a mere annoyance; Sly was in fact a *serious* threat to humanity.

"*What about Sly?*" asked Genesis curtly. He felt annoyed speaking *to* Sly in the past. And now he grew impatient—being dragged into a conversation *about* him.

More than that, Genesis held an absolute abhorrence for gossip. As Overcompensate began speaking, Genesis prepared himself to halt the conversation if it proved a mere childish chiding between Earthlings.

"Sly is up to *something*," teased Overcompensate. "I ordered an investigation. And I prepared a report for your review, Genesis."

Overcompensate removed some documents from his coat.

Genesis motioned to Kai at his side. He stepped forward to take the papers from the politician.

"What's the gist?" Genesis asked—looking for a verbal rendering of the *Cliffs Notes*: "What did the investigators find?"

"Nothing for certain, Genesis—"

"Then they are not very good investigators," interrupted Genesis with a scoff. "You should have told me about this earlier. I could have sent Zeg-E to spy."

"Who is Zeg-E?"

"Exactly!" answered Genesis, "Although you have been *in her sights* many times, you have no idea who she is. Now *she's* a *real* spy!"

307

Kai chuckled. However, the light jesting of the moment was quickly overtaken with horror…

Overcompensate whispered—eager to return to his discussion of Sly:
"Genesis, we think Sly's plan has *something* to do with *breaking minds*. According to the reports, Sly has this machine. They put people into the machine. Then the machine *breaks the minds of people until they see hidden things*…disturbing, otherworldly things."

"What!?"

"It is hard to explain, Genesis, but on Earth there was a conspiracy called the *Montauk Project*. We think Sly's machine might be *something* like this. The machine shakes people so their minds become something *different*. We found a couple people—" Overcompensate trailed off as Genesis' heart sunk.

The pilgrim's shoulders fell—as if a great burden was placed *upon* him. His mind swirled—being dragged to the realization of his greatest fear…a twisted, physical person *like Sly* gaining supernatural power beyond imagination.
Genesis' mind flashed back in pictures—remembering how he discussed *spirituality* with the

political council, specifically how a normal human could gain access to the 4th Dimension and Beyond. Now, being brought to the Luminary Watchhand itself for this party, Sly *could* have set an ethereal anchor for his return—even making other Luminary Systems vulnerable to his fell designs.

Previously Genesis had not pieced together similarities with the *Montauk Project*—although he was aware of it. But now the pilgrim was horrified at the thought Sly *might have* made the connection. Genesis' vision waned with the realization that Sly could use *his testimony* as a *missing piece* in the *Montauk Project*, learning to shake himself into the dimensions beyond the Earth. Indeed, if Sly took for himself this power through a physical means of mental fragmentation, he would gain for himself a magic beyond the reckoning of all Earth's inhabitants. He could declare himself "God" or a prophet—and hold within himself the ability to perform miracles by pulling and pushing things from the dimensions beyond.

Sly could be the anti-Christ!

The pilgrim's mind collapsed under the weight of the walls around him. But refusing to relegate itself to Perception Overload and the abandonment of the Luminary Watchhand to the darkness of chaos, Genesis moved the walls in his mind down and out—forcing them back into their holdings.

"*Where is Sly!?*" shouted the re-balanced pilgrim as he gazed at the party behind Overcompensate.

But Sly was *gone*.

Thus, the seemingly harmless politician, *Mr. Sly*, became in a moment, *Montauk Sly*—a man of hidden, ethereal power, which Earthlings would be incapable of discerning. He became the twisted, physical man with supernatural power beyond the lower dimensions. And, with that power he purchased for himself boundless intrigue—performing "miracles" through the veil of dimensions. And, with that intrigue he became capable of Great Deception through sleight of hand. And, finally, through that Great Deception he stole the hearts of all those imprisoned in the Earth—declaring himself "God."

Chaos would not permit the Earth respite. As soon as the Earth was repaired, Chaos found for itself a man to represent its fell purpose. And, being restored, the forces of evil moved quickly to corrupt the Earth as they did at first. Montauk Sly was the first step, but there were many more to follow.

However, that is another tale. With that, the party ended for Genesis. Searches were made throughout Earth. But Montauk Sly had hidden himself.

From the Watchhand, Genesis gazed down upon the jewel of the Earth. Whereas the pilgrim's heart was captured by her beauty—holding reverence for her as a marvel of the Creator; Chaos desired to seize that jewel as a possession—to *pluck* her for himself.

<u>16</u>:
Earth Plucked

Now I must tell you what happened to Earth. But in order to do this, I need to back up a bit to explain how "time" works…

Mind you, in Mahanaim, we *do not* think of time in the same anxious way it is reckoned on Earth. With the exception of certain projects which require specific timelines, no one in Mahanaim stresses over time. We have loose schedules where it is common to say to another, "*I will meet you in the morning, on the 5ᵗʰ day.*" That would simply mean *five days from now we will meet when the Greater Light rises*. Not so on Earth—where all things are mixed with anxious clock-watching.

To further separate ourselves from the conception of time on Earth, in Mahanaim we only think of time in the general term of the *century*. You may have noticed this in Genesis' books—which often mention "5000 A.D." Whereas readers on Earth may wonder *when* the year number will click up to "5001;" here in Mahanaim, the next *click up* would be "5100 A.D." This may seem most bizarre to humans on Earth; however, this is how we in Mahanaim prefer to think of time—and it works best for us, helping us to live with much less day-to-day anxiety.

Surely this explanation will lead to *further* questions. Especially the question of *how* we arrived at the number "*5000*" and the definition of "*A.D*" in Mahanaim. But for the sake of relevance and to avoid confusing readers with *red herrings*, we will move on.

So, how does *time* work in the *4ᵗʰ Dimension*?

When one is on the Luminary Watchhand in the 4ᵗʰ Dimension it appears all Luminary Systems run off similar chronological time. The Greater Light in each Luminary System is *synchronized* with all other Luminary Systems (at least as far we can tell based on our "charted" Luminary Systems). This means the duration of a "day" and "year" are the same for them all—simply put. Of course, I could be faulted for an oversimplification here, but suffice it to say that all the Luminary Systems "tick" time the same.

So, what happened to Earth?

On routine checks of our *microscopic machines* during the duration of our mission, some of the data reported was bizarre…*very bizarre* in fact. Of course, this wasn't noticed *during* the Earth mission, but *after* the disappearance of the Earth and a subsequent analysis of data. Data indicated small *glitches* in the microscopic machines. Simply put, their "clocks" were somehow altered from the "clocks" of the Luminary Watchhand camp.

In other words, the Earth was gradually *glitched* off Luminary Watchhand *time*, until finally it disappeared altogether!

Now, I am sure I have you quite befuddled with discombobulation in my discussion of time. However, let me assure you, this is not an easy topic for anyone…even time-traveler(s)!

"Time" is a difficult animal to wrangle—and to truly understand how it works, you would need to have the ability to *bumble* through its many layers to mitigate trickledown effects. Or at least that is what I have heard from our time-traveler! In other words, *even if* you *could* change something in the past, you would be most unwise to attempt this—as it would cause a cascade of unforeseen trickledown effects…

That is unless you happen to be a *Bumble master*, of course.

Perhaps in Earth culture one of the best ways to communicate this is through the concept of the *Butterfly Effect*—where the manipulation of past events alters the future. I mention this to help frame your understanding.

So, back to the issue at hand:
The disappearance of Earth…

Since the Mahanaim task force is from Mahanaim, we were never overly focused on *specific years* on Earth. And, indeed, it is not wise for us to be bogged down by *exact* years, because the *year* of an event can be altered. Think of this through the lens of the *Butterfly Effect*.

For example, if you are reading this book in A.D. 2500 on Earth, it would not be wise to state definitely that the events of this book *have not* already occurred. Suffice it to say, time *rolls out* in bizarre fashion onto the lower dimensions from the 6th Dimension and Beyond. So, in many cases, if an event is not directly tied to the higher dimensions, it could be removed entirely. The only things which *need to stick* are the things which are *required* from higher dimensions. Think of this as "prophecy."

Understanding this, it will make sense why members of the Mahanaim task force were *never* interested in recording the *time and date* of their Earth missions. Of course, we took copies of Earthling newspapers and things like that, but you must understand to us the *number of years* are quite arbitrary, and therefore neglected—much as you might neglect details which bear no relevance to yourself. After all, Genesis is a 5th Dimension time-traveler, so why would he or his task force be concerned with how 3rd Dimension Earthlings reckon their physical time?

So, after Earth's disappearance, a careful search was made among *all* records kept in the Luminary Watchhand camp—including copies of Earthling newspapers. And, in the re-reading of Earth newspapers, we came a conclusion: Throughout our mission Earth time was somehow…*fluctuating*. On one newspaper we noted time somehow jumped back—*many, many* years…even before our arrival!

Are you confused?

So am I.
But I am doing my best to let you know *what happened*—however bizarre it may seem.

In other words, even when the Earth was still on the Luminary Watchhand with all the other Luminary Systems, the Earth began *falling out of sync* with the shared timeline.

After examining the newspaper discrepancies, even Boggles, the Luminary expert, confirmed the time disruption was like nothing she ever recorded. Thus, the entire *Mahanaim task force* was distressed—having worked diligently to repair Earth, yet nevertheless incapable of saving her.

So, there stood the pilgrim—utterly perplexed on the Luminary Watchhand. The moment passed—as Genesis, Kai, Boggles, Lewis and Mage stood in silent reflection, bereft of sense, filled with grief.

Genesis felt dizzy and took a knee to center his mind. He was lost.

Just then, the Goat rushed upon the group, drawing them from grief with a glimmer of hope…

"Genesis! I have a report!"

With a mechanical whirring, Goat abruptly stopped before the pilgrim. The machine shell which housed portions of Goat's body creaked and snapped as they came to rest. Goat was a master tinkerer—constantly creating various gadgets and using them for nearly every purpose.

Although it was bizarre to witness the ungainly *running* of Goat, it could not be denied the machinery enhanced his locomotion. Although Goat *lost a step* in his old age, he was now *spry as ever* with his machinery enhancements. And, certainly, during this time, Goat's machine enhancements were a great blessing—allowing him to *quickly* cover distances on the Luminary

Watchhand as he moved to gather reports on the Earth's recent disappearance.

"Genesis, I received a report from one of our furthest observation posts! He saw something before Earth disappeared!" Goat said—huffing as if out of breath.

Mage had a great sense of humor—which she now wielded to lighten the mood of her fellows…

"Come on now, Goat!" Mage interrupted, "*You* can't be out of breath! We see *the machinery* is doing the running *for you*!"

Goat held his breath—taken aback from Mage's jest.

Why am I out of breath? Goat thought to himself with a scoff…

"*A n y w a y*," retorted Goat in a drawling dismissal, waving his hand in Mage's direction.

Genesis looked up at Mage with a nod of appreciation:

"Take us to the observation post, Goat. I want to hear what the watchman saw."

And, in this way, this story came to a close. Genesis and his team stood in dismay as the watchman recounted what he saw. The watchman told them of two posh, suited Earthlings—standing in the distance upon the Watchhand. Around the pair was an ethereal orb—matching in hue to the blackness of the Outer Darkness plane. Before the watchman could radio to base to question if they were aware of personnel in that location, the pair disappeared. And, upon closer inspection of the location of their appearance, nothing remained…that is nothing which could be *perceived* by the watchman. Thus the arrival and departure of the two men was left shrouded in mystery, now seen as a foreshadowing of the Earth's doom.

Genesis' mind quickly made sense of the watchman's testimony. Clearly, the appearance was none other than Montauk Sly along with a close associate. The ethereal orb—matching in hue to the Outer Darkness—was doubtlessly the endowment of the forces of Chaos below, choosing to move Sly as its Earthling puppet. And, the appearance upon the Watchhand was doubtlessly the last step needed to shroud the Earth from it. Genesis reckoned the quick appearance and disappearance was to set some otherworldly anchor—allowing Chaos to shake Earth free from the Watchhand through dark magic, concealing Earth in her despair, separating her from Mahanaim's interference. Thus, Chaos and Sly moved to lock away Earth in grief—beyond the reach of Mahanaim.

The hearts of the Mahanaim task force sank at the realization of their loss. Genesis wept and his fellows wept. They embraced one another in mourning. They wrote and recited laments for the Earth—making mention of her beauty and blessing, crying out for her loss, giving full vent to their despair.

Nevertheless, pain persisted—leaving a void as real as the darkness which now occupied the empty filigree setting below. By some powerful magic—far beyond the capability of Genesis, and even Ketu—the Earth was now completely beyond reach. In many moons past, the Luminary Watchhand bathed in the nearby light of the Earth's Sun and Moon. Now, as darkness settled upon the Luminary Watchhand camp in the absence of the Earth's light, the Mahanaim company was silenced in grief.

In this time, Kai emerged as a leader—so accustomed to pressing forward during times of despair. He seized the books of the pilgrim from within his backpack. Kai spread the books atop a table. One by one, the members of the Mahanaim task force joined with Kai to examine the writings. Truly, they knew not what they *might* find in the books. However, they busied themselves in the examination of the pilgrim's notes and accounts—searching for some clue or pattern which might bring remedy.

Happening upon one book, titled <u>How to Keep the Law of Moses</u>, Goat addressed the group…

"Genesis, in this book, you mention the original purpose of Moses' tabernacle was to serve as a pattern of the *Heavenly* tabernacle—citing Hebrews 8:5."

Genesis looked up from his reading with weary eyes, "What's your point, Goat?"

The other leaders fell silent, giving Goat audience.

"My point: Since the tabernacle was intended to be a *direct* copy of the Heavenly tabernacle, maybe we could use the tabernacle?" offered Goat. "Since the Earth was somehow hidden by a magic beyond our own, what magic can resist the *magic of Heaven* itself!?"

Goat added, "Even if all the power of Hell is focused upon the Earth, the power of Heaven would blaze upon it—like a firestorm in a darkened room."

As Goat spoke, his words gained in cadence—as if empowered to deliver a grand call to the Mahanaim task force:

"*If Earth is hidden by dark magic, we need the radiance of the Creator to dispel it!* The *original tabernacle* could do that because in its original form it bore the power of the *Heavenly pattern* itself! What in all of Creation could resist it!?"

And, with those words, Goat kindly guided the pilgrim back to truths locked within writing he penned long ago. As is the case with such things, the empowering of the Creator dispersed throughout the task force at once—enabling each for the mission ahead. Now they were reunified in purpose. They were revitalized with a new mission. The thought immediately clicked into place—like a key into a formidable lock. Truly, all things jostled and were moved powerfully into place. Just as the Earth needed to be moved back into its filigree setting, so also the Mahanaim task force needed to be moved into its next mission.

And, beyond the vision of the Mahanaim task force, the chains of the anchor set by the two mysterious men were broken. The darkness of Chaos no longer held captive the minds of those upon the Watchhand.

Goat's words echoed throughout the halls of the pilgrim's mind. As the words passed through each corridor, each in turn gave its consent—as the tabernacle presented within itself an answer to *every* question and objection within Genesis' mind. Finally, *the thought*—having gained the approval of all channels within—found its way to Genesis' lips as he offered his verdict . . .

"Yes, we will go back in time to rescue the tabernacle…
Then we will rescue Earth."

Convinced, the company closed the books upon the table, each facing toward the darkness which once held fast the jewel of the Earth. A strong breeze spread throughout the camp, jostling the pages of the books upon the table and rushing down the Watchhand into the void which stole Earth's setting. The members of the *Mahanaim task force* bowed their heads as fire blazed in their hearts. The tears, which moments earlier, streamed down their faces traced themselves back to the wells within. Then the wells broke free—swirling, sweeping, rejuvenating.

With the words of the pilgrim, the chains which were placed upon the Watchhand slithered in haste to the Outer Darkness below, falling as single broken shackles in a disheveled trail of retreat. Upon reaching the darkness below, they brooded and festered in a gathering swarm.

Meanwhile above, a path of light opened before the Mahanaim task force, pushing back darkness in waves of brilliance.

The pilgrim opened his eyes.

<u>Epilogue 1</u>:
Faith Super Power

"But Genesis, I do have a problem with it."

"What do you mean, Kai?"

"Well, it's hard for me to be here," Kai paused as his shoulders fell. He let loose an exasperated sigh as tears welled in his eyes. His head dropped—concealing his face beneath his brow.

Genesis felt deeply for Kai. Yet in his empathy, the pilgrim restrained himself from placing his hand upon Kai's shoulder. The pilgrim knew all too well the good process of grief. And he did not want to pull Kai from it in an untimely fashion. Keeping his distance, Genesis gently guided Kai…

"Finding purpose can be challenging, Kai."

"Well it isn't *purpose* that is the challenge. I know I have *a* purpose here—being a part of this mission and looking after you, Genesis," Kai paused, then continued. "My problem is that it is hard to be in a place where everyone has *super powers*, yet I am just a plain person."

"Oh, I see."

Kai was quick to seize Genesis' seeming concession: "Yeah, think of what it would be like to be around time-travelers, explorers, and these people with abilities I cannot even explain!" Kai lifted his head, "It wears on me. I feel like a scrub."

Genesis chuckled within himself at Kai's use of the word "scrub." He wasn't sure what Kai *meant by it*—and then debated within himself whether or not Kai even knew what *he* meant with that word. A moment passed as the pilgrim mused on *where* Kai would have picked up that word: *Certainly not from anyone on Mahanaim. So, maybe during his time on Earth?*

Kai broke the silence—staring at the blank pilgrim, "Get what I mean, Genesis? This is a big deal for me."

Genesis emerged from his mind, bringing with him a helpful thought:
"Kai, you said you feel different from everyone else—as if people like me have special abilities."

"Yeah."

"Kai, I am an *ordinary* man."

"You can do time-travel!" Kai objected, "And you can pass into different points on Earth. And you somehow found a way to *move beyond your own lifetime.* So, how in the world can you say you are an *ordinary man*, Genesis!? Bonkers!"

"Well, that is all a matter of perspective. From *your* perspective—and from the perspective of people on Earth and Mahanaim—you might be inclined to view me as a *multi-dimension time-traveler.* But at my core—in my spirit—that is not who I *really* am."

"Huh?"

"I am an *ordinary* man with faith."

"I don't get it."

"Kai, we are all in a journey of self-discovery. And none of us have *all* the answers. But I can share with you what I have learned *about myself*. Perhaps it could help you reframe how you view *yourself*?"

"Yes, please explain, Genesis."

"Well… The way I do time-travel and move within different dimensions is *through faith*. So, although you might view me as having *super powers*, any power I possess is really just *an effect of my faith*."

"What do you mean?"

"My ability to believe—that is to have faith— causes my mind to *set aside physical barriers*. I set my mind where I need to go, and then the physical worlds shift to make room for my mind to move. And where my mind goes, my body follows. So, really, time-travel for me isn't a super power. Time-travel and moving to different places is just *an effect of my faith*. My mind fixes itself on an experience or reality, then I move to it."

Kai's head swirled, "What do you mean '*faith*?'"

"Kai, in the Bible, the Lord Jesus said if a person has the smallest amount of faith, that person can move mountains. It is a very basic principle. Faith has the ability to *bend* physical things. Physical things are not solid for a person of faith. Faith can set aside things which need to be set aside."

Kai scoffed gently, restraining himself:
"You can move *mountains!?*"

"Yes."

"*Any* mountain?"

"Only a mountain which *needs* to be moved. Faith is not to be trifled with. Nor is it a parlor trick done for the amusement of people. But when the time comes to bend physical things by faith, it happens all the time," Genesis finished, "That is how I bend physical time— allowing me to move to different locations. I believe in my mind. Then my mind moves my body."

"Interesting. But how isn't that a *super power*? It sounds like a super power to me!"

"Certainly, faith is supernatural. But faith isn't something exclusive to a *special* person. Christ offers faith to *all* people who follow Him."

"But not all those people can do stuff like time-travel," Kai challenged.

"There could be many reasons for that, Kai. *First*, it might not be the right time for their faith to do certain things. In other words, they might not have encountered a 'mountain' which the Creator wants to be moved. *Second*, a person who believes in Christ might not have the ability to do great things because he fails to understand the gift granted to him. Or, *third*, a person of faith may be so trapped by his thoughts of the physical that he cannot see anything beyond the impressive physical barriers around him. In those cases, the believer—although he has faith—would be quite incapable of moving anything physical. *Fourth*—"

"What makes *you* different?" Kai interrupted.

"Nothing."

"That's not what I mean," Kai clarified further, "Why is *your* faith capable of bending physical things while the faith of others is not?"

"I get what you mean—although I know *all* people with faith *are capable* because Christ said so! But to answer your question, my faith is capable of bending physical reality because I am grounded in the Gospels. I read and I *choose* to believe."

Kai looked puzzled, so Genesis continued…

"When reading the Bible, and carefully considering the miracles therein, I was brought to the realization that faith has power over physical reality. Of course, this is a simple thing to declare, and one could do it with a reference to 2 Corinthians 5:7. However, my faith reaches further than a surface understanding."

"Tell me more."

"If you remember, Kai, during my time on Earth—when you visited—atheism had taken root in many cultures. The problem of atheism is that it taught people to be *merely physical* in their minds—forfeiting their spirituality. And, the problem went much further—where even Christian leaders would peddle *physical* things…speaking about stuff like outer space, evolution, and so on. They even began to list physical *proofs* for everything—effectively rendering 'belief' obsolete. They taught people they should 'believe' in the resurrection of Christ on the basis of '*physical proofs*' rather than simply encouraging people to 'believe' in the resurrection on the basis of *heartfelt faith*. Indeed, Kai, faith was never designed to be *based on physical things*. It was always designed to be based on *simple, heartfelt belief*. This is all explained in my book, <u>Faith: No Proof Required</u>."

331

Genesis pressed further, "Faith is defiant of physical reality. Faith is powerful. When physical reality declares something to be so, faith is the means of shattering physical barriers. But by Christian leaders teaching 'physical proofs,' they undercut the true power contained within faith. So, Christians of the 21st Century resolved themselves to *never moving mountains*. Led by their apologists they became *completely physical* in their minds. However, I took a different path—bypassing people who established their own teachings, *choosing* to simply follow Christ's teaching. And, whereas the others during that time developed knowledge and lists of 'physical proofs,' I developed something quite different— and quite forgotten throughout the millennia of history."

Around Genesis an aura snapped. With a crackle, a thread of blue light zipped from the pilgrim's hands— passing back into obscurity as quickly as it appeared.

"What was that!?" exclaimed Kai, attempting to capture the fleeting moment.

"That happens all the time. I guess it is just a byproduct of faith. I focus so much on moving *beyond the physical* that the physical at times seems to move itself around me," Genesis laughed, "No big deal."

Kai shook his head. He held his breath as he blinked his eyes in dismay. He lifted his hands—gesturing to Genesis, as if to present the occurrence as an exhibit in demonstration of his point:

"And ... You say you have no special powers! Ridiculous!"

"W h a t e v e r, Kai!" Genesis scoffed, dismissing his comment with a laugh. "It is what happens when you immerse your mind upon *the Christ*—who bent the physical world around Himself—healing people, cleansing lepers, raising the dead and even *raising Himself*! When one fixes his mind upon the Christ, it is *natural*—no *supernatural*—to do likewise. Whereas one might talk about a mountain or a wall as an impossible barrier, I just set it aside so I can move around it. Physical things have no hold on the person of faith. They just don't."

"What about death? Or injury?"

"What about *them*?"

"A person of faith can die."

"Not really, Kai. A person of faith can reach his *physical end*, but his spirit bypasses death. In fact, death is no barrier at all. The person of faith lives on. And his body is resurrected by faith. Hence…" Genesis held out his arms.

"I get it," Kai answered.

The pilgrim continued: "Because Christ lives, we live in Him. We find resurrection *in Him*. Then we gain understanding. Sure, a person of faith might have *died* from a snake bite, but in the grander scheme the snake bite was just something he needed to endure in his physical lifetime. No big deal," Genesis concluded, "We don't *really* die. If you show me my grave, I will show you a place where my physical body only *rested temporarily*. The grave is an easy thing for the person of faith. The Holy Spirit easily brushes it aside. It is meaningful for the person, yet is a thing conquered by the lightest breeze of the Almighty. When you live in the presence of the Christ, you are going to pick up your mat and walk. No matter what has kept you there in the past, *The Teacher* calls you forth from it."

Kai smiled as his heart warmed. He wiped tears from his face.

"There is much about faith, Kai. Of course, a person of faith possesses within himself the ability to *time-travel*—even if he never does it. Faith is not a linear history thing. Faith is defiant of the physical world. Whereas physical events can be placed on a timeline, faith supersedes time," Genesis paused, "I can tell you more if you like."

"Yes please."

"Well, as I said, faith supplants time. Just as a physical mountain poses no barrier to faith, so also 'years' are not a barrier to faith. We can pray for things in the past just as readily as we can pray for things in the present. And the Creator can touch different points just as easily. When a person gets this concept, things should start clicking for him. And, since our faith is not bound by time—or physical history for that matter—why should a person of faith care about whether or not atheists deny the *history* of the Bible? After all, since my faith can move mountains, my faith in Christ also possesses the ability to do *other things* throughout *past* history."

"Like what?"

"For example, let's say an atheist doubted the historicity of Moses parting the Red Sea. My position—as outrageous as it may seem," Genesis said as he stomped his foot, "Is that *I* can part the Red Sea *for Moses* from *right here*."

Kai chuckled—yet convinced of Genesis' veracity. Kai raised his hand to his chin. Indeed, it was most profound to consider—that the pilgrim could *somehow* be a part of the process of parting the Red Sea from thousands of years in the future. And it did make sense to Kai, since God is unbounded by time. Christ did say His followers could move mountains. So, a mountain in the *past could* be moved just as easily as a mountain in the *present.*

"I see," answered Kai.

"You get it?" Genesis asked, his eyes surveying Kai's face—unsure whether or not he was really *getting it.* "It is important you understand this, Kai. Then you *could* understand how I am able to move throughout time. Once you feel this for yourself, the shackles fall."

Kai smiled. The thought of having ethereal handcuffs removed from his arms was empowering. He breathed deeply—as if drawing strength from the words of the pilgrim, hanging in the air.

"And, extending this thought further, Kai, we can consider the claims of atheists concerning the cross of Christ. During my lifetime—as you witnessed—atheists would posit *counter claims* against Christ's historicity, death, burial, resurrection, appearances and ascension. Atheists would dispute many things in the Gospels. *Yet*—"

"*Yet*, what?"

"Well, as I have said, time is no barrier to the person of faith. This means faith exists—like a giant orb resting upon the threads of every timeline which has existed. Faith is the same regardless *where* you exist in time. Therefore, you must understand, faith has no need for human explanations of the past. Sure, it is interesting to study history and archaeology. But if an atheist claims archaeology defies my faith, then I will go back to that place in time and move whatever mountain needs to be moved. If an atheist claims Christ was buried in a *mass grave*, my faith will send a man named Nicodemus to bury Him in a tomb. If an atheist claims Christ wasn't raised from the dead, my faith will move to unroll the stone from the tomb. Therefore, just as Christ said, our faith can move mountains. So, I will move those mountains by faith. In fact, I will move *any* mountain which needs to be moved. Easy."

Kai burst into laughter. The thought of Genesis going back into time to remove barriers to faith was defiant indeed—stating he would reconstruct history to put all things in order based on his faith, if required. It was a profound absurdity to consider—which Kai mused was best for Genesis to share in secret, as if he should feel ashamed of his words.

The pilgrim, however, was not ashamed. He merely declared what he knew and how he had a habit of relating to *all* physical things.

"So, you see, Kai: I am not shaken by *anything physical*. Mountains, time and even death itself are no barrier to faith. Sure, I can be physically hurt, but whenever there is a mountain to be moved, I guarantee it will be moved!"

"Well then what about this, Genesis… Let's say although you rolled back the stone to the grave by faith, an atheist said he would go back in time to *undo* what you did?"

"Think about what you just said, Kai," Genesis laughed. "An atheist doesn't believe in the *supernatural*, so how would he have the ability to *defy the physical*? So, you are saying the *natural-minded* atheist would use a *supernatural* ability of time-travel just to deny the *supernatural!?*"

Genesis teased, "I'd like to see him try."

"Alright!" Kai said with a hand wave—as if in surrender, "I get it. *Faith is your superpower.* And faith should be my superpower."

"Yes!" Genesis answered with an enthusiastic nod.

"I understand."

Kai quickly withdrew from his concession, inviting further discussion: "Though it still doesn't help me with the mismatch between *my abilities* and the *abilities of others* on the task force."

Genesis smiled to foreshadow the impending demise of Kai's thought. Kai sauntered into Genesis' trap and the pilgrim laughed inwardly at the realization of the truth bombs he prepared to drop upon his companion.

"What do you mean?" Genesis said with a smirk.

"The other team members are *more special* than me."

"Example?" queried Genesis with a wince—as if to drag out Kai's demolition.

"Boggles."

"Kai, Boggles is a common house spider."

"Huh?"

"You mean you didn't get that—with the goggles, the thread and the web patterns?" Genesis laughed.

"I don't get it."

"You will though. It will just take some time, dear Kai."

Kai scratched his head—

"What about Red!? She is a giant shape-shifting bird!"

Genesis shook his head in jest: "Kai, *Red is a mosquito*. ... You mean you didn't figure that out from her appearance!?"

"Actually, no I didn't."

"Kai, how would *a bird* have knowledge of all the lifeforms within a Luminary System?"

Kai kicked the ball back into Genesis court, parroting his words: "Well, *Genesis*, how would *a mosquito* have knowledge of all lifeforms?"

"I don't know, *Kai*, maybe because a mosquito spends its entire life taking drops of DNA from just about everything!" Genesis laughed. "You've got to think there is a reason for mosquitos in Creation! And clearly over time a big mosquito would have ample opportunity to catalogue a bunch of stuff about animals, right? Therefore, *mosquito* makes sense; much more sense than *bird*!"

Kai sighed heavily, feeling the weight of Genesis' point.

"Kai, you should know by now I have a habit of pointing out the major blessings in the mundane. It is kind of my schtick. Don't overlook the things which are of low-esteem. In the common things we often find the greatest blessings. And despised things can hold within them cures for great evil. We can use even the *smallest* things to un-do the *greatest* evil. The gates of Hell can be undone with the smallest speck of the Creator's light. So, whereas humanity may despise the tiniest critters, I will magnify the light of the Creator within them."

"What about the others? What about *their* super powers?" asked Kai with a puzzled look.

"I'll leave you to figure that out. Perhaps the biggest mystery of all, Kai, is *you*. You have much to discover about *yourself*. Indeed, it is most profound that you view yourself in low-regard. There is something quite grand which escapes your vision. And, in time, you will see it," Genesis smiled—feeling blessed to offer encouragement to his friend.

"Alright, Genesis," answered Kai.

He shifted his weight upon his legs—sensing he grew taller *somehow*. It felt as if he were drawing strength from Genesis' words.

"If you don't mind, Genesis, I will hold onto copies of your books. I won't let your words fall away,"

Kai said as he gestured to his heavy backpack. "Who knows? Soon I might need to start some libraries."

"I expect you would!" said Genesis. "There are a lot of people stuck on their mats. We are going to command a whole lot of people to *stand and walk*. So, surely, if you find ways to empower people *anywhere*, feel free to do so through those writings."

Kai and Genesis spoke further as they drew nearer to the Luminary Watchhand camp. Pink and blue threads crackled upon their steps.

Epilogue 2:
The Spider &
The Lord of the Castle
A Tale of Mahanaim

Once there was a great lord of a mighty castle in Mahanaim.

One day the lord of the castle found in his megaron a small spider. The spider scurried about on the floor—searching for her place in that vast space.

The lord of the castle, being a man accustomed to warfare and battle, now sat in restful peace upon his elevated seat in the secluded hall. The spider, on this day, his only company as the sunlight beamed from the portholes above.

Now, many at the sight of a spider would be squeamish—recoiling from the creature as something most despised. But, as I have said, this great lord of the castle was a man accustomed to battle—bearing in his past horrors much more intimidating than a gentle spider.

And, many others at the sight of a spider would be inclined to take *its* life. However, the lord of the castle recoiled from such a thought. In his previous life upon Earth, the lord of the castle oft witnessed brutality. Now, however, within the security of his *fortress* and *stronghold* of *refuge*, there was no need for the taking of life. He alone decided the rules of his courts. And, his rule was mercy. Thus, within those courts of the mighty fortress, the heart of the lord was warmed, banishing the chills which once held him captive.

In a most noble feat, the lord stepped down from his throne. He struggled and stooped *low*, extending his hand to the gentle spider. Rather than force himself upon the spider, the lord granted her consent—merely placing his hand nearby.

The spider saw the hand and paused—as if in reflection. She twitched—feeling the air near the hand which appeared from above. Sensing the kindness of the lord, she clambered into his hand, then rested her legs beneath her. Her feet gently pressed into the grooves of his skin—giving her a newfound sense of balance compared to the slippery floor of the megaron.

The lord of the castle slowly stood upon his unsteady legs, with eyes fixed upon his new friend. He stepped backward, carefully retracing his path up the stairs to his throne.

The lord sat carefully, as if to avoid jostling the spider in his hand. As he slid into his seat, the spider remained motionless—content in his palm. He wondered as he peered closely at the spider—with her gentle blending of colors. The spider appeared a masterful work of art—carefully pieced together and painted with a gleaming camouflage. As the lord looked closely, he monitored the gentle breaths of the spider—her body now motionless save for that passive waxing and waning.

This gentle spider must be asleep, the lord of the castle thought.

Now, many may *recoil* at such thoughts—or become *squeamish* at such things. Yet the lord of the castle looked down at the spider with fondness and compassion. So, here the lord of the castle sat, spider in hand to greet a parade of his thoughts. His heart was pulled in many directions—reflecting upon times when *he* was likewise *scooped* from past battlefields by a hand from above. And, in this, the lord of the castle was thankful for this opportunity to *scoop* another in an act of compassion.

Then, the great lord considered the *fate* of the spider—if indeed *another* man were seated upon *this* throne.

Yet, here he was. And here was this spider.

At the thought, his eyes welled and the dam broke. Tears fell from the lord's face at the swirling of emotions within him. In part, the tears were drawn by his past battlefields; in part, they were drawn for *this spider*—so narrowly rescued by his grace, now safely asleep in his palm.

You see, this *lord of the castle* was not like lords of *other* castles.

Thus, the lord of the castle kept silent vigil— carefully holding the spider in his hand as his thoughts both comforted and afflicted him. Over time, affliction was assuaged as the gentle breathings of the spider lured his body to adopt the steady patterns of waxing and waning. The lord of the castle, as he slipped deeper into relaxation, dozed while his palm remained open. As he opened his eyes from time to time, he found the spider— still motionless and sleeping in the palm of his hand.

Many moments passed.

The lord of the castle opened his eyes—seeing the spider motionless, then beginning to twitch and stir herself from slumber. The lord of the castle smiled. He saw in the spider and himself a *kinship*—having shared these moments of respite together.

Not desiring to be parted from his new friend, the lord of the castle spoke…

"Dear spider, would you like to live in my castle? There are many rooms for you to find your place."

The lord's eyes surveyed the spider. He sensed within her a desire for rest and seclusion. He felt *somehow* that this dear spider had experienced much hardship in her short life. His heart broke for the spider as he offered consolation…

"My dear spider, I think I know how you feel. Your legs must ache from your journey—having walked across this grand hall. And who knows how you even arrived in this castle in the first place?"

The lord smiled in compassion. He gazed closely upon the spider—his eyes blanketing the spider in light. Reflections of his gaze were found in the darkened bulbous eyes of the spider as she gazed back upon him— perhaps with similar thoughts. Although the spider might not have understood his *words*, the light passing between them became in itself a much more capable language.

The lord of the castle wondered as he peered into the spider's eyes:

Perhaps this spider was sent to save me? the lord thought.

The lord of the castle was suddenly struck with a thought…

"Oh! I know, dear spider. I know the *perfect* place in my castle for you to make your home!" the lord paused, "Would you like to see it?"

The spider, being deprived the gift of speech, twitched—sending forth light from her bulbous eyes.

The lord of the castle roused himself from his seat, stretching his legs. Grasping a nearby light, the lord began his trek through the vast halls with his new friend. As he passed different parts of the castle, the lord spoke gently to the spider of each area.

After a long journey, the lord of the castle arrived in a corridor. The light of the day had now passed— giving way to the breezy dark of evening. As he walked, the lord and the spider alike drew strength from the moonlight which passed through the portholes.

At the end of the corridor, the space opened into a breathtaking orb-shaped room with a dizzyingly high, vaulted ceiling. In fact, this grand room would be best described as a tower—so high did it press into the sky above. The tower room felt sterile and lifeless—save for the light of the Luminaries above.

"I see you need rest, dear spider. And you need somewhere safe," the lord said as he held up the spider in his hand, offering her a better view of the tower space above them.

"This is a good place to rest, dear spider. I can offer to leave you here if you like, or if you prefer another room, I can bear you hence."

With that, the lord of the castle stood—awaiting the spider's consent. The spider slowed clambered to the edge of the lord's hand—peering at the tower room around her. Suspending herself from his fingertips, the spider signaled she found her new home. The lord of the castle made his way to the wall—finding a suitable place for the spider to begin her journeyings throughout the tower.

"Farewell, dear spider," said the lord of the castle as the spider crabbed her way up the tower wall.

"I will be back to visit you, spider," the lord said with a smile. His eyes traced the departure of the small spider in the heights above.

Many moons passed. The lord of the castle ever returned to visit the spider. In a natural progression of events, the spider became ever more comfortable within the tower heights. The lord of the castle ever enjoyed his daytime visits—seeing the vast accomplishments of the spider.

"What massive webs you have made above, kind spider!" the lord exclaimed in compliment to the tiny creature he once held in the palm of his hand.

"How you have grown!" declared the lord of the castle when from time to time his eyes caught a glance of the spider dancing in the heights above.

At times the spider would pause when the lord would pronounce such kind compliments from below in the daylight. Nevertheless, the spider, reluctant to move freely in the sunlight, would dart quickly out of sight. From her hiding spots, the spider would look down at the kind lord—enjoying his kind words. The lord of the castle would smile and the spider would smile in return—at least if spiders *could* smile, then she would, so satisfied was she in her friendship with the kind lord of the castle. But, since they could not exchange language, they practiced exchanging light with one another.

Thus, was the nature of their exchanges during the visits of the lord to the spider's tower. Some visits were brief, but many visits lingered—for the lord of the castle found comfort in the presence of his friend above. The lord of the castle ever spoke; the kind spider ever listened.

Once, in his regular visits, the lord of the castle tarried long—remaining past the ending of the Sun's watch as the Moon removed her veil. To the lord's surprise, in the gentle glow of moonlight, the webs above appeared to take new form. He peered closer, rubbing his eyes from disbelief. The webs above somehow *reached beyond* the walls of the castle—*through* the vast porthole above. As the lord of the castle traced each thread of the web, he saw clearly how they seemed to *touch* the light of the Luminaries! The lord of the castle wondered most ponderously, shaking his body free from the ground where he lay…

"My goodness, dear spider! How did you do that!?" he cried out in awestruck excitement. "It is beautiful, dear spider! How did you make such threads? With what magic did you touch the Luminaries!? I have never seen something like this before. You certainly are special, dear spider… Just as special as you were on the day we found one another in the throne room."

Although unsure of the kind spider's location, the lord of the castle bowed in humble adoration of the spider's miraculous work above. He placed his hand on his heart as tears welled in his eyes and his face formed a smile.

So great was the smile it seemed to the spider above to reflect the gentle moonlight—bathing her in radiance from below as well as from the Luminaries above. The spider had great respect for the lord of the castle—the man who saw grace within her when others would have been moved to despise her humble form.

Yet, the kind lord of the castle always saw further—always loved, always spoke tenderly, always cared.

With that, the kind spider descended on a thread to the kind lord of the castle. No longer harassed by the daylight, the dear spider found the boldness to reveal herself to her friend below. She twisted her way downward upon threads—longing and overjoyed at once to be brought to this moment where perhaps she could once again be near her friend. Although she would no longer fit in the palm of his hand, the kind spider longed to share her story of the webs above—how they touched the Luminaries.

The kind spider's two feet found the floor of the tower. She stood before the lord of the castle, eyes beaming and heart glad.

Then she spoke.

Index

Hungry for more Genesis Pilgrim?

Check out these other titles…
*Interview with the Time Traveler

*Faith: No Proof Required…How to Share your Faith with Zero Proof

*Survival of the Superstitious: How Religion Helped Ancient Humans Survive

*How to Keep the Law of Moses: The Step-by-Step Guide to the Old Testament Torah

*Dear David: Learning to See God through PTSD, Anxiety and Depression

*Heart of the Warrior: Learning the Combat Skills of King David

For a full listing of books, visit www.genesispilgrim.com